MANDARINS

Stories by

Ryūnosuke Akutagawa

Translated from the Japanese by Charles De Wolf

archipelago books

Archipelago Books
232 Third Street, #A111
Brooklyn, NY 11215
www.archipelagobooks.org

Library of Congress Cataloging-in-Publication Data
Akutagawa, Ryūnosuke, 1892–1927.
Mandarins : Stories / by Ryūnosuke Akutagawa ; translated from the
Japanese by Charles De Wolf.
p. cm.
ISBN 978-0-9778576-0-9 (alk. paper)
1. Akutagawa, Ryūnosuke, 1892–1927 – Translations into English.
I. De Wolf, Charles. II. Title.
PL801.K8A6 2007
895.6'342—dc22 2007015994

Distributed by Consortium Book Sales and Distribution
www.cbsd.com

Cover art: Auguste Rodin: *Femme à demi-nue, assise sur les talons*
(D. 4626), pencil and watercolor on paper, Musée Rodin, Paris.

Printed in Canada

This publication was made possible with support from Lannan
Foundation, the National Endowment for the Arts, and the New
York State Council on the Arts, a state agency.

CONTENTS

Mandarins   *9*

At the Seashore   *14*

An Evening Conversation   *25*

The Handkerchief   *35*

An Enlightened Husband   *46*

Autumn   *69*

Winter   *85*

Fortune   *94*

Kesa and Moritō   *105*

The Death of a Disciple   *114*

O'er a Withered Moor   *127*

The Garden   *139*

The Life of a Fool   *149*

The Villa of the Black Crane   *171*

Cogwheels   *190*

Notes   227

Additional Terminology   247

Translator's Afterword   253

MANDARINS

MANDARINS

Evening was falling one cloud-covered winter's day as I boarded a Tōkyō-bound train departing from Yokosuka. I found a seat in the corner of a second-class coach, sat down, and waited absentmindedly for the whistle. Oddly enough, I was the only passenger in the carriage, which even at that hour was already illuminated. Looking out through the window at the darkening platform, I could see that it too was strangely deserted, with not even well-wishers remaining. There was only a caged puppy, emitting every few moments a lonely whimper.

It was a scene that eerily matched my own mood. Like the looming snow clouds, an unspeakable fatigue and ennui lay heavily upon my mind. I sat with my hands deep in the pockets of my overcoat, too weary even to pull out the evening newspaper.

At length the whistle blew. Ever so slightly, my feeling of gloom was lifted, and I leaned my head back against the window frame, half-consciously watching for the station to recede slowly into the distance. But then I heard the clattering of dry-weather clogs coming from the ticket gate, followed immediately by the cursing of the conductor. The door of the second-class carriage was flung open, and a young teenage girl came bursting in.

At that moment, with a shudder, the train began to lumber slowly forward. The platform pillars, passing one by one, the water carts, as if left carelessly behind, a red-capped porter, calling out his thanks to someone aboard – all this, as though with wistful hesitancy, now fell through the soot that pressed against the windows and was gone.

Finally feeling at ease, I put a match to a cigarette and raised my languid eyes to look for the first time at the girl seated on the opposite side. She wore her lusterless hair in ginkgo-leaf style. Apparently from constant rubbing of her nose and mouth with the back of her hand, her cheeks were chapped and unpleasantly red. She was the epitome of a country girl.

A grimy woolen scarf of yellowish green hung loosely down to her knees, on which she held a large bundle wrapped in cloth. In those same chilblained hands she clutched for dear life a red third-class ticket.

I found her vulgar features quite displeasing and was further repelled by her dirty clothes. Adding to my irritation was the thought that the girl was too dimwitted to know the difference between second- and third-class tickets. If only to blot her existence from my mind, I took out my newspaper, unfolded it over my lap, and began to read, still smoking my cigarette.

All at once the light from outside was eclipsed by the electric illumination within; now the badly printed letters in some column or other stood out with a strange clarity. We had entered one of the Yokosuka Line's many tunnels.

Yet the better lighting for my perusal of the pages was of no help in distracting me from my melancholy; instead I was only weighed down all the more by the myriad commonplace matters of the world: peace treaty issues, weddings, some sort of bribery scandal, death notices. For a moment after the train entered the tunnel, I had the illusion that we had somehow reversed direction, as my eyes moved almost mechanically from one tiresome article to another. At the same time, I was, despite myself, rather conscious of the girl sitting in front of me, as though she were the personification of coarse reality.

The train in the tunnel, this country girl, this newspaper laden with trivia – if they were not the very symbols of this unfathomable, ignoble, and tedious life of ours, what were they?

In disgust, I tossed aside the paper I had hardly read and again leaned my head against the window frame. My eyes closing as though I were dead, I began to doze.

Minutes later, I was startled from my half slumber and instinctively looked about me with a feeling of alarm. At some point the girl had come over to my side of the train and was now next to me, feverishly endeavoring to open the window, the glass apparently proving to be too heavy for her. At intervals, I could hear her sniffling and gasping, her chapped cheeks redder than ever.

All of this should have been enough to evoke some measure of sympathy, even in the likes of me. Yet surely she could have seen that the hillsides, their dry grass alone illuminated in the twilight, were moving inexorably closer toward the glass panes – and known that at any moment we would again be in darkness. Still, quite incomprehensibly to me, she continued her attempt to lower the closed window. I could only imagine it as sheer caprice and so inwardly nurtured my original malice. Gazing coldly at her desperate struggle as she fought with chilblained hands, I hoped that she would be forever doomed to fail.

Then, with an enormous groan, the train plunged into a tunnel, and at that very moment the window at last came down with a thud. A stream of soot-laden air came pouring in through the square opening. Instantly, the carriage was filled with a cloud of suffocating smoke. Already suffering from an impaired throat, I had not even the time to put a handkerchief to my face and was now coughing so violently that I could scarcely catch my breath. Yet the girl, without the slightest pretense of concern for my plight, had poked her head out of the window and was staring relentlessly ahead, her side-locks disheveled by the breeze sweeping through the darkness. When at last my cough had eased, I peered at the figure through the smoke-dimmed light and would surely have barked at this strange creature to shut the window, had it not been for the outside view, which now was growing ever brighter, and for the smell, borne on the cold air, of earth, dry grass, and water.

Already the train was gently gliding out of the tunnel and approaching a crossing at an impoverished *banlieue* surrounded by withered hills. Near the road lay clumps of thatch- and tile-roofed houses, each shabbier than the next. Fluttering in the dying light of the day was a white flag, perhaps being waved by a flagman. *Finally!* I thought to myself, and just then saw standing behind the barrier of that desolate crossing three red-cheeked boys pressed up against one another, so small of stature that they seemed to have been crushed under the weight of the oppressive sky, the color of their clothing as drab as these urban outskirts. Looking up to see the train as it passed, they raised their hands as one and let out with all the strength of their young voices a high-pitched cheer, its meaning quite escaping me. And at that instant the girl, the full upper half of her body leaning out the window, abruptly extended her ulcerated hands and began swinging them briskly back and forth. Five or six mandarin oranges, radiating the color of the warm sun and filling my heart with sudden joy, descended on the children standing there to greet the passing train.

Quite involuntarily, I held my breath and knew immediately the meaning of it all. This girl, perhaps leaving home now to go into service as a maid or an apprentice, had been carrying in her bosom these oranges and tossed them to her younger brothers as a token of gratitude for coming to the crossing to see her off.

Everything I had seen beyond the window – the railway crossing bathed in evening light, the chirping voices of the children, and the dazzling color of the oranges raining down on them – had passed in a twinkling of an eye. Yet the scene had been vividly and poignantly burned into my mind, and from this, welling up within me, came a strangely bright and buoyant feeling.

Elated, I raised my head and gazed at the girl with very different eyes. Without my noticing when, she had resumed her place in front of me, her chapped cheeks buried as before in her woolen scarf of yellow-green. Again she held a large bundle on her lap, her hand still clutching a third-class ticket . . . And now for the first time I was able to forget, at least for a moment, my unspeakable fatigue, my ennui, and, with that, this unfathomable, ignoble, and tedious life.

AT THE SEASHORE

1

. . . It went on raining. We finished lunch and began talking about our friends in Tōkyō, turning many a Shikishima cigarette to ashes.

We were sitting in a two-room cottage of six tatami mats each. The windows, shaded by marsh-reed blinds, looked out on a yard where nothing grew – or rather nothing other than the seashore's ubiquitous sedge, here in only scattered clumps on the sand, their spikes already drooping. Those spikes had not yet fully emerged when we first arrived, and the ones we saw then were for the most part bright green. Now they were all a vulpine brown, with drops of rain on their tips.

"Well now, I think I shall get a bit of work done."

M was sprawled out on the mats, wiping the spectacles he wore for his myopia with the sleeve of the inn's heavily starched *yukata*. The work to which he referred concerned the monthly contribution that each of us was obliged to write for our literary magazine.

He moved into the next room, while I used one of the floor cushions for a pillow and read *Nansō-Satomi-Hakkenden*. The day before I had reached the part where Shino, Genpachi, and Kobungo are going off to rescue Sōsuke.

> *Now Amazaki Terubumi reached into his bosom pocket and took out the five packets of gold dust he had prepared. Of these, he placed three on his fan and said: "Now, you three warrior dogs, each of these contains thirty ryō of gold, and though that is no great amount, I hope that it will be of use to you for the journey on which you are about to embark. Please deign to accept these, not as a parting token from me but rather as a gift from Lord Satomi."*

As I read this passage, I remembered the royalties I had received two days earlier for a manuscript: forty *sen* per page . . . In July, M and I had completed our university studies in English literature. Now we faced the task of finding a means to support ourselves. Gradually putting aside the eight dogs, I found myself considering the idea of becoming a teacher. But then it seemed I had fallen asleep and had the following brief dream:

It was, it appeared, quite late in the night. In any case, I was lying down alone in the sitting room, having closed the shutters. Someone had suddenly knocked, calling out to me: "Hello, hello?" I was aware that beyond the shutters there was a pond, but I had no idea who might be calling to me.

"Hello, hello? Please. I have something to ask of you," I heard the voice saying. I thought to myself: *Aha, it's K.* He was a class behind us, a hopeless student in the philosophy department. Without getting up, I called out in reply:

"It's no use putting on that plaintive tone for me. I suppose it's about money again."

"No, no, it's not about that. I merely wish to present to you a woman of my acquaintance."

Somehow it did not seem to be K's voice after all. It was rather that of someone genuinely concerned about me. My heart pounding, I jumped up to open the shutters. There was indeed an immense pond below the veranda, but I found neither K nor anyone else there.

For some time I gazed at the moonlit pond. The flow of seaweed told me that the tide was coming in, and now there were wavelets sparkling silver immediately before my eyes. As they edged closer to my feet, a crucian carp slowly came into view, leisurely moving its tail and fins in the transparent water.

Ah, so it was the fish that was calling me, I thought to myself with a sense of relief . . .

When I awoke, the pale light of the sun was seeping through the reed blinds at the front of the cottage. I took a basin and went down to the well in back to wash my face. Yet even when I returned, the dream lingered curiously in my mind. A half-formed thought occurred to me: *Then the crucian carp I saw in my dream is, in fact, my subliminal self!*

2

An hour later we put on our swimming caps, wrapped towels around our heads, slipped into clogs on loan from the inn, and went off to swim in the ocean, some sixty meters away. Stepping off the veranda and walking through the garden, we descended the gentle slope and immediately found ourselves on the beach.

"Do you think we can swim?"

"It seems a bit chilly today."

Even as we chattered of such things, we were at pains to avoid walking through the sedge. (We had already learned to our astonishment of the terrible itch in the calves that comes from carelessly walking through those rain-soaked weeds.) The coolness in the air did indeed preclude a dip. And yet we felt a wistful attachment to this beach in Kazusa – or rather to the waning summer.

During our first days here, there were boys and girls merrily riding the waves, and even until yesterday there had been seven or eight. Today, however, there was no one to be seen, and the red flags marking the swimming area were not flying. Now there were only the waves crashing endlessly against the vast seashore. Empty too were the reed enclosures that served as the changing area. There was only a brown dog chasing a swarm of gnats, and no sooner had we seen it than it had run off in the opposite direction.

I had taken off my clogs but was in no mood to swim. M, on the other hand, had already left his *yukata* and spectacles in the changing area, wrapped his towel over his swimming cap, tying the loose ends under his chin, and plunged into the shallows with a loud splash.

"You're going to swim after all?"

"Well, isn't that why we're here?"

M was bent forward in the water, which came up to his knees. His smiling face, tanned with the sun, was turned toward me.

"Come on in!"

"No, thank you!"

"What? I dare say you would if Enzen the Charmer were here!"

"Nonsense!"

The Charmer was a middle-school boy of fifteen or sixteen whom we had seen during our stay here and casually greeted. He was not a particularly beautiful lad; it was rather that he was possessed of a youthful freshness that made one think of a sapling tree. On an afternoon some ten days before, we had just come up from the water and thrown ourselves down on the hot sand when he arrived, likewise wet from the waves, briskly pulling behind him a plank. When he saw us lying there at his feet, he broadly smiled at us with a set of dazzling teeth.

When he was gone, M gave me a wry grin and remarked:

"Now there's one with the smile of a charmer!"[1] And so, between us, he had acquired the name.

"So you're determined not to come in?"

"Quite."

"*Quel égoiste!*"

M got himself wetter and wetter and was now gliding out to sea. Paying no further heed to him, I walked to a low dune a slight distance from the changing place. Sitting on my clogs, I tried to light a Shikishima. The wind was stronger than I thought, and the flame did not easily reach the tip.

"Hello there!"

I had not seen M return, but there he was in the shallows. He was calling to me, but unfortunately my ears could not catch his words for the incessant roar of the waves.

"What is it?"

He came and sat beside me, his *yukata* draped over his shoulders.

"Oh, I was stung by a jellyfish."

For the last several days, the jellyfish had seemed to be multiplying. In fact, the morning before last I had found myself covered with their pinprick marks, running from my left shoulder to my upper arm.

"Where?"

"On my neck. I was thinking, *Oh, they've got me!* – and then saw them all around."

"That's why I didn't go in."

"Fine talk coming from you! But now we're finally done with swimming."

The sun had bathed the shore, as far as the eye could see, in a white haze, obscuring all but the seaweed brought in on the tide. Only the shadow of a cloud would sometimes pass swiftly by. With cigarettes dangling from our lips, we paused to gaze in silence at the incoming waves.

"Have you been offered that teaching position?" asked M suddenly.

"Not yet. What about you?"

"I? I, well . . ."

As he started to speak, we were startled by laughter and the thud, thud, thud of footsteps. They belonged to two girls of similar age, in swimming suits and caps. They passed us with an indifference bordering on insolence, running straight toward the water. The suit of the one was scarlet, that of the other a tigerlike blend of black and yellow. Our eyes followed these happy, fleeting figures, as the two of us simultaneously found ourselves smiling, as though on cue.

"So they haven't left yet . . ."

For all his air of irony, there was something in his voice that betrayed a touch of emotion.

"Well then, are you going back for another dip after all?"

"I don't know. I might if she were by herself. But she's with Singesi . . ."

As with the Charmer, we had given the girl in the black-and-yellow suit a name – for her *sinnliches Gesicht*.[2]

Neither of us found the girl easy to like. And neither did we find the other one . . . No, M felt a certain interest . . . And he had no qualms about making such self-seeking suggestions as: "You take Singesi; I'll take her friend."

"Go ahead. Take a swim for her sake!"

"Yes, such a display of self-sacrifice! But she's perfectly aware that she's being watched."

"But why not?"

"Well, it does rankle a bit . . ."

Hand in hand, they were already in the water. Wave after wave sent foam and spray swirling toward their feet, but each time they invariably jumped, as though anxious not to get wet. It was a blithe and brilliant picture, a strange contrast to the desolate beach in the lingering heat of summer, a beauty indeed belonging less to the realm of humans than to that of butterflies. We listened to the sound of their wind-borne laughter and watched them as they waded away from shore.

"You have to admire them for their pluck!"

"The water's not yet over their heads."

"No, they're already . . . No, no, they're still standing."

They had long since released their hands and were moving separately out to sea. The girl in the scarlet suit had been swimming briskly onward when she suddenly stopped in the water, which came up to her breasts, and beckoned to the other, crying out in a piercing voice. Even encased in her enormous cap and at this distance, her vibrantly smiling face could still be seen.

"Jellyfish?"

"Perhaps."

Yet they went on, one behind the other, paddling ever farther into the offing. When the two dots that were their swimming caps became all that we could still see of them, we got up at last from the sand. We hardly spoke, for now we were getting hungry, and ambled back to the inn.

. . . Even the twilight was as cool as in autumn. When we had finished supper, we went again to the beach, this time in the company of our friend H, who was home for a holiday visit, and N-san, the young proprietor of the inn. We had not intended to go out for a walk together, but as it happened H and N-san each had errands to run, H to visit his uncle in a nearby village, N-san to go there himself to order a chicken coop from the local basket-maker.

The way to the village led across the shore, around the base of a high dune, and then continued on, the swimming area directly behind us. The dune naturally blocked any view of the ocean, and even the roar of the waves was muffled. There were nonetheless sparse patches of weeds, their black spikes poking out of the sand, and a sea breeze was still ceaselessly blowing.

"The plants here are not very much like sand sedge. Do you know what they call them, N-san?"

I plucked a clump that lay at my feet and handed it to him. He was dressed for the season in casual jacket and shorts.

"It isn't knotweed. I wonder what it is. H-san should know. He's a native, not like me."

We had heard that N-san had come from Tōkyō to be adopted into his wife's family and that sometime around the summer of the previous year she had abandoned home and hearth to run off with a lover.

"H-san also knows much more about fish than I do."

"Oh? Is H really so learned a scholar then? I would have thought he knew nothing other than *kendō*."

H, who was using a piece of an old bow as a walking stick, responded to the provocation with no more than a smirk.

"What about you, M-san?"

"I, I only swim."

N-san lit a cigarette, a Golden Bat, and told us the story of a stock-broker in Tōkyō, who the previous summer, while swimming, had been stung by a scorpion fish. He adamantly insisted, however, that it was preposterous to think that anything of the sort could have stung him and that instead it must have been a sea serpent.

"Are there really sea serpents?"

H was the only one to respond. He was tall and wore a swimming cap.

"Sea serpents? In the ocean here there certainly *are* sea serpents."

"Even now?"

"Yes, but they're rare."

The four of us burst out laughing. Now coming toward us were two men, fish baskets dangling from their hands. Their prey was *nagarami*, a variety of spiral shellfish. Clad in red loincloths, they were sturdy and muscular. Glistening wet from the sea, they also seemed less pitiable than simply wretched. As they passed, N-san replied to their perfunctory greeting by calling out: "Come for a bath at the inn!"

"What a dreadful occupation!" I exclaimed. It occurred to me that I myself might very well wind up becoming a diver for *nagarami*.

"Yes, dreadful indeed!" said N-san. "First, you have to swim out into the offing, then dive again and again to the bottom."

"And to make it all the worse," added H, "if you get caught in a channel, the chances are eight or nine to ten that you won't come back again."

Waving his walking stick in the air, H told us many a tale about the channels, even of the one that extends from shore for a full league and a half.

"Tell us, N-san. When was it, the matter about the ghost of the *nagarami* fisherman?"

"Last year. No, it was in the autumn, the year before last."

"There really was one?"

N-san's voice was already betraying a chuckle as he responded.

"It wasn't a ghost. But where the said ghost supposedly appeared was in a cemetery at the back of a slope that reeks of the sea, and when, to top it all, the remains of the fisherman in question came to the surface, they were covered with shrimp, so even though no one would have taken the story at face value, it was certainly an eerie one. But then finally a retired naval officer who had been keeping watch in the cemetery after dusk made a positive sighting. He pounced on the phantom, but when he took a good look, it was nothing of the sort – just a teahouse strumpet the fisherman had promised to marry. But even so, it had for a time stirred up talk of will-o'-the-wisps and ghostly voices, all in all, a total madhouse!"

"So the woman hadn't any intent to frighten people?"

"No, not in the least. She merely would go visit the grave of the fisherman around midnight and stand in front of it as though lost in a daze."

N-san's story was a splendidly appropriate comedy of errors for this seaside setting, though none of us laughed but rather, for whatever reason, merely walked on in silence.

"Well now, perhaps it's time to turn back," said M.

There had already been a lulling of the wind as he spoke; we were walking a now utterly deserted shore. It was still light enough that on the broad expanse of sand the footprints of the plovers were faintly visible. Yet even as the sea drew along the shore its vast arc of foam, stretching as far as the eye could reach, the entire horizon was slipping away into darkness.

"We shall take our leave then."

"*Sayōnara.*"

Having parted company with H and N-san, M and I made our way unhurriedly back along the chilly edge of the waves. Their roar was in our ears – and then from time to time the clear tone of the evening cicadas'[3] singing in the pine wood that lay more than three hundred meters away.

"What do you say?" I asked M. At some point, I had fallen five or six steps behind him.

"What do you mean?"

"About us going back to Tōkyō too?"

"Hmm . . . Can't say that would be a bad idea."

And then he began whistling ever so cheerily: "It's a long way to Tipperary . . ."

AN EVENING CONVERSATION

"One can't be too careful these days. Even Wada's taken up with a geisha."

Fujii, a lawyer, drained his cup of *lǎojiǔ*, and, with an exaggerated flourish, looked around at the faces of his listeners. Sitting at the table were the six of us, middle-aged men who had once lived in the same school dormitory. It was a rainy evening in June, on the second floor of the Tōtōtei in Hibiya. I need hardly say that by the time Fujii had made this remark, his cheeks, as well as our own, were ruddy with drink.

"Having made that shocking discovery," he continued to declaim, apparently warming to the subject, "I was struck by how times have changed.

"Back in the days when Wada was studying medicine, he was a *jūdō* champion, a ringleader in the room-and-board protests, a great admirer of Livingstone, and the sort of stoic who could go coatless in the dead of winter. In other words, he was quite the dashing young man, was he not? The very idea that he would become acquainted with a geisha! And apparently she's from Yanagibashi and goes by the name of Koen."

"Have you changed your drinking haunts?"

This shot from the dark came from Iinuma, a bank branch manager.

"Changed drinking haunts? Why do you ask?"

"Didn't you take him to wherever it was? Wasn't it then that he met this geisha?"

"Now let's not jump rashly to conclusions! Who said anything about *taking* Wada anywhere?"

Fujii haughtily arched his eyebrows.

"It was – let me see – what day last month? In any case, it was on a Monday or a Tuesday. I hadn't seen Wada in some time. He suggested going to Asakusa. Now, mind you, I'm not that keen on Asakusa, but as I was with an old friend, I immediately agreed. We set out in broad daylight for Rokku . . ."

"And you met her in the cinema?" I interrupted.

"*That* would have been preferable. As it happened, it was at the merry-go-round. And to make matters worse, we each wound up astride a wooden horse. Looking back, I'm struck by the absurdity of it all! I didn't suggest it, but he was so eager . . . Riding a merry-go-round isn't easy. Someone like you, Noguchi, with your weak stomach, should stay off altogether."

"We're not children. Who at our age would ride a merry-go-round?" remarked Noguchi, a university professor. He laughed scornfully, his mouth full of Sōnghuā eggs, but Fujii continued nonchalantly, glancing occasionally at Wada, a look of triumph in his eyes.

"Wada sat on a white horse; mine was red. *What* is *this*? I thought,

as we began to go around in time with the band. My rump was dancing, my eyes were spinning, and it was only quite fortuitously that I did
not go tumbling off. But then I saw that outside the railing there was a
woman in the crowd who appeared to be a geisha. With pale skin and
moist eyes, she had a strange air of melancholy about her."

"At least you were in such a state as to understand that much,"
interjected Iinuma. "Your claim to dizziness sounds a bit dubious."

"Am I not telling you what I saw in the midst of it? Her hair was, of
course, drawn up into a ginkgo-leaf bun, and she was wearing a pale-
blue striped serge kimono, with some sort of multipatterned obi. In
any case, there she stood, a woman as delicately lovely as one might
imagine in any illustration from a novel set in the demimonde.

"And now what do you suppose occurred? She happened to catch
my eye and offered me an exquisitely demure smile. *Uh-oh!* I thought
to myself, but it was already too late. We were still riding our horses,
and before I knew it, we had turned, so that all I had in front of my
red wooden mount was that blasted music band."

We all burst out laughing.

"The next time round, she smiled again – but then was gone. And
after that it was nothing but the jumping horses and the bouncing
coaches – or else the trumpeting bugles and banging drums . . . I
turned the matter over in my mind and thought that this was a fitting symbol of life. Our all-too-real humdrum existence puts us on a
merry-go-round, and when perchance we encounter 'happiness,' it
passes us by ere we can grasp it. If we really wish to seize the opportunity, we should jump off . . ."

"Jump off? Oh, surely not . . ."

This was said mockingly by Kimura, head of engineering at an
electric company.

"Don't be ridiculous!" protested Fujii. "Philosophy is philosophy;

life is life . . . But now imagine that as I was mulling it over, I came round the third time, when it suddenly dawned on me, much to my astonishment, that it was not, alas, I at whom she had smiled but rather, yes, that same room-and-board protest ringleader and Livingstone admirer, ETC. ETC: Wada Ryōhei, M.D."

"Still, it's fortunate you weren't so philosophically consistent as to leap off after all."

Normally taciturn Noguchi chimed in with his own joke. Fujii, however, was zealously forging ahead.

"And when the woman appeared before that Wada, he took great delight in bowing to her, though as he was still astride his white horse, he could only do so timorously, so that it was really only his dangling necktie that did the honors."

"Nothing but a pack of lies!"

Wada had at last broken his silence. For some time now he had been imbibing *lǎojiǔ*, a wry smile on his face.

"What? How should I be telling lies?" retorted Fujii. "And that was the least of it. When we finally got off the merry-go-round, I found Wada chatting with her, as though suddenly quite oblivious to my very existence. 'Sensei, Sensei!' she kept saying . . . And there I was, left holding the sack."

"Indeed!" said Iinuma, extending a silver spoon into the large pot of shark fin soup as he glanced toward Wada sitting next to him. "A most curious story . . . Look, old man, in light of what we've heard, I'd say that you're the one to be treating us all tonight!"

"Nonsense! That woman is the mistress of a friend of mine."

Wada was leaning on both elbows as he spat out these words. As seen from across the table, he was more swarthy than the rest of us, and his features were hardly those of an urbanite. Moreover, his closely cropped head was solid as a rock. In an interschool competition, he had once felled five opponents despite a sprained left elbow. For all of his accommodation to current fashion, with his dark suit and striped trousers, there clearly lingered something of the titan from days gone by.

"Iinuma! Is she *your* mistress?"

Fujii posed the question with a tipsy grin, though without looking Iinuma directly in the eye.

"Perhaps she is." Iinuma coolly parried the thrust and turned once more to Wada. "Who is this friend of yours?"

"The businessman Wakatsuki . . . Isn't there someone here who knows him? He graduated from Keiō, it seems, and now works in his own bank. He's about our age. He's light complexioned and has a gentle sort of look. Sports a short beard . . . In a word, a handsome man with, one may expect, a keen appreciation for the finer things of life."

As I had just been to a play with that same businessman four or five days before, I now entered the fray myself.

"Wakatsuki Minetarō? The haiku poet who goes by the nom de plume of Seigai?"

"That's right. He's published *Seigai-kushū*[1] . . . He's Koen's patron – or rather was until two months ago. They've now made a clean break of it."

"What? So this Wakatsuki fellow . . ."

"He and I were classmates in middle school," said Wada.

"Well, well," exclaimed Fujii merrily, there's more to you than I thought. Quite behind our backs, you and your middle-school chum have been off plucking the flowers and climbing the willow tree!"

"Nonsense! I met her when she came to the university hospital. I was simply doing Wakatsuki a bit of a favor. She was having some sort of operation for sinusitis . . ."

Wada took another sip of *lǎojiǔ*, a strangely contemplative look in his eyes.

"But, you know, that woman is an interesting one . . ."

"Are you smitten with her?" asked Kimura, quietly teasing him.

"Perhaps I am indeed – and perhaps not in the least. But what I should like to talk about is her relationship with Wakatsuki."

Having provided his remarks with this preface, Wada issued what was for him an unusual burst of oratorical eloquence.

"Just as Fujii has said, I recently ran into Koen. I was surprised as we talked to learn that she had ended her liaison with Wakatsuki some two months before. When I asked her why, she gave me nothing that could be called a reply, though she said with a lonely sort of smile that she had never been the person of refinement that Wakatsuki is.

"I had already pried enough and so took my leave. But then just yesterday . . . in the afternoon . . . It was raining, as you all remember, and just as it was coming down hardest, I received a note from Wakatsuki, asking me whether I might come round for a bite to eat. Having some time on my hands as well, I arrived early at his house and found him, as always, in his stylish six-mat study, quietly reading.

"I am, as you see, a barbarian, with not the slightest notion of refinement. Yet whenever I enter that library of his, I get some sort of inkling of what it's like to live the artistic life. For one thing, an old scroll hangs in the alcove – and the flower vases are always full. There are shelves of books in Japanese and, next to these, shelves of books in Western languages. To top it off, next to an elegant desk, he sometimes displays a *shamisen*. And then, of course, there is Wakatsuki himself, cutting a dashingly sophisticated figure, as though having stepped forth from some sort of up-to-date *ukiyoé* print. Yesterday too he was wearing a strange garment, and when I asked him about it, what do you think he called it? A *chanpa*! Now I can lay claim to a wide circle of friends, but I don't suppose there is anyone other than Wakatsuki who wears such a thing . . . Anyway, that certainly typifies his entire way of living.

"As we were filling each other's cups before dining, he told me about Koen. She had, it appeared, another lover, but that was, he said, not particularly surprising. No, but the man in question, it turned out, was a lowly ballad recitation apprentice.

"Hearing this, my friends, you will find it impossible not to laugh at Koen's folly. At the time, not even a bitter smile would have passed my own face.

"You will, of course, not be aware of it, but Koen over the last three years has benefited greatly from what Wakatsuki has done for her. He provided not only for her mother but also for her younger sister. He saw to it that she was trained in reading and writing, in the traditional performing arts, and in whatever happened to strike her fancy. Koen had been granted a dancing name by one of the masters. She is also said to be preeminent among Yanagibashi geisha for the *nagauta*. She can compose *hokku* and is a skillful *kana* calligrapher in the Chikage style. And that is again thanks to Wakatsuki . . . As I knew all this, I could not help feeling, I am sure more than any of you, utterly dumbfounded by the absurdity of it all.

"Wakatsuki told me that he had given no great thought to the breaking of ties with the woman. And yet he said that he had spared no effort in supporting her education and shown understanding for whatever it was she wished to do. He had sought to train her as a woman of broad interests and tastes . . . Such had been his hopes, and now they had been dashed. If she had to take up with a man, it should hardly be a balladeer. If even after all manner of devotion to performance art, a person's fundamental character has not improved, it is truly a loathsome thing . . .

"Wakatsuki went on to say that over the last half year, the woman had also become prone to hysterical fits. For a time, she would exclaim – 'Today I have played the *shamisen* for the last time!' – or some such and then burst into childish tears. And when again he asked why she was weeping, she would argue quite irrationally that he did not love her and that that was why he was having her trained in music and dancing. At such times, she gave no indication of hearing anything he had to say but instead would merely bitterly and endlessly accuse him of heartlessness. Eventually, of course, such paroxysms would cease, the entire episode made a laughing matter.

"Wakatsuki also said that he had heard that Koen's lover, the ballad singer, was an unmanageable ruffian. When a waitress in a chicken-brochette restaurant with whom he had a liaison took up with some-one new, he seems to have got himself into quite a scuffle with the woman, causing her considerable injury. Wakatsuki had also heard various ugly rumors about the man: that he had been involved in a failed double-suicide pact, that he had eloped with the daughter of an arts teacher . . . What possible discernment on Koen's part, he asked, could be seen in her willingness to become involved with someone like this . . . ?

"As I have said, I could not help feeling disgusted at Koen's dissolute conduct. And yet as I listened to Wakatsuki, I felt a growing sympathy for her. Of course, it may well be that in him she had a patron of a sophistication that is quite rare in today's world. And yet did he not himself admit that separating from her was of no consequence to him? Even if we assume that in saying so he was endeavoring to spare himself humiliation, it is clear that he felt no fierce passion for her.

Now 'fierce' is the word to describe the balladeer, who, out of sheer odium for the heartlessness of a woman, inflicted serious bodily injury on her. Putting myself in Koen's place, I think it perfectly natural that she would fall for the vulgar but passionate balladeer over the cultured but phlegmatic Wakatsuki. The fact that he had her trained in all the arts is evidence that he had no love for her. In all of this, I saw something more than hysteria: between the two, I detected a chasmic difference in perception.

"Yet I do not intend to bestow for her sake my blessing on the liaison with the balladeer. No one can say whether or not she will achieve happiness . . . But if unhappiness is the result, then the curse should fall not on the other man but rather on Seigai the Sophisticate for driving her into his arms.

"Now Wakatsuki, like the men of the world he personifies, may, as individuals, be charming and lovable. They understand Bashō; they understand Tolstoy. They understand Ike no Taiga and Mushanokōji Saneatsu. They understand Karl Marx. Yet what is the result? Of fierce love, the joy of fierce creativity, or fierce moral passion they are ignorant. All in all, they know nothing of the sheer intensity of spirit that can render this world sublime. And if they are marked by a mortal wound, they surely also contain a pernicious poison. One of its properties is direct, enabling it to transform ordinary human beings into sophisticates; another works by way of reaction, making them all the more common. Someone such as Koen is a case in point, is she not?

"As we know from time immemorial, thirst will drive one to drink even from muddy water. That is to say, if Koen had not been in Wakatsuki's milieu, she might not have wound up with the balladeer.

"If, on the other hand, she finds happiness . . . Well now, I suppose to the extent that she has her new lover in place of Wakatsuki, she has already found it. What was it that Fujii said just now? We all find ourselves riding the same merry-go-round of life and, at some moment as we turn, encounter 'happiness,' only to have it pass us by in the very moment that we reach out for it. If such is truly our desire, we should jump off . . . Koen has, as it were, dared to do just that. Such fierce joy and sorrow is something that the likes of Wakatsuki and other men of the world do not know. As I contemplate life's value, I shall willingly spit on one hundred Wakatsukis, even as I honor and revere a single Koen.

"What say you all to that?"

Wada's tipsy eyes shone round the silent room, but Fujii at some point had put his head down on the table and was now blissfully and soundly asleep.

THE HANDKERCHIEF

Hasegawa Kinzō, professor in the Faculty of Law at Tōkyō Imperial University, was sitting in a rattan chair on the veranda, reading Strindberg's *Dramaturgy*. Such might come as something of a surprise to readers when informed of the professor's specialized field of research: colonial policy. He was, however, renowned as an educator as well as a scholar, and so to the extent that leisure allowed, he took it upon himself at least to glance through works which though not immediately useful to his discipline were nonetheless in some way relevant to the thoughts and feelings of today's students. Being at the time the headmaster of a higher professional school, he had even endeavored to peruse Oscar Wilde's *De Profundis* and *Intentions*, his sole motivation being their popularity among his pupils.

Thus, there would really have been no cause for astonishment in seeing him absorbed in the world of modern European plays and actors. Indeed, among his charges there were not only those who wrote commentaries on Ibsen, Strindberg, and Maeterlinck but even some passionately seeking to follow in the footsteps of these up-to-date dramatists and to devote themselves to the theater.

Whenever the professor finished a chapter, each filled with penetrating insights, he would put the book with its yellow cloth cover down on his lap and throw a desultory glance at the Gifu lantern that hung on the veranda. Curiously, his mind would then wander from Strindberg to his wife, with whom he had gone to buy it.

The professor had studied in America, where he had first met her; naturally enough, she was an American. Yet she, no less than he, was enamored of Japan and of the Japanese people. She was particularly attached to Japan's exquisitely wrought handicrafts. It would thus seem reasonable to assume that the lantern was more a reflection of his wife's taste than of his own.

Such moments invariably set him to thinking – about his wife and about the lantern as representative of Japanese civilization. It was his belief that for all the considerable material progress made over the preceding half century, there had been almost nothing that one could truly call spiritual advancement. Indeed, in some sense there had been degeneration. It was thus, he thought, urgently incumbent upon the nation's contemporary thinkers to consider a remedy. He had further concluded that such could only lie in traditional *bushidō*. This should not, he insisted, be viewed as simply the moral code of a blinkered island people. On the contrary, it contained elements that were consistent with the spirit of Christianity in the nations of the West. If *bushidō* could provide a beacon for contemporary Japanese thought, it would not only contribute to Japan's spiritual culture; it would also facilitate greater understanding between Western peoples and the Japanese and thereby promote the cause of international peace . . . In this respect, he often imagined himself becoming a bridge between

East and West. To such a scholar, it was in no way unpleasant to bear in mind that his wife, the lantern, and the Japanese civilization were all quite in harmony with one another.

As he repeatedly savored his satisfaction, it slowly dawned on Professor Hasegawa that even as he was reading, his attention was indeed straying from Strindberg. Feeling somewhat annoyed at this, he shook his head and again single-mindedly fixed his eyes on the fine print before him. Just where he had left off, he found this passage:

> "When an actor discovers an appropriate means for conveying a perfectly ordinary emotion, one that gains him success, he comes, gradually and habitually, to resort to it, regardless of its suitability, both because of the facility he enjoys with it and because of that same success. This is what is called a Manier." [1]

Professor Hasegawa was by nature indifferent to the arts, especially to drama. He had not even been to the Japanese theater more times than he could readily count. A student of his had once written a story in which Baikō was mentioned. Yet for all the erudition of which the professor boasted, the name was quite unknown to him. When the opportunity arose, he took the student aside and asked him: "Who is this Baikō?"

The young man, dressed in a pleated *hakama*, replied courteously.

"Baikō? Why, he is currently playing the role of Misao in the tenth act of the *Taikōki* at the Marunouchi Imperial Theater."

Understandably then, the professor had utterly no opinion concerning the pithy criticisms that Strindberg had contributed to the discussion of dramaturgy. His interest was limited to mental associations with those few theater pieces he had seen while studying abroad. He was, so to speak, hardly different from those secondary-school English teachers who read the scripts of George Bernard Shaw for the sole purpose of finding idiomatic expressions. Yet an interest, however imperfect, is still an interest.

Readers will readily imagine the length of that early summer afternoon when told that the Gifu lantern suspended from the ceiling on the veranda was still unlit and that Professor Hasegawa Kinzō was still sitting in his rattan chair, reading Strindberg. This should by no means suggest that he was suffering from boredom. Any reader inclined to think so would be willfully assigning an all too cynical interpretation to the writer's intentions.

In any case, the professor was obliged to abandon his reading when the maid interrupted his refined pursuits by announcing a visitor. However long the day, it would seem that a professor's work is never done.

Professor Hasegawa laid his book down and glanced at the small calling card the maid had brought. Imprinted on ivory paper was the name Nishiyama Atsuko. She appeared to be no one he had met before, but as he associated with a wide range of people, he took the precaution, as he got up, of searching his mental name register. Even so, he could not picture a face to match a single entry. Uneasily, he placed the card between the pages of Strindberg's *Dramaturgy* as a provisional bookmarker, placed the volume on his chair, straightened his summer kimono of Meisen silk, and glanced once more at the Gifu lantern, now directly in front of his nose.

Now it is certainly the general rule that the host who keeps his guest waiting feels greater impatience than the waiting guest. Moreover, it hardly needs to be said that Professor Hasegawa was at all times conscientious, even on this day in regard to a woman visitor he did not know.

At last, with conscious timing, he entered the drawing room. No sooner had he released the doorknob than a woman in her forties stood up from the chair on which she had been sitting. She was of a refinement that was well beyond the competence of the professor to measure. Over her blue-gray summer kimono she wore a black *haori* of silk gauze, open slightly in the front to reveal a coldly glistening, rhombic obi pin of nephrite. Though he was usually insensitive to such trivialities, he noted that her hair was arranged in *marumage* style. With her round, quintessentially Japanese face and amber complexion, she had a wise, motherly air about her. A single glance was enough to suggest to him that he might have seen her before.

"Hasegawa," he said affably with a bow. He thought that if he greeted her in this manner, she would remind him of where, if ever, they had previously met.

"I am the mother of Nishiyama Ken'ichirō," she replied in a clear voice, and bowed politely in return.

Now he recognized the name. Nishiyama Ken'ichirō was a student of his. Though specializing, he was fairly certain, in German law, he was among those who had written essays for him on Ibsen and Strindberg. Since his matriculation, he had taken an interest in philosophical trends and had often come to consult with him. Then after the young man's admission to the university hospital for peritonitis in the spring, he had gone to visit once or twice when other business took him in that direction. It was no coincidence that he seemed to recognize the woman's face, for she and that spirited youth, with his handsomely thick eyebrows, bore an amazing likeness to each other – as though, to fall back on the old saying, they were two gourds from the same row.

"Ah, yes, Nishiyama-kun's . . . I see . . ."

Half muttering as though to himself as he nodded his confirmation of this, he pointed to a chair on the other side of a small table.

The lady first apologized for the sudden visit, then, having bowed again, accepted his invitation and sat down. As she did so, she took from her sleeve pocket a white object that appeared to be a handkerchief. Seeing this, he immediately offered her a Korean fan that lay on the table and then took his own seat across from her.

"You have a most pleasant house," she remarked, looking about the room in what appeared to be a somewhat forced manner.

"Oh, it's large enough," he replied, accustomed to such conversational conventions. "I'm afraid we have left it quite unattended."

At this moment, the maid brought iced tea. He had her place the glass in front of his guest and then turned without delay to the subject at hand.

"And how is Nishiyama-kun? Have you any news to report of him?"

"Yes."

The woman fell silent for a moment as she modestly crossed her hands on her lap. She then spoke evenly and matter-of-factly.

"As it happens, it is regarding that son of mine that I am now imposing on you. I regret to say that it has all come to naught, though I thank you for all the trouble you took on his behalf while he was still studying . . ."

Thinking his visitor too reserved to drink the tea set before her and not wishing to appear an aggressive but somehow at the same time halfhearted host, he had just resolved to set an example by sipping his own rather than risk appearing importunate. The edge of the cup had not yet touched his soft mustache when her words fell upon his ears. Quite apart from his consternation at hearing of the young man's death was the momentary concern: should he or should he not now drink his tea?

He could not, however, go on holding the cup indefinitely. In a single gulp he emptied half of the contents. Knitting his eyebrows ever so slightly, he said in a choked voice: "What a pity!"

"...While in the hospital he often spoke of you, and so it is that I have presumed to interrupt you in all your work to inform you of this. Again, I express my gratitude."

"No, please . . . ," he replied glumly, setting down his teacup and picking up the blue waxed fan. "So this was the unfortunate end to it . . . He showed such promise . . . I failed to go to the hospital again and simply assumed that he was on the mend . . . And now . . . When was it?"

"The seventh-day observance[2] was yesterday."

"So he was still in the hospital when . . . ?"

"Yes."

"I had no idea!"

"All was done that could be done, so that there is nothing to do but accept it. Yet I cannot help lamenting that having come so far . . ."

As the professor was engaged in this exchange, he became aware of something quite extraordinary: there was nothing in her attitude or behavior that would suggest that she was speaking of the death of her own son. She spoke in a normal tone of voice, without a tear in her eyes, and the corners of her mouth even showed a trace of a smile.

To judge from her outward appearance, without hearing her words, no one would have assumed that she was engaged in anything other than everyday talk of household affairs. This he found baffling.

. . . Many years before, while he was studying in Germany, Wilhelm I, father of the present Kaiser, had died. Not being greatly affected by the news, which he heard while sitting in his favorite coffee shop, he later returned to his lodgings, his cane under his arm and a cheerful expression on his face. He had scarcely opened the door when two of the children living there threw their arms about his neck and burst into tears. One of them, a girl of about twelve, was wearing a brown jacket; the other, a boy of about nine, was dressed in navy-blue knee breeches. The professor, who was quite fond of children, stroked their light-colored hair and earnestly tried to console them:

"What has happened?" he asked them repeatedly, but they only went on weeping, until between sniffles they exclaimed:

"They say that our beloved grandfather, His Majesty the Emperor, has died!"

The professor was amazed that sadness at the passing of the head of state should affect even children. Yet it was not merely the matter of the bond between the imperial house and the people that gave him pause to think. Since his first experience of living abroad, he had often been struck by how readily and openly Westerners manifested their emotions. Once again, as a Japanese and a firm believer in *bushidō*, he was astounded. He had never succeeded in putting aside the mélange of suspicion and sympathy he had felt at the time. And yet he was now mystified by something quite the opposite – by this woman who did not weep.

Immediately in the wake of this first discovery came a second. The topic of their conversation had moved to details of the deceased youth's daily life and was on the verge of shifting back to general reminiscences when the professor's fan happened to slip from his hand, falling immediately to the parquet floor. The pace of their exchange naturally being not so intense as to permit no interruption, he leaned forward in his chair to retrieve it.

The fan lay under the table, next to the lady's split-toed socks, hidden in the house slippers she now wore. And now by chance the professor's eye caught the handkerchief clutched in the hands that were still resting on her knees. This by itself was, of course, without significance. But in that same instant he also saw that her hands were violently trembling and that, perhaps in a desperate effort to suppress this turbulent manifestation of her inner feelings, she was pulling at the handkerchief so tightly that she seemed close to tearing it. The embroidered edge of this wrinkled piece of silk cloth pinched between her lithe fingers was shaking as though stirred by a light wind. Despite the smile on her face, her entire frame had from the beginning been convulsed with weeping.

The professor picked up the fan and raised his head, but his face bore a very different and most complex expression. Somewhat theatrically overplayed, it reflected pious circumspection at a sight he ought not to have witnessed, mixed with satisfaction at his own awareness of the same.

"I have no children of my own, but I can well understand your anguish." He said this in a low, emotion-filled voice, throwing his head back with an exaggerated flourish, as though he had just experienced a blinding flash of light.

"I am grateful for your words," she replied, "but there is nothing that can bring back what has gone."

She bowed her head slightly, her buoyant face still radiating the same abundant smile.

Two hours later, having taken a bath, finished his evening meal, and nibbled on some after-dinner cherries, the professor settled comfortably into his rattan chair. The drifting twilight of the long summer evening lingered; the glass doors of the broad veranda had been left open, with no sign of falling night. The professor had been reclining there for some time, his legs crossed and his head leaned back against the chair, absently staring in the dim light at the red tassel of the Gifu lantern. In his hand he held the book by Strindberg, but he seemed not to have read another single page of it . . . And such was no wonder:

his mind was still preoccupied with the nobility displayed by Madame Nishiyama Atsuko.

Over dinner he had told his wife the entire story and praised the mother of Nishiyama-kun as an exponent of Japanese *bushidō* among women. His wife, with her great love for Japan and the Japanese people, no doubt lent a sympathetic ear. The professor himself was pleased to note how ardently she was listening. His wife, Madame Nishiyama, and the Gifu lantern . . . It now occurred to him that the three formed a sort of moral and ethical backdrop.

The professor had been immersed in such pleasant retrospection for some indeterminate time when he remembered that he had been asked to write an article for a magazine soliciting contributions to a series entitled "Thoughts for Today's Youth"; the topic was general morality, the writers being prominent figures from all over Japan. He resolved to respond immediately that he would relate his experience of today.

He paused to scratch his head, using the hand that had held the book he had been neglecting. He now opened it again and looked at the page he had been reading, marked by the woman's calling card. At that moment the maid came in to light the lantern, so that he had little difficulty making out the finely printed letters. Though no longer in a mood to read, his eye happened to fall on one particular passage. Strindberg had written:

"In my youth, one told a story, perhaps originating in Paris, of Madame Heiberg's handkerchief and her 'double plays,' whereby she tore it, even as she smiled. Such we now call mätzchen . . ."[3]

The professor laid the book down on his knee. Between the pages, Madame Nishiyama Atsuko's calling card was still there, but his thoughts were no longer on her; for that matter, they were no longer on his wife or on Japanese civilization. Something beyond his ken had threatened the tranquil harmony of those three elements. Needless to say, Strindberg's critical comment on theatrical performance was distinct from the issues of practical morality. There were nonetheless implications in what he had just read that impinged on his *après-bain* serenity. *Bushidō* and its *Manier* . . .

The professor shook his head several times, as though displeased. Then, without raising his head, he once more looked upward to gaze at the bright Gifu lantern and the grasses of autumn painted upon it.

AN ENLIGHTENED HUSBAND

When was it now? On a cloudy afternoon, I had gone to a museum in Ueno to see an exhibition of early Meiji-era culture. I moved methodically from room to room until I came to the final display: engravings dating back to the period. In front of glass-enclosed shelves stood an elderly gentleman looking at worn copper-block etchings. Slender, with an air of fragile elegance about him, he was dressed entirely in black, with neatly creased trousers and a stylish bowler. I immediately recognized him as Viscount Honda, to whom I had been introduced at a gathering some four or five days earlier. I started to approach him but then momentarily hesitated, unable to decide whether to greet him, for I had known from before that his was a personality disinclined to social relations. Then, however, as though having heard my footsteps, he slowly turned toward me, a smile flitting briefly across lips draped with a half-white mustache. "Well, well," he said gently, slightly lifting his hat. Feeling somewhat relieved, I wordlessly acknowledged the salutation and timidly made my way to him.

In his hollow cheeks there lingered, like the last glimmerings of evening light, traces of the handsome features that had been his in the prime of youth. At the same time, it was a face over which a pensive shadow fell, a reflection, unusual for a man of the aristocracy, of inner suffering. I remembered staring on the day of our first encounter, just as I was doing now, at his large pearl tiepin, a dismal light shining out of a sea of black, as though it were the heart of the viscount himself.

"What do you think of this etching? It is a map of the Tsukiji settlement, is it not? A brilliantly done sketch, wouldn't you say? The contrast between light and shadow is quite extraordinary."

He spoke in a soft voice, gesturing with the silver knob of his slender cane toward the enclosed prints. I nodded my head.

Tōkyō Bay engraved with micaceous waves; flag-waving steamships; foreigners, men and women, walking the streets; pine trees à la Hiroshige, their branches reaching toward the sky beyond Occidental-style buildings . . . This eclectic blend of East and West, in both subject and technique, exemplified the beautiful harmony that characterized the art of the early Meiji era, a harmony now forever lost, not only from our art but also from everyday life in the capital.

I again nodded my head, remarking that the plan of the Tsukiji settlement interested me both as an etching and for the heightened sense of nostalgia it evoked, recalling "modern enlightenment": two-seat rickshaws, decorated with a Chinese lion and a peony, competing with glass-plate photographs of geishas . . . Viscount Honda smiled as he listened but even now was stepping quietly from the display and slowly moving on to the next: *ukiyoé* by Taiso Yoshitoshi.

"Well then, look at this: Kikugorō in Western dress and Hanshirō wearing a ginkgo-leaf-shaped wig, just as they are about to perform a tragic last scene beneath the light of a lantern moon. It recalls the times all the more . . . It appears, does it not, with such vividness, Edo and Tōkyō indistinguishably blended, as though night and day had formed a single era!"

Whatever his current aversion to further social intercourse, I was aware that Viscount Honda, having been sent abroad for study, had earned an oft-lauded reputation, both within the halls of power and among the people, as a man of great talent. As I now stood listening to him in this nearly deserted exhibition room, surrounded by those glass-encased prints and etchings, I was thus struck by how fitting his words were – indeed, all too fitting. At the same time, this very feeling engendered within me something of a counter-sentiment, so that I hoped he would end his remarks and allow us to move our discussion from times past to the general development of *ukiyoé*. But with that same silver knob on his cane he continued to point to one print after another, commenting as ever in a low voice:

"When I find myself looking at such prints, that era of three or four decades ago appears before me as if it were yesterday. It is as if I might open the newspaper and find an article about a ball held at the Rokumeikan. To tell you the truth, ever since entering this display room, I have had the feeling that all of those from that time have come to life again and, though invisible to us, are here walking to and fro . . . And those phantoms sometimes put their mouths to our ears and whisper of days gone by . . . That queer idea continues to haunt me. Particularly as I see Kikugorō in Western clothes, I almost have the impulse to apologize for my long silence, for, you see, he closely resembles a friend of mine. It is a nostalgia mixed with a sense of the macabre. How would it be? . . . If you would not mind terribly, I should like to tell you something about him."

Viscount Honda spoke in an agitated tone, deliberately looking away from me, as though uncertain of my response. At that moment I remembered that on first meeting him some days before, the acquaintance who had gone to the trouble of introducing us had said, "He is a writer. If you have any sort of interesting story, please relate it to him."

Even if that had not transpired, I was now so caught up in the viscount's sighs of longing for things past that I had already wished it possible to ride a horse-drawn carriage with him into lively avenues lined with stylish red-brick buildings, enshrouded in the mists of lost time. I bowed my head and happily agreed to his proposal.

"Ah, well then, let us go over there . . ."

Complying with his suggestion, I followed him to a bench in the middle of the room, where we sat down. We were alone, surrounded only by the glass cases and the rows of antiquated copper-block etchings and *ukiyoé*, all looking rather forlorn in the cold light of the cloudy sky. The viscount rested his chin on the knob of his cane and gazed about the room, as though surveying a catalog of his own memories. At last, however, he turned toward me and began to speak in a subdued voice.

"My friend's name was Miura Naoki; I happened to make his acquaintance on the ship that brought me back from France. We were the same age, twenty-five years old at the time. Like Yoshitoshi's Kikugorō, he was fair-complexioned and slender-faced, his long hair parted in the middle. He was indeed the epitome of early Meiji culture. Over the course of the long voyage we found ourselves on quite friendly terms, and on our return to Japan the bond had become such that we would hardly let a week go by without one of us visiting the other.

"Miura's parents, it seems, had been large-scale landowners in the Shitaya area. When they died, one after the other, just as he was on his way to France, he would, as their only son, have already become a man of considerable means. By the time I knew him, he was favorably situated, performing a few nominal duties at a certain bank but otherwise enjoying an unbroken life of idle pleasure. Thus, from the moment he returned to Japan, he lived in the mansion he had inherited, located near Hyappongui in Ryōgoku, where, having built an elegant new Western-style study, he basked in luxury.

"Even as I speak, I have that room as vividly before my eyes as one of the etchings over there. The French windows overlooking the Great River, the white ceiling with its gold fringe, the red chairs and sofa covered in morocco, the portrait of Napoleon on the wall, the large, engraved ebony bookcase, and the marble fireplace, on which stood a mirror and his late father's beloved pine bonsai . . . There was a sense of antique newness about it all, an almost sepulchral splendor. Or, to describe it in another way, it was like a musical instrument that is out of tune – and so very much a library of its time. And when I tell you how Miura was ensconced under the portrait of Napoleon, wearing a kimono suit made of Yūki silk with double collars and reading Victor Hugo's *Orientales*, you will see how the scene was all the more from the copperplate etchings there across the room. Hmm . . . Now that I think of it, I believe I even remember sometimes looking out on passing white sails so immense that they filled the French windows.

"Though Miura lived extravagantly, he was, in contrast to other young men of his age, not the least inclined to venture into the licensed quarters of Shinbashi or Yanagibashi, preferring to shut himself up every day in his newly constructed library, absorbed in reading more suitable to a young retiree than to, let us say, a banker. Of course, such was in part the consequence of his frail health, which permitted no deviation from regular and wholesome habits. It was also, however, a reflection of his character, which, in direct opposition to the materialism of the times, naturally inclined him, with abnormal intensity, toward pure idealism and thus to the acceptance of his solitary existence. Indeed, Miura, otherwise the model of the modern, enlightened gentleman, differed from the mood of the age only in his idealistic disposition, and in that he somewhat resembled the political dreamers of a generation before.

"Let me tell you, for example, of going with him one day to the theater to see a dramatic presentation of the Jinpūren Rebellion. As I recall, the curtain had closed on Ōno Teppei's ritual suicide, when Miura suddenly turned to me and asked, a serious expression on his face: 'Can you feel sympathy for them?'

"As a proper returnee from study abroad, I was inclined at the time to loathe anything smacking of the discredited past and so icily responded: 'No, I cannot. It seems to me a matter of course that those who fomented insurrection all because of an ordinance forbidding the wearing of swords should have brought about their own destruction.'

"Miura shook his head with an air of dissatisfaction: 'Their cause may have been mistaken, but their willingness to die for it deserves sympathy – and more.'

"To this I retorted with a laugh: 'Well then, would you not begrudge throwing away your one life on the childish dream of turning the Meiji generation back to the Divine Age?'

"Even so, his own reply was both serious and decisive: 'I could wish for nothing more than to die for a childish dream in which I truly believed.'

"At the time, I paid little heed to his words, taking them to be no more than fragments of ephemeral conversation. I now know on reflection that in them lay, coiled like hidden smoke, the shadow of the piteous fate that awaited him down the years. But I must proceed step-by-step, in the natural sequence of the story.

"In any case, Miura was a man who clung to his principles, even in the matter of marriage. He had no qualms about declining even the most promising offers that came his way, having made clear that he would not wed without *amour*. Moreover, his was no common understanding of the term, so that even when he met an eligible young lady who quite struck his fancy, it never led to any talk of eventual matrimony, as he would remark to the effect: 'My feelings are somehow still muddled.'

"Even from my vantage point as a disinterested third party, I found it quite vexing and so for his own good would occasionally resort to meddling: 'To examine the nooks and crannies of one's heart, as you do, should make it all but impossible to live a normal life. You must simply resign yourself to a world that does not conform to your ideals and content yourself with a less than perfect match.'

"But Miura would only give me a pitying look and say quite dismissively: 'If that were so, I should not have endured so many years as a bachelor.'

"Yet though able to ignore a friend's admonitions, he had also to contend with his relatives, who, mindful of his frail health, could not help being concerned that he might not produce an heir. They had apparently gone so far as to encourage him at the very least to take a concubine.[1] Needless to say, Miura was not inclined to give heed to such advice. Indeed, the very word disgusted him, and he would often catch my ear to remark derisively: 'For all our talk about modern enlightenment, Japan is still quite openly a land of kept women.'

"Thus, for the first two or three years after his return from France, he devoted himself to reading, with Napoleon as his sole companion. Not even those of us who were his friends could speculate concerning his prospects for a *mariage d'amour*.

"Meanwhile, I had been dispatched to spend some time on government matters in Korea. I had not been there a month, having just become accustomed to my new quarters in Keijō, when, lo and behold, I received a marriage announcement from Miura.

"You can well imagine my astonishment. Yet I could not but be amused as well as surprised at the thought that he had at last found his heart's desire.

"The content of the message could not have been simpler: nuptial arrangements had been concluded between Miura Naoki and one Fujii Katsumi, the daughter of a purveyor to the imperial household. According to the letter that followed, he had taken a walk to Hagidera in Yanagishima when he happened to meet an antiquarian who had frequented Miura's mansion on business. With him on his visit to the temple were a father and daughter. As the four were strolling through the precincts, Miura and the young woman had quite spontaneously fallen in love.

"The gate of the temple in those days still had its straw-thatched roof, and in the middle of the bush clover is even now a stone monument on which Bashō's famous verse is inscribed:

> *Gracefully alike:*
> *Traveler and bush clover,*
> *Damp with autumn rain*

"Such elegant surroundings were undoubtedly the perfect setting for this juxtaposition of intelligence and beauty. Nevertheless, the idea of Miura having been so smitten – the self-professed epitome of the modern gentleman, who never went out without donning his tailor-made Parisian suit – suggested much too conventional a pattern. Reading the announcement alone had brought a smile to my lips, as though I had been subjected to a veritable tickling.

"As you may readily suppose, it was the antiquarian who managed all the arrangements. Fortunately, someone was found to act as a pro forma matchmaker for this sudden fait accompli, and with that, all proceeded smoothly to their marriage in the autumn of that year.

"I hardly need to tell you that the newlyweds lived happily. What particularly amused me, even as I felt a twinge of envy, was the buoyancy and cheerfulness emanating, to judge from subsequent letters informing me of his latest news, from a man nearly entirely transformed from the dispassionate, deskbound scholar he had been.

"I have kept all of those letters, and whenever I read them one by one, it is as though I see his smiling face before me. With a childlike joy, he persevered in his missives, telling in great detail of his daily life. The morning glories he had attempted to cultivate that year had died . . . He had been requested to make a donation to a Ueno orphanage . . . Most of his library had mildewed during the rainy season . . . His rickshaw puller had suffered an infection . . . He had gone to see a performance of Occidental jugglers and sleight-of-hand artists at the Miyakoza Theater . . . There had been a fire in Kuramae. One could go on endlessly . . . Yet, in all of this, he seemed to have found the greatest joy in commissioning the artist Gozeta Hōbai to paint a portrait of his wife. This he put on the wall to replace Napoleon, and I myself later saw it.

"Madame Katsumi had been portrayed in profile, standing in front of a full-length mirror; with her hair swept back in a Western-style bun, she was wearing a black kimono embroidered in gold thread and holding a bouquet of roses in her hand. Yet though I did indeed see that portrait, I was never to see the buoyant and cheerful Miura . . ."

Viscount Honda uttered a faint sigh and was silent for a moment. I had been listening intently but now involuntarily threw him an anxious look, as his words gave me reason to wonder whether by the time of his return from Keijō, his friend Miura was no longer living. He appeared immediately to perceive this and in response slowly shook his head.

"I do not mean that during my year's absence Miura died, only that when I saw him again he was, though still self-composed, inclined toward pensiveness. I could see this already at Shinbashi Station, where he had come to meet me, as I cordially took his hand to signal the end of our long separation. No, perhaps I should say that I was struck instead by what seemed to be an excessive equanimity. In fact, such was my feeling that something was amiss that no sooner had I seen his face than I exclaimed: 'What is it? Are you ill?'

"For his part, he appeared quite taken aback by my concern and assured me that both he and his wife were in the best of health. I thought to myself that, after all, the mere space of a year, whatever the effects of a *mariage d'amour*, his fundamental character could not have changed so radically. With that, I put my worry aside by saying jocularly: 'It must have been an odd refraction of the light that made me think that your facial coloring was not what it should be.'

"It took two or three months more for me to discern little by little that here there was nothing to be dismissed with laughter, that behind the melancholic mask lay a terrible anguish. But now I am once again getting ahead of the story. To proceed properly, I must tell you something about his wife.

"I first met her shortly after my return, when Miura invited me to dine with them at their home along the riverbank. Though I had heard that they were approximately the same age, she would have appeared to anyone, perhaps because she was so small and slender, to be several years younger than he.

"She had rich eyebrows and a round face, with a fresh and rosy complexion. That evening she wore a classic kimono, decorated, as I remember, with traditional images of butterflies and birds and secured with a satin obi. To resort to the thinking of the time, I should say that there was something about her that suggested *le haut niveau*.[2]

And yet when I compared her with the person I had imagined as Miura's bride, the very personification of his *amour*, I sensed a vague discrepancy. I say 'vague' – for I could not explain even to myself the source of this intuition.

"The shadows that fell on my expectations were no more than the flickering thoughts that had passed through my mind on various encounters, including that initial reunion with Miura and, of course, the evening spent together; they were certainly not such as to dampen the exuberance with which I congratulated the couple. On the contrary, I could only be filled with admiration at the sheer vivaciousness of his wife, as we lingered at the table, sitting around the light of the kerosene lamp.

"Her repartee was as swift and sure as the proverbial reverberations of a tolling bell. 'Okusan,' I was even moved to exclaim in all seriousness, 'you really should have been born in France rather than Japan!'

"'Well, you see now,' interjected her husband, sipping at his cup, 'isn't this just what I've long been telling you?' This he said to his wife, as though gently teasing her, but it cannot have been merely my imagination that even as I heard these words, I detected a disagreeable edge to them. Nor can it have been merely unjust suspicion on my part to have seen in her half-reproachful sideways glance at him a revelation of what lay beneath her brazen coquettishness.

"Be that as it may, I could not help seeing their life together illuminated in that ever so brief exchange, as though by a bolt of lightning. In retrospect, I see myself as having been present as the curtain rose on the tragedy of Miura's life. At the time, however, it was only a slight shadow of anxiety momentarily dimming my spirits; immediately thereafter all had been set aright, as he and I began a lively exchange of cups. Thus, having spent a truly delightful evening, I took my leave in a state of mild inebriation, and as I rode the rickshaw home over the river, exposing my flushed face to the wind, I repeatedly offered for his sake silent words of congratulation on having succeeded in finding *amour*.

"About a month later, during which time I had, of course, paid frequent visits to the couple, I was invited to the Shintomi-za by a doctor friend of mine. As it happened, the play being performed was *O-den no Kanabumi*,[3] and there, sitting in the middle tier of boxes directly across from us, was Miura's wife. At the time, it was my habit to take opera glasses with me whenever I went to the theater, and it was she who first caught my eye as I looked through those round lenses. She was seated in front of a flamboyantly colorful tapestry. With her white double chin resting on a decorative collar of sedate hue, she had inserted in the knot of her hair what appeared to be a rose. At the very moment I recognized her, she nodded to me with those same provocative eyes. As I lowered my opera glasses and returned the greeting, I was surprised to see her looking back at me with a flustered expression. This time, however, her salutation was strikingly more formal and deferential. I now understood that her initial greeting had not been intended for me. Quite without thinking, I glanced about to discover who this other acquaintance of hers might be. I saw sitting in the box next to me a young man dressed in a loud striped suit. He too seemed to be looking for his counterpart. He stared in our direction, a strong-smelling cigarette in his mouth, until his eyes caught mine. There was something about his dark complexion that I found unpleasant, and I immediately averted my gaze, again picking up my opera glasses and idly looking across to the opposite side of the theater.

"In the box with Miura's wife sat another woman. When I tell you that it was a certain Narayama, an advocate for women's rights, I think it unlikely that you will not have heard of her. She was at the time the wife of the rather well-known lawyer Narayama. An outspoken promoter of judicial equality between the sexes, she was also the perennial subject of unpleasant rumors. Seeing her sitting there, stiff-shouldered, in a black crested kimono and gold-rimmed spectacles, next to Miura's wife as though she were her guardian, I was overwhelmed by an ominous sense of foreboding. As she adjusted and readjusted her collar, the feminist was pointing her angular, lightly powdered face in our direction – or rather, I think, throwing meaningful glances at the man in the striped suit.

"It is no exaggeration to say that all during the performance I gave far greater attention to him and the two wives than to the actors on stage, Kikugorō or Sadanji. Filled as it was with repugnant thoughts and images, my mind was utterly incapable of relating to the world before me: the lively musical accompanists to the left of the stage or the artificial cherry sprigs hanging from above.

"Thus, when the two women went out immediately after the end of the middle piece, I experienced a genuine sense of relief. Of course, the man in the striped suit had remained. Constantly puffing on his cigarette, he would glance at me from time to time, but now that two of the three were gone, his swarthy face did not trouble me as much as before.

"It will strike you as absurdly groundless suspicion, but his features did indeed inspire in me a strange aversion, so that between him and me – or rather between him and us – I felt an intractable hostility. Thus, when less than a month later I was introduced to him in Miura's study, overlooking the Great River, I could not help feeling something close to perplexity, as though I had been confronted with a riddle.

"It seemed he was the cousin of Miura's wife and held a position of some responsibility, relative to his youth, in a certain textile company.

He again puffed on a cigarette as we sat round the table at tea, engaged in desultory chatting. It soon became apparent to me that he was a man of some talent, though, needless to say, none of this changed in the least my opinion of him. Yet when I appealed to my own reason, I saw that inasmuch as he was the cousin of Miura's wife, there was nothing the least extraordinary in their exchange of greetings at the theater. I therefore did my utmost to engage him. Yet whenever I appeared to be on the verge of success, he would invariably do something annoying – slurping his tea, casually dropping cigarette ashes on the table, laughing uproariously at his own jokes. And so my antipathy for him was only rekindled.

"When after some thirty minutes he excused himself, saying that he had to attend some sort of company banquet, I found myself impulsively going to the French windows overlooking the water and opening them wide, as though to purge the room of vulgar air. Seated as was his custom under the portrait of his wife with her bouquet of roses, Miura said to me reproachfully: 'My goodness, how you do dislike him!'

"'I cannot help finding him unpleasant. That he is your wife's cousin is astounding.'

"'Astounding? Why?'

"'He is of an altogether different sort . . .'

"Miura fell silent for some time, staring fixedly at the river, the light of the evening sun having already begun to play on its surface. When he spoke again, it was with an unexpected proposal:

"'What would you say to going off on a fishing expedition, the two of us?'

"Being only too happy to have the subject of the cousin behind us, I responded with an immediate show of spirit: 'A splendid idea! I have a bit more confidence in angling than in diplomacy.' Miura smiled for the first time and said: 'Than in diplomacy, you say. As for myself . . . Well, to begin with, I suppose I feel more competent in matters piscatorial than amatorial.'

"'Have you then a prize catch in mind to surpass your wife?'

"'Now wouldn't that be good – something more with which to make you jealous!'

"His words seemed to pierce my ears like a needle. Peering at him through the penumbra, I saw a cold expression on his face as he continued to gaze at the light on the water below.

"'When should we go?' I asked.

"'Whenever it suits you.'

"'Then I shall inform you by post.'

"I slowly rose from the red-leather chair in which I had been sitting, silently shook his hand, and quietly left his somber study, the whiff of secrets in the air, and stepped into the even darker corridor. Near the door, I quite unexpectedly met a black figure, quietly standing there as though having eavesdropped on our conversation. Seeing me, the person immediately approached me, exclaiming in a most charming tone: 'Oh, are you leaving so soon?'

"Madame Katsumi was again wearing a rose in her hair. For a moment I felt breathless but then gave her a glacial stare and a wordless salutation before moving with rapid strides to the entrance, where a rickshaw was awaiting me. My mind was in such a state of confusion that I myself was hardly aware of it. All that I remember is that as I was crossing Ryōgoku Bridge, I found myself repeating over and over the name of Delilah.

"It was from that moment that glimmerings of the secret behind Miura's melancholic demeanor began to make themselves clear to me. I need hardly say that this secret was seared into my mind in the form of those abhorrent characters that represent the word *adultery*.[4]

Yet if my assumption was correct, why did not Miura, idealist that he was, resolve to divorce her? Did he, for all his suspicions, lack sufficient evidence? Or was he, despite everything, hesitating out of love?

"As I relentlessly pondered these hypotheses, turning them over one by one, I soon forgot about the fishing trip, and though over the next fortnight I continued on occasion to write, my heretofore frequent visits to the Miuras' house on the riverbank ceased altogether. It was then, however, that I had another unexpected chance encounter. It was this that gave me the resolve to use our talk of going fishing as a partial reason for a direct meeting and there to lay open to him my anxieties.

"I had gone with my doctor friend to the Nakamura-za to see a play. We were on our way back when we happened to meet a familiar face, a journalist for the *Akebono*, writing under the name of Chinchikurin-shujin. It had started to rain on this late afternoon as we went for a drink at the Ikuine, located at the time in Yanagibashi.

"We were seated on the second floor, enjoying moderate imbibing, as we listened to the faraway sound of a *shamisen,* evoking long-ago Edo. Now our journalist friend arose, caught up in the merriment, and, like a popular writer of fiction from that era, sprinkling his remarks with *jeux de mots*, began to entertain us with scandalous stories about Madame Narayama. It seems the woman had been a foreigner's concubine in Kōbe. Then for a time she had had San'yūtei Engyō as her kept man.

"She had been then in her heyday and wore six gold rings, but in the last two or three years had been up to her neck in debts of legally dubious provenance . . . Chinchikurin-shujin had much else to tell us concerning her dissolute conduct behind the scenes, but for me the most disturbing shadow that he cast with his account concerned the recent appearance in her company of a certain young lady, who, rumor had it, had become for the other an accessory as inseparable as her kimono pouch. Moreover, it was said that she sometimes stayed overnight with the women's rights advocate in Suijin – and in the additional company of men.

"When I heard this, I saw, amidst the jolly exchange of cups, the pensive figure of Miura flicker hauntingly before my eyes, and found it impossible to join, even out of a sense of duty, in all the boisterous laughter. Fortunately, the good doctor quickly became aware of my subdued spirits and adroitly steered the raconteur in another direction, completely away from the topic of Madame Narayama. Now I could breathe again and continue to converse without marring the conviviality.

"Yet that evening had been made to bring me naught but bad luck. Disheartened by the gossip concerning the women's rights advocate, I had stood up with my two companions to leave and was standing in front of the Ikuine, about to step into a rickshaw, when another, this one designed for two passengers, suddenly and forcefully swept by, its rain-covered canopy glistening. I had one foot on the running board when, almost exactly at that moment, I saw the oilcloth hood of the other rickshaw raised and someone bounding out in the direction of the entrance. Glimpsing the figure, I threw myself into the safety of the canopy. As the puller lifted the shafts, I felt strangely agitated and involuntarily muttered: *"That* one!" It could be no other than the dark-complexioned, stripe-suited cousin of Miura's wife. Thus, as I sped along the illuminated boulevard of Hirokōji, the rain streaming from the canopy, I was pursued by dread anxiety at the thought of who might have been his fellow passenger. Might it have been Madame Narayama – or Madame Katsumi, a rose in her hair?

"Even as I agonized over the irresolvable uncertainty of my suspicions, I was fearful of solution – and angered at my own cowardice in having hurriedly jumped into the rickshaw to conceal my identity. To this day, the question of which woman it had been remains for me an enigma."

Viscount Honda drew out a large handkerchief and, discreetly blowing his nose, looked round again at the contents of the display cases, now bathed in evening light, before quietly resuming his story.

"Of course, I earnestly thought all these matters, particularly what I had heard from Chinchikurin-shujin, to be of extreme interest to Miura, and so the next day immediately sent a letter to him, offering him a date for our fishing jaunt. He immediately replied, saying that as the day would be the sixteenth day in the lunar calendar, we might instead go out in a boat on the river at twilight and view the moon. I had, needless to say, no particularly strong desire to go fishing and so readily consented to his proposal. On the appointed day, we met at the boathouse in Yanagibashi and, before the moon was up, rowed out toward the Great River in an open, flat-bottomed barque.

"Even in those days, the view of the water in the evening may not have been worthy of comparison with the elegance of the more distant past, but something of the beauty that one sees in old woodblock prints remained. When on that evening too we rowed downstream past Manpachi and entered the Great River, we could see the parapet of Ryōgoku Bridge, arching above the waves that flickered in the faint mid-autumn twilight and against the sky, as though an immense black Chinese ink stroke had been brushed across it. The silhouettes of the traffic, horses and carriages soon faded into the vaporous mist, and now all that could be seen were the dots of reddish light from the passengers' lanterns, rapidly passing to and fro in the darkness like small winter cherries.

"'Well, what do you think of it?' asked Miura.

"'I think one would look in vain for such a view anywhere in Europe,' I replied.

"'Ah, then you apparently see no harm in enjoying a bit of the discredited past when it comes to scenery.'

"'Yes, when it comes to scenery, I concede.'

"'I must say that recently I have grown quite weary of all that is called modern enlightenment.'

"'If you're not careful, you too will be stung by Mérimée's acerbic tongue. You must remember how that sneering rogue allegedly said to Dumas or someone, standing next to him, when a delegate from the shogunate was walking down the boulevard in Paris: "Tell me, who could have bound the Japanese to such an absurdly long sword?"'

"'Yes, but I prefer the story of Hé Rú Zhāng, who, during his stay in Japan as a diplomat, expressed admiration for the sleepwear he saw in a Yokohama hotel: "Here in this country are relics of the Xia and Zhou dynasties!" No, there is nothing that one may ridicule simply on the grounds that it is a thing of the past.'

"Surprised at the sudden deepening of the darkness as the tide rose, I glanced round and saw that having greatly quickened our pace, we were now south of Ryōgoku Bridge, approaching *Shubi-no-matsu*, its trunk and branches appearing in the night to be of an even deeper ebony.

"Eager to broach the subject of Madame Katsumi, I quickly pursued Miura's comment:

"'If you yourself are so attached to older ways, what will you do about your modern wife?' I asked, testing the waters.

"For several moments, as though he had not heard my question, Miura gazed at the still moonless sky above Otakegura. Finally, he fixed his eyes on me and said softly but firmly: 'I shall do nothing. As of about a week ago, we are divorced.'

"Quite taken aback by this unexpected reply, I gripped the gunwales of the boat.

"'So you knew?' I asked in a strained voice.

"Miura continued with the same air of calm as before:

"'So you knew it all too?' he asked, throwing the question back at me, as though by way of confirmation.

"'Perhaps not everything. I did hear about her ties to Madame Narayama.'

"'And about my wife and her cousin?'

"'I had some glimmerings of it . . .'

"'Then surely I need say no more.'

"'But, but . . .When did *you* become aware of the relationship?'

"'Between my wife and her cousin? About three months after our marriage – just before commissioning her portrait with the painter Gozeta Hōbai.'

"This response too, as you can well imagine, was quite astonishing.

"'But why, until now, have you tacitly accepted the outrage of it all?'

"'I did not accept it tacitly – but rather quite openly.'

"For the third time, I was dumbfounded. For several moments I merely stared at him in stupefaction.

"'Mind you,' he said without the slightest trace of insistence, 'the relationship of which I approved between my wife and her cousin was the one that I had painted in my imagination, not the one that presently exists. You will remember that I insisted on a marriage based on *amour*. This was not to satisfy my own egotism; it was rather the consequence of my having placed love above all things. Thus, when once we were married I came to understand that the bonds of affection between us were less than genuine, I regretted my precipitancy and at the same time felt pity for her, now that she was obliged to live with me. As you know, I have never been in the best of health. Moreover, despite my efforts to love my wife, she has been unable to love me – or perhaps it may be that my notion of *amour* was from the beginning such a paltry thing that it could never have inspired passion in her. If therefore there was such true affection between my wife and her cousin, who have known one another since childhood, I would gallantly sacrifice myself to their happiness. Not to do so would be, in effect, to renounce the supremacy of *amour*. It was for that eventuality that, in fact, I intended the portrait of my wife – to hang in my study as a replacement for her.'

"As he spoke, Miura again looked to the sky above the opposite bank. It was as though a black curtain had fallen from the sky, enveloping the towering chinquapins of the Matsuura estate in gloom, with no sign of a cloud from out of which the moon might appear. I lit a cigarette and urged him to continue: 'And then?'

"'I learned soon thereafter that the love between my wife and her cousin was something impure. To put it bluntly, I discovered that he also had a liaison with Madame Narayama. I am sure that you will not have any particular desire to know how I acquired such knowledge, and I myself do not wish to elaborate. Suffice it to say that it was by pure chance that I found them together.'

"I let the ashes of my cigarette fall over the gunwale as I vividly recalled the memory of the rainy evening at the Ikuine. Miura immediately continued: 'That was the first blow. Having largely lost whatever grounds I had for approving of their relationship, I naturally found it impossible to maintain my previous air of benignity. That must have been about the time you returned from Korea. I was daily tormented by the question of how to separate my wife from her cousin. However false might be his love for her, there was no doubt in my mind that her feelings for him were sincere . . . Such was what I believed. At the same time, for the sake of her happiness as well, I thought it necessary for me to act as a negotiator. But when they – or at least she – perceived my state of mind, she seemed to have reasoned that I had just become aware of their relationship and was now overcome with jealousy. She thus began to keep a wary and hostile watch over me; perhaps she even exercised the same wariness toward you.'

"'Now that you say that,' I replied, 'she was standing outside your study, listening to our conversation.'

"'Yes,' he remarked in return, 'she is the sort of woman who is quite capable of that.' For several moments we remained silent, staring at the dark surface of the water. Our boat had already passed under what was then Oumayabashi, leaving a faint wake in the night water as we edged toward tree-lined Komakata.

"Miura spoke in a subdued voice: 'Even then I did not doubt my wife's sincerity. Thus, the knowledge that she did not grasp my true feelings or rather that I had only earned her hatred caused me all the more anguish. From the day I met you at Shinbashi until today, I have constantly been in the throes of that distress. But then about a week ago, a maid or one of the other servants carelessly allowed a letter that should have gone to my wife to find its way to my desk. I immediately thought of her cousin . . . Well, I eventually opened the letter and found to my astonishment that it was a love missive from yet another man. In a word, her love for her cousin was no less impure. Needless to say, this second blow was of vastly more terrible intensity than the first. All my ideals had been ground to dust. At the same time, I was sadly comforted by the abrupt lessening of responsibility.'

"Miura ceased speaking, and now from above the rows of grain storehouses along the opposite bank we saw just beginning to rise the immense, eerily red globe of the autumn moon. When just a few minutes ago I saw Yoshitoshi's *ukiyoé* of Kikugorō in Western dress and was reminded of Miura, it was particularly because that red moon was so similar to the lantern moon mounted on the stage.

"Miura, with his thin, pale face and his long hair parted in the middle, gazed at the rising of the moon and then suddenly sighed, remarking sadly even as he smiled: 'Once, some time ago, you dismissed as a childish dream the cause of the Jinpūren rebels and their willingness to fight to the death. Well, perhaps in your eyes my married life too . . .'

"'Indeed, perhaps so. But then it may also well be that in one hundred years our goal of achieving modern enlightenment will likewise seem no less a childish dream.'"

Just as the viscount had finished speaking these words, an attendant appeared to inform us that the museum was about to close. We stood up slowly and, giving one last look at the *ukiyoé* and copperplate prints all around us, silently walked out of the darkened display hall, quite as though we ourselves had emerged from those glass cases as phantoms from the past.

AUTUMN

1

From the time she began her studies, it was well known that Nobuko was a gifted young writer. There was scarcely anyone who doubted that sooner or later she would make her way into the literary world. It was even widely reported that while yet a student at her women's university she had written more than three hundred pages of an autobiographical novel. Upon graduation, however, she found herself in circumstances sufficiently strained as to leave no room for idle self-indulgence: with her widowed mother resolved not to remarry and her sister, Teruko, still attending a girls' school, she was obliged, in conformity to social custom, to set aside her creative endeavors and seek a marriage partner.

Their cousin Shunkichi, enrolled in the literature department of his own university, appeared to have likewise set his sights on a writer's career. Nobuko had long been on friendly terms with him, and now their common interest in literary topics made for even closer ties. He did not, however, share her unbridled enthusiasm for Tolstoyism, then very much in vogue. He was forever making ironic comments *à la française* or speaking in aphorisms. His sardonic manner sometimes angered the intensely earnest Nobuko, but despite herself she was unable to be entirely contemptuous of his manner. Thus, even while still in university, they would not infrequently attend exhibits and concerts together, usually in the company of Teruko.

In their comings and goings, the three laughed and chattered freely. When, as they strolled along, the talk turned to matters beyond her ken, Teruko would peer childlike into the show windows at the parasols and silk shawls, without appearing to feel in the slightest neglected. Whenever Nobuko noticed this, she never failed to change the subject and to bring her sister immediately back into the conversation. Yet it was she herself who was the first to forget her sister. Shunkichi appeared to be oblivious to it all, tossing off clever comments as he swung his way slowly through the pell-mell of pedestrian traffic . . .

In the eyes of everyone, needless to say, the relationship between Nobuko and her cousin gave more than enough reason to suppose that the two would wed. Her classmates were filled with envy and spite at her prospects, and, as foolish as it may sound, it must be said that it was among those who knew Shunkichi the least that such emotions were the most intense. For her part, Nobuko denied – and yet by insinuation deliberately encouraged – the speculation. Thus, for as long as they were still in school, the image lingered in their minds, as clear as a wedding photograph, of Nobuko and Shunkichi as bride and groom.

Nobuko had scarcely completed her studies when she confounded the expectations of all by marrying a young commercial high school graduate. Within two or three days of the nuptials, they had gone to live in Ōsaka, where he had recently joined a trading company. The well-wishers who saw them off at Tōkyō's central railway station later said that Nobuko was her usual cheerful self, ever with a smile on her face, even as she tried to console her lachrymose sister, Teruko.

In their bewilderment and amazement, Nobuko's classmates found themselves filled with ambivalent feelings: a strange sense of contentment on the one hand, a new and entirely different sense of envy on the other. Those with full confidence in her attributed the decision to her mother's wishes; other, less trusting, souls let it be known that she had simply had a change of heart. Yet all of this, as the tongue-waggers themselves were well aware, was mere conjecture.

Why had not Nobuko married Shunkichi? For some time thereafter, such was the inevitable focus of conversation. Then two months went by; Nobuko was quite forgotten, to say nothing of any novel she had been rumored to be writing.

Meanwhile, on the outskirts of Ōsaka, she set about the task of becoming a new and presumably happy homemaker. The couple's two-story rental house was situated in what even for the locality was a particularly quiet neighborhood, surrounded by a pinewood. Sometimes on lonely afternoons, amidst the smell of resin, the light of the sun, and the overpowering stillness that reigned whenever her husband was out, Nobuko, for no apparent reason, would find her spirits sinking. It was then that she invariably reached into a drawer of her sewing box to take out a letter lying folded up at the bottom. Written on pink stationery, it read:

My Dear Elder Sister,
    . . . Even as I write, the thought that after today we shall no longer be together fills my eyes with an endless flood of tears. I beg you for

forgiveness. As I contemplate the sacrifice that you have made for me, your unworthy sister, Teruko, words quite fail me.

You have accepted this marriage proposal for my sake, and though you have denied it, I know very well that such is true. The other evening, when we were together at the Imperial Theater, you asked whether I held a special place in my heart for Shun-san, saying that if I did, you would spare no effort on my behalf to see that we were married.

You must have read the letter that I intended to send to him. I confess that at the time of its disappearance, I felt terribly resentful. (Forgive me. Again, I scarcely realize myself just how inexcusable my conduct has been.) When I heard your kind offer of assistance, I could only understand it as ironically intended. You will not, of course, forget that I angrily responded by hardly responding at all. When several days later you suddenly agreed to be married, I should happily have died, so great was my desire to make amends.

As much as you may seek to conceal it, I know that you too care very much for Shun-san. Had you not been concerned for me, you would surely have married him. Now, having told me again and again that you had no such feelings, you have wed a man who is not of your heart.

My beloved elder sister, do you remember that I held the chicken in my arms and told her to bid you farewell? I wanted even that hen to join me in seeking your pardon. Our mother too, though she knows nothing of this, could only weep.

So tomorrow you will depart for Ōsaka. I implore you not to abandon Teruko, who every morning as she feeds her hen, out of sight and hearing of all, will be shedding tears as she thinks of you.

Whenever she read this girlish letter, Nobuko too would weep. Particularly on recalling how Teruko had quietly handed it to her as she was boarding the train, she was moved beyond words, even if, at the same time, she also wondered whether her marriage had really been entirely the sacrificial act that Teruko imagined it to be. When her tears had dried, the suspicion weighed heavily upon her. For the most part, to dispel the gloom, she would will herself to bask in pleasant reverie, as she watched the sunlight falling on the pines beyond her window slowly turn to evening gold.

2

Three months went by. Nobuko and her husband spent their days contentedly, as is the wont of newlyweds. There was a hint of feminine reserve in his taciturn manner. On his return from the office, they would sit together for some time after supper. As she knitted, Nobuko would describe a recent novel or play that had become the talk of the town, her comments sometimes evoking an outlook on life colored by the Christian background of her university. His cheeks red with the sake he had drunk, the evening newspaper he had just begun to read spread out on his lap, he would listen without comment or opinion, a look of bemused curiosity on his face.

On Sundays they would generally go off on a sightseeing jaunt to Ōsaka or the vicinity. Whenever they rode the train or streetcar, Nobuko was struck by the vulgarity of her compatriots in western Japan, eating and drinking even on public conveyances without constraint. In that regard she was pleased at how remarkably refined her husband was. From his hat to his suit to his red-leather lace-ups, his clean-cut appearance, as though he might smell faintly of bathing soap, made for a refreshing contrast. Particularly during the summer holidays, when on a trip to Maiko they encountered his colleagues in a teahouse, she could not help feeling all the more proud of her husband, though she also noted that he seemed to be on oddly intimate terms with his crude companions.

It was during this time that Nobuko returned to the writing she had long since put aside, spending an hour or two in front of her desk when her husband was away. Hearing of this, he remarked with a slight smirk on his lips: "Well now, you're to be an authoress after all."

To her surprise, the ink did not flow. She would catch herself, chin in hand, staring out at the wood, ablaze in the sunlight, listening quite unconsciously to the whine of the cicadas.

The lingering heat of late summer gave way to early autumn. One morning as Nobuko's husband was preparing to leave for work, he sought to change his sweat-stained collar, only to find unhappily that all the others had been sent to the laundry. Fastidious as he was, a look of displeasure clouded his face. As he drew up his suspenders, he said in an unusually biting tone: "We can't have you spending all your time writing fiction." Nobuko lowered her eyes and brushed the dust from his jacket.

Several days later, he looked up from reading a newspaper article about current food problems and remarked that Nobuko might think about ways to economize from month to month, adding: "You're not going to be a college girl forever, you know."

Nobuko made a halfhearted reply as she embroidered the gauze for her husband's collar. "Rather than bother with all that needlework," he nagged at her with uncharacteristic persistence, "it would be less expensive simply to buy ornamented collars." Nobuko fell silent. Her husband eventually picked up a trade journal with an air of ennui. Later that evening, as she switched off the electric lamp in their bedroom, Nobuko turned her back to him and whispered: "I shan't be writing anymore." He did not reply. A few moments later, she repeated the same words, more softly still; soon there was the sound of muffled weeping. Her husband tersely scolded her, but though she went on sobbing, she found that before she knew it she was tightly clinging to him.

The next morning they were again a happy couple. Soon, however, there was another incident when, on returning home from work after midnight, reeking of drink, he was in no condition even to take off his raincoat. Nobuko knitted her eyebrows and diligently set about helping him change his clothes. He nonetheless spoke to her sarcastically, slurring his words: "With my having stayed out so long, you must have made considerable progress with your novel." Thus, with his womanish mouth, he nagged at her.

As Nobuko lay down to sleep, she again wept in spite of herself: "Ah, if Teruko could only see me, what tears would we shed together! Teruko, Teruko, on you alone can I depend!" With such thoughts, calling out again and again to her sister, she tossed and turned all night, forced to endure the smell of sake on her husband's breath.

Again the next day harmony had been restored, quite of its own accord. Yet other scenes would follow, even as the autumn deepened.

It was now rare for Nobuko to sit at her desk, pen in hand, and her husband too seemed less inclined to listen to her speak of literature. Sitting across from each other at the long brazier, they began to pass away the evenings talking of mundane household expenses. Moreover, at least after his evening drink, he apparently found this topic of greatest interest. Nobuko would sometimes look sadly into his face, but he seemed to take no notice, chewing on the whiskers he had recently grown and speaking more animatedly than usual. "And what if we were to have children?" he would ask, wondering aloud to himself.

Meanwhile Shunkichi's name began to appear in a monthly journal. Nobuko had had no contact with her cousin since her marriage, as though she had quite forgotten him. All she knew was what Teruko had written to her – that, for example, he had completed his studies in the literature department and had launched a literary coterie magazine. She had not wished to know more, but now that she was reading his stories, fond memories returned. As she turned the pages, she often smiled and laughed to herself. Even in his fiction, she could see, Shunkichi was a literary Miyamoto Musashi,[1] a sword in each hand – a sardonic quip in one, a witticism or pun in the other. Still, it occurred to her, perhaps as no more than a fleeting thought, that behind her cousin's easygoing irony there was something she had previously not known in him: a sense of lonely desperation. She felt a vague twinge of guilt.

She became more solicitous of her husband. Sitting across from her at the brazier in the chill of the evening, he would constantly stare into her bright and cheerful face, which appeared more youthful than ever, now invariably touched with cosmetics.

As she sat with her sewing work spread out before her, she would recall their wedding day. Her husband seemed both surprised and pleased at the precision of her memory. "So you remember even that, do you!" he would exclaim, whereupon she would fall silent, replying only with an endearing look in her eyes. She too sometimes wondered why indeed she had not forgotten such things.

Not long thereafter she received a letter from her mother informing her that Teruko was betrothed; for his bride-to-be, she noted, Shunkichi had found a new house on the outskirts of Tōkyō. Nobuko immediately sent a long congratulatory message to both her mother and her younger sister.

"As it happens, I have no domestic help and so must most reluctantly decline to attend the ceremony . . . ," she wrote. More than once, without knowing why, her hand faltered, as she looked up and turned her gaze ineluctably to the gray-blue thicket of pine trees under the early winter sky.

That evening she discussed the news with her husband. He listened amused, a familiar thin smile passing across his face, as Nobuko imitated her sister's manner of speaking. Yet somehow she had the feeling that it was to herself that she was making the announcement.

"Well, time for sleep I suppose," he said several hours later, stroking his soft mustache, as he listlessly stood up from the brazier. Nobuko, who had not decided on a wedding gift, sat with the tongs, idly writing letters in the ashes. Suddenly she raised her head and exclaimed: "How strange to think that now I shall be gaining a brother!"

"Of course," her husband replied, "just as I have a sister." In her eyes was the look of one deeply lost in thought, and though she heard his words, she did not reply.

Teruko and Shunkichi were married in the middle of December. Light snow began to fall just before noon of that day. Nobuko finished her solitary lunch, a lingering aftertaste of fish in her mouth. "Perhaps it is also snowing in Tōkyō," she wondered as she sat ruminating at the brazier in the dark sitting room. The snow fell ever more heavily, and still the taste of fish remained.

3

In the autumn of the following year, Nobuko accompanied her husband on a business trip that brought her for the first time since her marriage to Tōkyō. With much to accomplish in a short time, he had no opportunity to go out with her, except for a visit to her mother just after their arrival. Thus, it was alone that she rode the streetcar to the terminal stop, drearily typical of the newly developed urban areas, and from there took a rickshaw the rest of the way, swaying back and forth.

Not far from the house, the residential area gave way to spring onion patches. The neighboring buildings were clusters of newly constructed rental dwellings, indistinguishable, one from the other: the door under the eaves, the photinia hedge, and the clothes hanging on the laundry pole. Nobuko was rather disappointed at how commonplace it seemed.

When she called out to announce herself, it was to her surprise that Shunkichi himself appeared. "Aha!" he exclaimed cheerily, welcoming the rare visitor. He looked much the same, though she saw that he had let his once closely cropped hair grow.

"It's been a long time."

"Well then, come in, come in. Unfortunately, I happen to be alone."

"Where is Teruko? Is she out?"

"She went on an errand – along with the maid."

Nobuko felt strangely uncomfortable as she stepped into the hallway and quietly took off her somewhat flamboyantly lined coat.

He invited her to sit in the eight-mat room that served as both library and drawing room. Everywhere there were heaps of books. The afternoon light that seeped through the sliding paper doors fell conspicuously on a small rosewood desk, about which lay an unmanageable mass of newspapers, magazines, and manuscript paper. The only evidence of a wifely presence was a new *koto* leaning against the wall of the alcove. Nobuko gazed long and curiously at what she saw before her.

"We knew from your letter that you were coming but not that it would be today." Shunkichi lit a cigarette, a look of fond reminiscence in his eyes. "How is your life in Ōsaka?"

"And how are you, Shun-san? Are you happy?"

As she offered this brief reply, Nobuko was conscious of happy moments from the past returning. The awkward memories of the last two years, with virtually no correspondence between them, now caused her surprisingly little anguish.

Warming their hands at the brazier, they found an inexhaustible variety of matters to discuss: Shunkichi's novel, news of mutual friends, similarities and contrasts between Tōkyō and Ōsaka . . . Yet, as though by tacit agreement, nothing was said of how each lived from day to day. For Nobuko, this only reinforced her keen sensation that she was indeed talking to him, her cousin of old.

Sometimes there was silence between them. Nobuko would simply smile, looking down into the ashes of the brazier. In those moments, she felt a vague sense of expectation. This was each time dispelled as Shunkichi, whether deliberately or coincidentally, plunged into a new topic of conversation. Little by little she found herself looking irresistibly into his face. For his part, however, he puffed nonchalantly on a cigarette, revealing in his expression nothing the least bit odd.

Teruko returned. She seemed on the verge of rushing to clasp her sister's hands, so happy she was to see her. Nobuko too was smiling, though already there were tears in her eyes. For a while they forgot Shunkichi as they plied each other with questions about their lives since the previous year. Teruko was particularly energetic, her cheeks flushed as she spoke, not neglecting to tell her sister all about the chickens that she continued to raise.

Shunkichi looked contentedly at the two as they talked, a cigarette in his mouth and all the while a smile on his face. When the maid returned, he took from her several postcards she had brought and, immediately turning to his desk, began to busy himself with his pen. Teruko appeared surprised to realize that the maid had been out:

"So no one was home when you arrived?" she asked.

"No, only Shun-san," her sister replied in a tone that seemed to emphasize that there was nothing in this to trouble her.

With his back still turned, Shunkichi remarked to his wife: "You should thank your master, for it was he who served the tea!" The two women exchanged mischievous glances and giggled, but Teruko intentionally did not reply.

They now gathered around the dining table for supper. Teruko explained that the eggs they saw before them had all come from her own hens, which she kept in the garden.

"Human beings," said Shunkichi, offering wine to Nobuko as he launched into a discourse of a socialistic hue, "sustain their lives through plunder. The eggs we see here are but one minor example."

"How strange of *you* to say so!" Teruko replied with a childlike titter, for it was clearly Shunkichi among the three who had the greatest fondness for eggs. As for Nobuko, the ambience there at the table could only remind her of a lonely sitting room in a distant pinewood at dusk.

The conversation topics were still unexhausted, well after the last of the dessert fruit had been consumed. Shunkichi, now mellow with the wine, sat cross-legged under the electric light of the long autumn evening, delineating with gusto a school of sophistry quite his own. The animated discussion once again brought Nobuko back to more youthful days. Her eyes gleamed as she exclaimed: "I think I might just write a novel myself!"

Shunkichi replied with Gourmont's aphorism: "The Muses are women, and you must be a man to possess them properly."[2] Nobuko and Teruko joined forces in refusing to accept the authority of such a pronouncement.

"If so," said Teruko in all seriousness, "must one be a woman to compose music? After all, Apollo is male!"

The hour was already late, and in the end it was agreed that Nobuko would spend the night. Before going to bed, Shunkichi opened one of the shutters on the veranda and, dressed only in his nightclothes, stepped down into the small garden. He called out, as if to no one in particular:

"Come. There's a fine moon out."

Nobuko alone followed him. Taking off her split-toed socks and slipping into the clogs that lay on the stepping-stone, she felt the cold dew on her feet.

The moon was shining over the top of a thin and withered cypress in a corner of the garden. Shunkichi stood under it and looked up at the faint light of the night sky.

"My, how high the grass is!" said Nobuko, walking gingerly toward him, as though repelled by the overgrown garden. Shunkichi continued to gaze at the sky.

"Hmm, Thirteenth Night,"[3] he murmured simply.

They had stood silently for some time when Shunkichi gave her a quiet look.

"Would you like to go look at the henhouse?"

Nobuko nodded silently. They walked slowly side by side toward the opposite corner of the garden until they reached the straw-mat enclosure. The smell of chickens was in the air. All lay in the faint moonlight or in shadows. Shunkichi looked inside.

"Asleep," he said softly to her, as though speaking to himself alone.

Hens robbed of their eggs . . . , thought Nobuko involuntarily.

When the two returned to the house, they found Teruko standing in front of her husband's desk, gazing vaguely at the electric light. Into the lampshade had crawled a green leafhopper.

4

The next morning Shunkichi put on his best suit and after breakfast made his way hurriedly to the threshold to go out, explaining that he had to visit the grave of a friend to mark the first anniversary of his death.

"All right? Please wait for me. I'll be back about noon."

He said this to Nobuko as he threw on his overcoat. She smiled but said nothing, holding out his trilby in her delicate hand.

Teruko saw him off and invited her elder sister to sit across from her at the long brazier as she dutifully busied herself with serving tea. She appeared to have still many a jolly topic to discuss: the housewife next door, the journalists who had come for an interview, the foreign opera troupe Shunkichi had taken her to see . . .

Nobuko's spirits sank as she listened, and she suddenly realized that she was giving only perfunctory replies to what her sister was saying. At last her state of mind was apparent to Teruko as well. She stared worriedly into her sister's face.

"What is wrong?" she asked. Nobuko herself did not know.

The wall clock struck ten. Nobuko listlessly looked up.

"It seems Shun-san won't be returning any time soon."

"No, not yet." Her sister's terse response struck her as somehow typifying that of a still contented bride. Again despite herself, she felt downcast.

"You *are* happy, aren't you, Teruko?" She intended to sound light-hearted as she made the remark, burying her chin in her kimono collar, but spontaneously and inevitably a note of genuine envy had crept in.

Seemingly guileless, Teruko merrily laughed with a playful scowl: "You just wait, dear sister. I'll get even for that!" She then added fawningly: "You say that knowing full well how happy *you* are!"

Nobuko heard the words as though she had been struck by a whip. She raised her eyelids ever so slightly.

"Do you really think so?" she asked in return, and was immediately sorry for her words. For an instant Teruko bore a strange look, and, as their eyes met, Nobuko saw that in her sister's face was an irrepressible expression of regret.

"Well, I am happy if you think I am," she said with a forced smile. The two fell silent, listening to the iron kettle as it simmered beneath the ticking wall clock.

Presently Teruko inquired quietly and ever so timidly: "But is he not kind to you?" Her voice clearly resonated with a sense of compassion, but Nobuko would have none of it. She lowered her eyes to the newspaper spread out across her lap and deliberately offered no reply. As in Ōsaka, the news was all about the price of rice.[4]

In the still sitting room could soon be heard the faint sound of weeping. Nobuko looked up from her newspaper and across the brazier to her sister, now holding a sleeve to her face.

"You needn't cry," she said. But it was no simple task to comfort her, and still her tears flowed. As she gazed wordlessly for some time at the shaking shoulders, Nobuko experienced a cruel sense of joy. Mindful that the maid should not hear the commotion, she looked into Teruko's face and continued in a low voice.

"If I've been wrong, I apologize. If you are happy, Teru-san, then I shall feel gratified. Truly . . . If Shun-san loves you . . ."

As she spoke, her own voice, moved by her very words, gradually took on a mawkish tone. Now Teruko abruptly lowered her sleeve and raised her tear-stained face. In her eyes was kindled a new and strange emotion, not of sadness or anger but rather of irrepressible jealousy.

"Then why, even last night, did you . . . ?" Before she could finish the sentence, she had buried her face in her sleeve and was convulsed with weeping . . .

Several hours later, Nobuko was jolting hurriedly toward the streetcar station in a canopied rickshaw. Her only view of the outside provided by a celluloid window in the front, she watched a slow but steady procession of drab suburban houses, together with thickets of brush and trees, their colors turning with the season. Only the cold autumn sky remained motionless, as fleecy clouds drifted by.

Nobuko's mind was tranquil – the tranquillity of bleak resignation. When Teruko's tearful paroxysms had subsided, peace between the two, though occasioned by renewed weeping, was easily restored. Yet Nobuko could not separate herself from grim reality. She had not waited for the return of her cousin, and as she stepped into the rickshaw, her heart congealed in spite: her sister was now forever a stranger.

She abruptly looked up and through the celluloid window saw Shunkichi coming along the squalid road, walking stick under his arm. Her heart began to palpitate: should she stop the rickshaw or go on? She tried to calm herself beneath the canopy, even as she vainly wavered. Within moments of meeting, she saw him, bathed in the soft sunlight, cautiously guiding his shoes around the many puddles in his path.

Shun-san! she thought for an instant of calling out. Indeed his familiar figure was just beside her carriage. But again she hesitated, and now, quite unawares, he had passed her by. The faintly overcast sky, the sparse rows of houses, the yellow tops of the tall trees . . . and then, as before, only the thin traffic of pedestrians along the streets of the dismal *banlieue* . . .

Autumn . . . , came the thought. Beneath the canopy she sat, chilled and pensive, overwhelmed by desolation.

WINTER

I put on a heavy overcoat, donned my Astrakhan hat, and set off for Ichigaya Prison, where my cousin had spent the last four or five days. My role was simply that of a family representative, offering cheer and comfort, but clearly mixed with my motives was curiosity.

It would soon be February. There were still post–New Year's sales banners along the street, but in all of the neighborhoods I passed, the pallor of the season had settled on trade and commerce as well. As I walked up a slope, I too felt an aching weariness.

An uncle of mine had died of laryngeal cancer in November, and another kinsman, a youth, had run away from home at the beginning of the new year. Yet what followed – my cousin's incarceration – was by far the greatest shock. I was now obliged, together with his younger brother, to conduct negotiations with which I had not the remotest experience. Moreover, the emotional problems among relatives that spring from such incidents tend to create complications of the sort that will hardly be comprehensible to anyone not born and bred in Tōkyō. I could not help thinking that once I had seen my cousin, I would go off somewhere to spend a tranquil and restful week . . .

Surrounding the prison was a high embankment covered with withered grass. The thick wooden bars in the door of the gate lent it a medieval appearance; looking through them, I glimpsed a gravel-strewn garden, with frost-burned cypress trees.

I presented my calling card to the gray-bearded guard, a seemingly good-natured soul, who led me to a visitors' waiting room close by, the elongated eaves covered with a thick layer of dried moss. There were others, sitting on rush-matted benches. Conspicuous among them was a woman in her midthirties, wearing a jacket of black silk crepe over her kimono and reading a magazine.

An extraordinarily brusque and sullen guard would come into the room to read out, in a monotonous voice, the numbers of the next visitors whose turn had come. Mine did not, though I had waited since about ten in the morning. My wristwatch now told me that it was ten minutes before one.

I was, naturally, beginning to feel hungry, but what was truly unen-durable was the cold, for the room was quite without any sign of heat-ing. As I continually stamped my feet, trying to keep my annoyance in check, I was surprised to observe that no one else in the crowd seemed perturbed. There was, for example, an apparent gambler, wearing two cotton-padded kimonos, who, instead of whiling away the time with a newspaper, slowly ate mandarins, one after another.

As the guard came and went, however, the crowd steadily dwin-dled. I finally walked out of the waiting room and began walking the graveled garden. There was, to be sure, the light of the wintry sun, but a wind had arisen and was blowing dust in my face.

Nonetheless resolved to defy Nature, I remained outside until four. Unfortunately, even then I was not called, although it appeared that others who'd arrived after me had been. The room had largely emptied.

I went back in and made my way to the gambler. With a deferential bow, I addressed him, seeking his advice. Without smiling, he replied in a voice that sounded as though he were reciting an old ballad, mixing harsh reality with a measure of compassion: "A fella's only allowed one visitor a day, you know. Yours may have had his already."

His words were, of course, quite distressing. When the guard returned to call more numbers, I decided to ask him whether I would be able to see my cousin. Without so much as glancing at me, he gave no reply and walked away, followed by the gambler and two or three others.

I stood in the middle of the bare earthen floor and mechanically lit a cigarette. As time passed I felt my loathing for the sullen guard growing stronger. (I am constantly surprised at my lack of immediate anger in response to such insults.) He returned about five. Doffing my hat, I tried to pose my previous question once again. He turned his face aside and briskly walked away. This was clearly the moment in which I sensed that enough was enough. I gave a toss to my cigarette butt and walked toward the prison entrance at the other side of the waiting room.

Several guards dressed in traditional Japanese clothing were on duty behind a glass window to the left of a stone staircase. I opened the window and spoke as softly as I could to a man wearing a crested jacket of black pongee. I was quite conscious of looking pale and nervous.

"I am here to visit T. Will that be possible?"

"Wait your turn."

"I have been waiting here since about ten o'clock."

"You'll be called in due time."

"Am I to wait even if I am *not* called, even though it is already nightfall?"

"Well, in any case, wait until you are called. Just wait."

He seemed to be worried that I might cause a disturbance. Though quite annoyed, I felt a measure of sympathy for him. I was also not unaware of an ironic similarity: I was the family representative, he the prison representative.

"It is already past five. Please try to allow me a visit."

With this as my parting shot, I decided to return for the time being to the waiting room, which by this time was already dark. The woman who had been reading the magazine now had it placed facedown on her lap and was looking straight ahead. Her hair was arranged in the fashion of one already married; her face somehow suggested a Gothic sculpture. I sat down in front of her, still filled with the antipathy that the powerless feel toward penal institutions as a whole.

It was nearly six o'clock before I was finally summoned. I was led to the interview room by a round-eyed, seemingly quick-witted guard. The "room" – such that it was – measured no more than a few square feet. There were other similar enclosures as well, each with its own painted door, giving one quite the feeling of being in a public lavatory. At the end of a narrow passageway was a half-moon window; it was through this opening that visitors showed themselves.

Through the dim light of the window I could see my cousin's plump, round face. It was heartening to see that he had undergone surprisingly little change. With no pretense of sentimentality, we had a terse and businesslike discussion. To my right, apparently there to see an elder brother, was a sixteen- or seventeen-year-old girl, whose ceaseless weeping we could not help noticing.

"Please tell everyone that I am entirely innocent of the charge."

My cousin spoke with stiff formality. I looked back at him in silence, my very lack of reply overwhelming me with a suffocating feeling. To my left, an old man with bald patches on his head was talking through the half-moon window to a prisoner who, it seemed, was his son:

"When I'm alone and haven't seen you for a while, I remember all sorts of things to say, but when I come here, I forget what they were . . ."

As I left the interview room, I felt that I had somehow failed my cousin – but also that in this there was a measure of shared responsibility. Again I was led by a guard and now found myself striding down the corridor toward the entrance in the bone-piercing cold.

At my cousin's house uptown, his wife, my blood relative, would be awaiting my arrival. I walked through the squalid streets to Yotsuya-Mitsuke Station and got on a crowded train. The words of the strangely enfeebled old man rang in my ears: "When I'm alone . . ." They struck me as ever so much more human than the wailing voice of the girl. Gripping the hand strap as I looked out through the lingering light of day at the electric lamps burning in the houses of Kōjimachi, I could not but be reminded of the term *charactres* [1] and of the sheer diversity of human personality.

Thirty minutes later I stood in front of the house, pressing the button of the bell on the concrete wall. I heard a faint ringing sound and saw the glass door at the entrance illuminated. An elderly maid opened it a crack, let out an exclamation, and then led me up to a room on the second floor, which looked out on the street.

As I threw my overcoat and hat onto the table, I felt myself yielding to the fatigue that for the time being I had forgotten. The maid lit the gas stove and left me there in the room alone. Being a bit of a manic collector, my cousin had two or three oil and watercolor paintings hung on the walls. As I gazed absentmindedly at them, I was again reminded of the various ancient words that point to life's vicissitudes.

My blood relative and her husband's younger brother had arrived within a few minutes of each other. Even she appeared to be in a calmer frame of mind than I had anticipated. I explained as accurately and precisely as I could what my cousin had told me and launched into a discussion of what measures might be taken, a subject in which she showed no burning interest. As I was speaking, she picked up my Astrakhan hat:

"Quite unusual. Foreign, I should think."

"This? It's the kind of hat that Russians wear."

For his part, my younger cousin had proved to be more "enterprising" than his imprisoned sibling in foreseeing obstacles in our way.

"Anyway, some sort of friend of his recently sent round a journalist in the society department of The X News, entrusting him with his calling card, on the back of which he'd written: 'I've paid half the hush money out of my own pocket. You pay the rest.' We looked into the story. It was, of course, the friend himself who had talked to the journalist in the first place. And naturally there hadn't been any hush money paid. He was merely trying to trick us out of the sum, with some newsman as his confederate . . ."

"Being a journalist myself, I'll thank you to spare me such hurtful comments."

I was resorting to levity as a means of rousing my own spirits, but the younger brother went on talking, as though delivering a speech, his eyes bloodshot from drink. He had a menacing look that would allow for no trifling.

"And to boot, my brother has a friend who, just to set the examining judge's teeth on edge, cornered him in order to offer his own rousing defense."

"Perhaps if you had spoken to him . . . ," I ventured.

"Of course, I did just that. I went bowing and scraping to him to say that while we are so grateful for his consideration, any remarks that antagonize the judge will, for all his good intentions, have a most adverse effect."

My cousin was sitting in front of the gas heater, playing with my Astrakhan hat, and it was to this, I must honestly say, that my attention was now solely directed, even as her brother-in-law was speaking. I could not bear the thought that she might drop it into the fire . . . I had already sometimes imagined that. A friend had searched the Jewish quarter in Berlin for such a hat and then, quite by chance, on a trip to Moscow, had at last been able to find it.

"And I take it that that was not to his liking . . . ," I remarked.

"That's not the word for it! He told me: 'I've gone to great lengths to help the two of you and find it most annoying to be treated rudely.'"

"So it really does seem that nothing can be done."

"I'm afraid not. It's a matter of neither legality nor morality. From the looks of it, the friend had expended much time and trouble, but only to help dig a deeper hole for my brother . . . I'm by nature the fighting sort, but with someone like that, I'm quite at a loss."

As we were talking, we were suddenly surprised by cries of *"T-kun banzai!"* [2] I parted the curtains with one hand and looked through the window down to the street. The narrow pavement was crowded with people, some carrying lanterns with the name of the local youth association written on them. I looked at my cousin and remembered that her husband was serving as a leader.

"I suppose we should go out to thank them."

My cousin, looking quite as though she had finally reached the limits of endurance, gave us alternating glances.

"Well, I'll be right back," he said.

He left the room nonchalantly. I felt envious of his combativeness, even as I avoided my cousin's face by turning to look at the paintings on the wall above me. Though painfully aware of my taciturn behavior, I thought that any perfunctory remark of mine would only reduce us both to sentimental insincerity. I silently lit a cigarette and looked at the portrait of my imprisoned cousin on the wall, studying the distorted perspective in it.

His wife finally spoke to me in a strangely hollow tone of her own:

"This is hardly a time for us to be greeted with *banzai*, though I suppose it's useless to say so . . ."

"The neighborhood doesn't know yet?"

"No . . . But what on earth has happened?"

"Happened?"

"I mean, concerning T, Otōsan . . ."

"Anyone who looks at T-san's side of things will see that there were various factors and circumstances."

"So it is, is it then?"

I was beginning to feel nervous and annoyed. I turned my back to her and walked to the window. The cheers from below continued, coming in waves of three: *Banzai! Banzai! Banzai!"* The younger brother was standing at the entrance, bowing individually to each of the many people holding lanterns. His elder brother's two small daughters stood next to him on each side, their hands in his, giving their pigtailed heads an occasional, oddly forced nod . . .

The years passed. One bitterly cold night I found myself in the living room of my cousin's house, sitting across from her and drawing on the peppermint pipe to which I had recently taken. We had just observed the seventh-day ceremony, the house eerily still. In front of her husband's plain memorial tablet, a single lantern wick was burning; in front of the table on which the tablet had been placed, the two daughters were buried under quilts in the bedding on the floor. My cousin had noticeably aged, and as I looked at her, I suddenly remembered the events of that long-ago day of torment. Yet my only remark was quite humdrum:

"Sucking on a peppermint pipe somehow makes it seem all the colder."

"Oh? I can feel the chill in my hands and feet."

Somewhat halfheartedly, it seemed, she poked at the charcoal in the long brazier.

FORTUNE

From inside the workshop, he could see the pilgrims through the roughly woven screen that hung down from the doorway. Indeed, he could see them quite clearly: an endless stream flowing to and from Kiyomizu. A priest passed, wearing a small metal gong round his neck; next came a suitably attired married woman in a broad-brimmed hat, and then a wickerwork palanquin drawn by a golden ox – a most unusual sight. He watched them through the thin cat-tail screen, abruptly appearing from his left and his right and just as quickly moving on. All was ceaseless change but for the narrow earthen-brown street baking in the sun of a spring afternoon.

Casually observing this scene was a young attendant to a lord.[1] As though struck by a sudden thought, he called out to the master potter:

"Lady Kannon has as many visitors as ever, has she not?"

"Yes, yes . . ."

The potter replied with an air of annoyance, apparently absorbed in his work. He was an old man, with small eyes, an upturned nose, and something rather droll about him; in both his features and his manner, there was not a hint of malice. Wearing what seemed to be a light hemp kimono and a wilted soft cap, he might remind us of a figure from Abbot Toba's now highly regarded scroll paintings.

"I wonder whether I might become a regular worshipper myself," remarked the attendant. "Having no prospects for advancement is unbearable."

"You are joking."

"Well, if it were to bring me good fortune, I'd be quite devout. Daily worship, devotional retreats . . . Such is a small price to pay . . . It's a good transaction to conduct with the gods and the Buddha."

He spoke with the flippancy of youth, licking his lower lip and looking about the workshop . . . With a bamboo thicket in back, the straw-thatched cottage was so cramped that one's very nose bumped up against the walls. Yet, unlike the dizzying tumult of travelers beyond the screen, it offered a peace and quiet that, to all appearances, had endured for a hundred years, the balmy spring breeze blowing over the reddish-brown surface of the jugs, the wine jars, and the other unglazed earthenware. Even the swallows, it seemed, were refraining from building nests along the ridge of the roof.

As the old man remained silent, the attendant resumed speaking.

"You have surely seen and heard a great variety of things in all your long years. Tell me now. Does Lady Kannon truly bestow good fortune?"

"She does. Years ago I would sometimes hear of this."

"Of what?"

"It is not something I can relate in a few short words. And even if I were to tell the whole story, it is unlikely you would find it much of interest."

"More's the pity for me! I am nonetheless a man with at least a modicum of faith. If, after all, I should be the beneficiary of her blessing, I would tomorrow . . ."

"A modicum of faith, you say. Or is it a nose for business?"

The old man laughed, wrinkling the corners of his eyes. Having molded the clay that he had been kneading into the form of a pot, he seemed at last to be in blither spirits.

"One of your tender years is not likely to understand whatever I might venture to say concerning the will of the gods and the Buddha."

"I suppose not. But it is precisely because I do not understand that I am asking you, venerable one!"

"No, no . . . The question is not whether they determine our fates but rather whether such is for good or ill."

"But surely it is perfectly known to those on whom either favor or disfavor has fallen . . ."

"Ah, but there you seem to be quite uncomprehending."

"It is not the matter of fortune or misfortune that I fail to grasp but rather your reasoning."

The day was waning, lengthening the shadows of the passersby – and of two in particular: women carrying their wares in tubs on their heads. One was holding a cherry sprig in her hand, apparently intended to be offered as a gift for those awaiting their return.

"The woman has a hemp-thread shop in the Western market . . . Now there's a case in point."

"So have I not been telling you that I am eager to listen?"

The two fell silent for several moments. Plucking at chin stubble with his fingernails, the attendant gazed vacantly out to the road, where seashell shapes were shining white, most probably fallen petals from the cherry sprig he had seen.

Finally, in a drowsy voice, he murmured:

"Let me hear the tale, old man . . ."

"Well then, by your leave, I shall tell you," began the other slowly. "It is, as ever, a story from times past." He spoke at the leisurely pace of which only those knowing neither the length nor the brevity of the day are capable.

"It is already some thirty or forty years hence. Still a young woman, she had gone to Kiyomizu to beseech Lady Kannon to grant her a life of ease. Her prayer was hardly without merit, for having lost her mother, she now found herself in such dire circumstances that it was all she could do to eke out a living from day to day.

"Her deceased mother had once been a sought-after medium at Hakushu Shrine, but then when rumor spread that she was availing herself of foxes,[2] the clientele had, it seems, abruptly fallen off. Moreover, she was quite a large woman, youthfully sensual for all the white spots on her face. There was, foxes aside, something about her that ordinary human males found beguiling."

"I should rather hear about the daughter than the mother."

"Now, that's a fine way to talk! . . .Well, the mother's death left the girl with meager means, and despite her efforts she was unable to support herself. She was a lovely and clever lass, but with her tattered rags she was reluctant to venture to the temple grounds for her devotional retreat."

"My, my, was she such a beauty?"

"She was. I confess to partiality, but there was surely nothing in either her features or her disposition that would have been cause for shame."

"Ah, what a pity that the story is of so long ago!" the young man exclaimed, tugging slightly on a sleeve end of his faded indigo robe. The old man chortled and resumed his story. Every now and then, in the grove behind the cottage came the mating song of a bush warbler.[3]

"She had spent twenty-one days in retreat at Kiyomizu-dera, and on the last evening, as the time for the fulfillment of her vow grew nigh, she had a dream. Now as it happened, there was among those lodged in the same temple a hunchbacked monk, who, it seems, was endlessly reciting a *dhāraṇī*. This most probably disturbed her, so that though she occasionally dozed, the sound remained in her ears. It was as if even the earthworms in the ground beneath the outer corridor were murmuring in the night . . . And then she suddenly heard a human voice that said: 'On thy return, a man shall approach thee. Hearken to him.'

"Startled, she awoke. The monk was still absorbed in his incantation, but no matter how she strained her ears to catch the words, she could understand nothing of their meaning. Suddenly she happened to turn and there saw dimly in a lamp kept burning throughout the night the face of Lady Kannon. It was the countenance she was accustomed to seeing in worship: wondrous and majestic. Yet as she looked, she had the uncanny feeling that someone was whispering in her ear: 'Hearken to him.' The lass had now thoroughly convinced herself that she had, in fact, heard the voice of the bodhisattva."

"Well, well . . ."

"The night was advancing as she left the temple. She walked down the gentle slope to the capital's Fifth Avenue, and there, as she might well fully have expected, found herself caught from behind in the arms of a man. It was a warm evening in early spring, but, alas, in the darkness she could neither see his face nor even distinguish his clothing. As she tried to break loose, her fingers touched his mustache. Ah, to have concluded her days of devotion in such a manner!

"Moreover, though she asked him for his name, he gave no reply, nor would he tell her where he resided. He merely said that she was to do as she was told and then led her along the avenue below the slope, holding her firmly in his grip, tugging at her as they went along, and heading ever toward the north. All her weeping and wailing were for naught, as they followed the deserted avenue."

"I see. And then?"

"At last they came to the Yasaka pagoda,[4] where, it seems, he took her inside and spent the night . . . I don't suppose there is any reason for an old man such as myself to elaborate."

Again the corners of his eyes wrinkled as he laughed. The shadows of the passersby had lengthened all the more. The scattered cherry blossoms had found their way toward them, perhaps blown across the road by an imperceptible breeze. They now lay between the rain-catching stones, filling the spaces with specks of white.

"You mustn't jest," said the attendant, then added, continuing to pluck at his chin stubble, as though having just remembered:

"And that was the end of it?"

"If that were indeed the end of the story, it would hardly be worth telling," replied the potter, his hands again on the clay utensil he had molded.

"When morning came, the man, apparently thinking that their encounter had been decreed by karma, earnestly entreated the woman to become his wife."

"Aha!"

"Whatever she might have said had she not had her oracular dream, she was in any case certain that this was the will of Lady Kannon and so finally nodded assent. When they had performed a perfunctory exchange of nuptial cups, the man brought out from the interior of the pagoda ten bolts of twilled fabric and ten bolts of silk, saying that such would serve as a provisional dowry . . . I should think it hardly likely that *you* could match him!"

The attendant's only reply was a smirk. The bush warbler too had fallen silent.

"The man now said that he would go and return in the evening. Leaving the woman behind, he hurriedly departed. Now she found herself doubly forlorn. However clever she was, her anxiety could, under the circumstances, have hardly been surprising. With nothing more in her mind than a desire for diversion, she went further inside. There, lo and behold, she found not only twilled fabric and silk but also gems, together with gold dust and other precious metals, heaped up in leather-covered boxes. The sight caused the heart of even this brave lass to skip.

"A man might acquire some of this wealth, but to have amassed such a fortune, there could be no doubt that he was, if not an armed robber, at the very least a thief . . . Adding to her loneliness was now, with this realization, great fear – and thus the desperate desire to remain there not another moment. Were she to fall into the hands of the authorities, what would become of her?

"She was about to turn round and run toward the door, when she was stopped by a hoarse voice calling to her from behind the leather-covered boxes. Utterly astonished by the mere thought of any other person in such a place, she looked and saw sitting among the gold-dust sacks a round figure which, though human, might just as easily have been taken for a sea slug . . . Blear-eyed, wrinkled, bent, and squat, this was a nun of some threescore years. Whether or not she knew of the lass's intention, she edged forward on her knees and, in a purring tone that quite belied her appearance, offered greetings of introduction.

"She was hardly in a state of mind to receive such, but fearful that she might be suspected of planning an escape, she reluctantly sat among the boxes, her elbow on one of them, and engaged the nun in empty chatter. From their talk, it seemed that the woman had served as the man's cook. Yet, strangely enough, when asked about his occupation, she gave no answer. And even at that, as she appeared to be rather hard of hearing, the lass was obliged to repeat the same comment or question so often that soon she was close to tears of vexation . . .

"This went on until about noon. But then, as she was talking of how the cherry trees of Kiyomizu were now in bloom and how the bridge at Fifth Avenue was being repaired, she saw that the crone, no doubt as a happy consequence of her years, had begun to grow drowsy. Then too, the lass had not been quick in her replies. Now seeing her drawing the deep and even breath of sleep, the lass seized her chance. Creeping quietly to the entrance, she cracked open the door and looked out. As luck would have it, there was no one outside . . .

"If she had run out right there and then, that might have been the end of it, but suddenly she remembered the twilled fabric and the silk that she had been given that morning. And so she stole back to the leather boxes, where somehow she stumbled over the sacks of gold dust, thereby accidentally touching the knees of the nun. The old wench awoke in surprise. For a moment she remained in a state of dazed annoyance but then suddenly, as though in a mad rage, began clinging to the young woman's feet, half weeping, half babbling. From what the other could make of her fragmented speech, she seemed to be bemoaning what dire punishment she would face should her captive succeed in escaping. Yet the lass was now sure that to remain in this place would endanger her life, and so the two went to furious battle, with slapping hands, kicking feet, and flying sacks . . . So great was the commotion that had there been mice nestling in the crossbeams, they would have come tumbling down.

"In this struggle to the death, the strength of the crone was no laughing matter, but in the end it was no match for her age. Soon, as the lass, with the twilled fabric and silk tucked under her arm, was breathlessly and stealthily slipping out the door of the pagoda, the nun was quite still. It was later reported that her remains were found lying faceup in a dimly lit corner, a bit of blood having dripped from her nose and her head awash in gold dust.

"The lass fled Yasaka-dera and made her way to the hovel of a friend in Kyōgoku, near the bridge at Fifth Avenue, for, not surprisingly, she was eager to avoid heavily residential districts. The friend was living no less precariously from hand to mouth, but having no doubt received a bolt of silk, she boiled water, made rice gruel, and, it seems, went to great lengths to care for her guest. Now at long last she could be at her ease."

"I too am relieved to hear it." The young attendant took out a fan from his sash and adroitly snapped it open and shut, as he gazed out through the screen at the evening sun. At that moment five or six servants, dressed in white, were strolling along the road, laughing raucously and merrily, trailing long shadows as they passed.

"And so that is the end of the story?"

"Ah, but wait!" said the old man with an exaggerated shake of his head. "While she was still in the house of her friend, there was suddenly a great tumult in the street. And now she heard a cacophony of voices, crying: 'There! There!' With her already troubled conscience, she was immediately seized with anxiety. Had the thief come to exact revenge? Or had the constables come for her? Such was her state of mind that she was unable even to sip her gruel."

"Yes, yes . . ."

"Peering through an opening in the door, she could see among the onlookers five or six officers of the law, accompanied by a bailiff, passing in stately procession. In their midst was a man bound with a rope. He wore a tattered outer robe with no cap and was being pulled along by his captors. It appeared that they had arrested a thief and were taking him to his place of residence to make inventory of all his stolen treasure.

"Moreover, this thief was the very same man who the previous night had accosted the lass on Fifth Avenue. Seeing him, she seems for some reason to have burst into tears. She later told me herself that it was not in the least out of love for him. It was rather that as she saw him so ignominiously bound, she felt pity for herself . . . Be that all as it may, so it was – and at the time the story quite stirred me."

"In what way?"

"As a cautionary reminder of what may happen when we pray to Lady Kannon."

"But tell me, old man. Did she not find the means to make her way through life thereafter?"

"She has done better than merely make her way; she now passes her days quite without hardship. I should assume that for one thing she sold the twilled fabric and silk. In that at least the bodhisattva was true to her promise."

"It would seem to me only just recompense for her ordeal."

Outside, the sunlight was turning to the color of evening gold; from the bamboo thicket, stirred by a breeze, came a faint rustling sound. The road now appeared to be quite deserted.

"If it was not her intention to cause a death or to wed a thief, there is, I suppose, nothing further to be said."

The attendant reinserted his fan and stood up, as the old man poured water from a pitcher to wash his clay-covered hands . . . Each seemed to be feeling a vague dissatisfaction, both with the waning light of the spring afternoon and with the disposition of the other.

"Well, whatever the matter, the woman is fortunate," said the younger of the two.

"You are joking!" replied his companion.

"Not in the least. Do you not agree with me, as a man of your years?"

"As for me, I would have no truck with such fortune."

"Really? For my part, I would not hesitate to accept such blessings."

"Then by all means trust in the mercies of Lady Kannon!"

"Yes indeed. Tomorrow I shall go on my own retreat!"

KESA AND MORITŌ

1

It is night. Outside the earthen walls of the palace, Moritō gazes at the rising moon, brooding to himself as he tramps his way through fallen leaves.

His soliloquy:

"So the moon is out. There was a time when I could not wait for it to appear, but now this very brightness has become a dread omen. I tremble at the thought that this night I shall lose my soul, that tomorrow I shall be a common murderer. How rightly the mind's eye sees my hands already crimson with blood! How damned I shall soon seem even to myself! It would cause me no such anguish if I were to kill a detested foe. Yet tonight I must take the life of a man I do not hate.

"I know him by appearance, though his name, Wataru Saemon-no-jō, I learned only recently. When, I wonder, did I first see his fair complexion, a face which, for that of a man, is much too delicate. I confess to having felt pangs of jealousy on being told that this was Kesa's husband. Yet now every trace of such has vanished, so that though he might be my rival in love, I neither loathe nor resent him. Indeed, I could even say that I feel a degree of empathy. When Lady Koromogawa recounted to me how ardently Wataru had courted her niece, I went so far as to feel genuine fondness for him. Why, it seems that in his desire to make her his wife he even took lessons in writing verse. As I contemplate how this deeply earnest samurai composed and sent love poems to her, I sense a smile stealing over my lips – and by no means one of scorn. I am moved to think that he would do so much for a woman. Perhaps it is the knowledge of the passion that drove him to woo her that gives me, her paramour, a sense of satisfaction.

"Still I wonder: *Do I truly love Kesa?* My longing for her falls into two phases: past and present. I was already in love with her before she was wed to Wataru – or at least I thought I was. On reflection I now realize that there was much in my feelings for her that was sordid. What did I want of her? Having never had carnal knowledge of a woman, I clearly desired her body. If I may exaggerate, my love for her was, in fact, nothing more than a sentimental frame of mind, embellishing ordinary lust. I submit that though indeed during the three years in which all ties were lost, I never forgot her, the question remains whether, had I once possessed her, I would have remained as steadfast in my infatuation. I confess with shame that I lack the courage to offer an acknowledgment.

"Thus, my attachment to that woman was in no small measure mixed with regret at never having embraced her. It was in that anguished state that I entered into the liaison that I at once both feared and desired. But now? Once again I pose the question: *Do I really love Kesa?*

"Before answering, I must recall, however painfully, a series of events. After meeting her by chance, for the first time in all those three years, at the dedication of the Watanabe Bridge, I spent the next six months scheming and contriving to meet her in secret. In this I succeeded – and in more. I was able to fulfill my dream of making her mine.

"Yet what possessed me was not merely my previously stated regret at not having had her in my arms. As I sat on a mat in the same room with her in the house of Lady Koromogawa, I was aware of how that feeling had diminished. This may have been in part because I had come to know women. The principal reason was, however, that her beauty had faded; she was no longer the Kesa I had last seen three years before. Her skin had quite lost its luster, and her eyes were encircled by dark rings. The abundant flesh of her cheeks and chin had vanished as though it had never been. All that remained unchanged was the fresh and spirited look of those same jet-black eyes.

"The alteration clearly dealt a terrible blow to my desire for her. Brought together with her again for the first time, I felt compelled to look away. Even now I vividly remember it all.

"How is it then that, my longing having so receded, I came to be involved with her? First there was a bizarre desire for conquest. Sitting across from me, Kesa had poured out her love for Wataru with deliberate exaggeration; it only struck me as hollow. I thought to myself that she had quite a vain opinion of her husband, though it also occurred to me that she might be trying to ward off any pity or compassion on my part. I became increasingly desirous to lay bare her lies. Should anyone ask me why I thought it deception or suggest that such might have been simply my own conceit, I could not refute the charge, though this was my belief then, as it is even now.

"But it was not merely the urge for conquest that ruled me; it was

– and I blush red to confess it – something more: sheer lust. It was not even regret at not having made her flesh mine; rather it was something far baser, something for which she was not even required. It was lust for its own sake. A man procuring the favors of a harlot could not, I suppose, be as coarse and common as was I.

"With such muddled motives, I came at last to make love to her – or rather to bring shame upon her. And so I return once more to the question – *do I truly love Kesa?* – and find that it is one that I need not direct to myself after all. There are times when I even hate her. Especially when the ultimate act was completed and I forcibly lifted her up from where she had lain weeping, she struck me as an even more shameless creature than I. There was nothing – whether her tangled hair or the paint and powder on her perspiring face – that did not suggest a hideousness of both body and spirit. If I had ever had any love for her, it was extinguished forever on that day. And if, in fact, I never loved her, then I may freely say that henceforth there was in my heart a new sense of loathing. And now tonight, for the sake of this woman I do not love, I am setting forth to put to the sword a man I do not hate!

"That too is no one's sin but my own, for it was I myself who brazenly put the words in Kesa's ear: 'Shall we not kill Wataru?' When I contemplate what I whispered, I wonder whether I was not already quite mad. But the words were nonetheless mine. I told myself that I would say no such thing but then, through clenched teeth, did so nonetheless.

"The why of it is to me, now in retrospect, utterly incomprehensible. Forcing myself to explain it, I might suppose that the more I despised and loathed her, the more eagerly I sought her further humiliation and disgrace. Nothing could better serve that purpose than to propose killing Wataru Saemon-no-jō, the imperial guard, the husband for whom she has made such a display of her love, and coerce consent to my plan. And so I found myself, like a man driven by a nightmare, persuading her to assist in a murder I myself did not want to commit. If my motive is not sufficiently clear, then all that remains by way of explanation is a power unknown to mortals – or, if one prefers, a demon bent on subverting my will and leading me down the path of evil. In any case, I persistently whispered the same words again and again into Kesa's ear.

"At last she suddenly raised her face to mine and gave her docile assent. The ease of her answer was more than surprising. As I looked into her face, I saw in her eyes a strange light I had never seen before: adulteress! A feeling close to despair instantly unfurled before my own eyes the full horror of what I intended. How her wanton, withered features tormented me I need not say. If it had been within my power, I would have renounced our pact then and there and sent the lascivious creature plunging into the very depths of disgrace. Though I had made her my plaything, my conscience might at least then have been able to take refuge in righteous indignation. And yet such leeway was not to be mine, for now, with an abruptly altered expression, her eyes were fixed on me as though penetrating my innermost thoughts . . . I confess that I fell into this conspiracy, setting the day and hour of Wataru's murder out of fear that should I make the slightest attempt to extricate myself from it, I would be at the mercy of her vengeance. Even now I am held firmly in the grip of terror. Those who would despise me for cowardice may do so, but then they will not be such who have known Kesa as I saw her then. As I watched her weep without tears, I thought despairingly that if I were now to refuse to kill him, she would not fail to kill me, even if not by her own hand.

"I would therefore carry out the deed. Even as I swore to her, did I not see on her pale face, to confirm my fears, the dimple of a smile?

Oh, because of this cursed oath, I shall add to all my other sins the crime of murder. If I could but evade the impending doom to which I am committed this very night! But I cannot. Fealty to my own oath and fear of her revenge conspire against me.

"All this is certainly true, but there is more to it. What might it be? It is something that drives even a coward such as me to murder. What overwhelming power is it? I do not know. And yet . . . But no . . . I despise, fear, and hate her. And yet perhaps it is also out of love . . ."

Moritō wanders on aimlessly but says no more. From somewhere the sound of a chant is heard:

> *Truly is the heart of man no other than an endless night,*
> *His life a raging, death-doomed fire of envy, lust, and spite.*

2

It is night. Kesa sits outside her bed curtains, her back to an oil lamp. Clenching a sleeve in her mouth, she is lost in thought.

Her soliloquy:

"Will he come or will he not? It is scarcely possible that he should not, and yet the moon is sinking, and still I hear no footsteps. Has he suddenly changed his mind? Oh, if he comes not, I must, like a harlot, raise my shameful face once more to the morning sun. How could I do anything so brazen, so wicked? I should be like a corpse abandoned at the side of the road, disgraced, trampled upon, and then brutally exposed to the light of day. And yet I would mutely endure it all, and were such to happen, not even death would bring an end to it. No, no, he surely will come. Looking into his eyes when we recently parted, I could not help but know that he would. He fears me. Even as he hates and despises me, that fear remains. In fact, if I were relying merely on myself, I could not say so, but on *him* I can rely, on his egotism, or rather on the ignoble fear that springs from it. Thus, I can be sure that he will indeed steal into this chamber.

"Yet what a wretched creature I am, not to be able to depend upon myself! Until at least three years ago I could count both on myself and on my beauty, perhaps until much more recently, indeed until that fateful day, when in that room in my aunt's house I met him and saw at a glance how my ugliness was reflected in his mind's eye. He acted as though it were nothing and even flattered me with kind words. But how can a woman's heart be consoled once her own repulsiveness has been revealed to her? I felt chagrin, fear, and sadness. I remembered as a child being seized with horror when, held in my nurse's arms, I saw an eclipse of the moon. Yet this was immeasurably worse. In an instant, all the fond illusions I had ever cherished were gone. I was enveloped in loneliness as bleak as a rainy dawn and thus, trembling in forlorn despair, yielded my body to a man I do not love, to a lecher who loathes and despises me.

"Was it that I had been unable to bear the desolation of having seen my unsightly appearance revealed? In pressing my face to his breast, was I attempting in one moment of heated frenzy to dull the pain of it all? If not, was I, like him, simply driven by lewd desire? The mere thought fills me with shame, with shame, with shame! What wretchedness I felt when, having been released from his arms, I was once again mistress of my own body!

"As much as I wanted not to weep, bitterness and loneliness brought an unending flood of tears to my eyes. Yet the cause of my misery was not merely my infidelity; above all, it was the disdain he heaped upon me in committing the act, quite as though I were a leprous dog, to be loathed and abused.

"What I did next I can now only recall as a dim memory, as though from the distant past. Yet I know that, as I was sobbing, I felt the whiskers on his upper lip touching my ear and his hot breath whispering in a low voice: 'Let us kill Wataru.'

"Hearing his words, I felt strangely, radiantly alive, in a manner I had never known before. Alive? If moonlight may be said to be bright, then such indeed was my state of mind, though a luminous moon would still be altogether different. Yet did not his terrible words bring comfort to me? Oh, can I, a woman, rejoice at being loved by a man, though such should mean her husband's murder?

"In this moonlight state of mind, forlorn and yet euphoric, I went on weeping. But then? Then? When did I at last agree to have him strike my husband dead? It was only in that moment that I first remembered him. Yes, I must honestly say, only then, for I had been thinking solely and entirely of my own disgrace. Now I thought of him, of my reserved and diffident husband, and yet not of him: what I saw clearly before my eyes was rather his smiling face when he speaks to me. And it was perhaps precisely then, as I remembered that face, that my plan came to me: as of that very moment I knew I was determined to die. The mere fact of having made so firm a resolution filled me with joy.

"But as I ceased my weeping, looked up into his face, and saw my ugliness reflected in his heart, that same joy instantly vanished, and I remembered the darkness of the eclipsed moon that I had seen with my nurse. It was as though, for all my exaltation, a host of demons had been hiding beneath and were now released.

"By dying in my husband's place, am I really doing so out of love for him? No, no. Behind that convenient façade lies my desire to atone for the sin of yielding my body to that man. I lack the courage to die by my own hand; in this way, I shall at least show myself to the world in a better light. It is admittedly a petty motive, but for that I might be pardoned. And yet I have been a far more miserable and monstrous creature than that. Is it not that I am feigning to die in my husband's place, so that I may take revenge on the man who has hated and scorned me and turned me into the object of his evil lust?

"I need no more proof than the loss, as I looked into his face, of that strange moonlight euphoria as my heart was instantly frozen in grief. It is for myself and not for my husband that I intend to die, for the pain of a wounded heart, for the chagrin of a body defiled. Ah, I have not only lived a useless life; I shall now die a useless death!

"Yet how much better to choose this useless death than to prolong my life! Forcing myself to smile despite my sorrow, I promised again and again that I would conspire with him. He is quick-witted enough to surmise with dread certainty the measures I will take if he should break his word. He solemnly swore an oath to me, and so indeed he will steal his way in to where I lie.

"Is that the sound of the wind? When I think that all my woe since that fateful day is now at last to end this night, I feel my anguished spirit ease. The morrow's sun will cast its chill rays on my headless corpse, and when my husband sees . . . No, I must not think of him. He loves me, but I have no strength to return that love. From long ago I have been capable of loving only one man, and that man will come tonight to kill me – me, for whom, tormented to the very end by my lover, even the glow of the lamp is now too bright."

Kesa extinguishes her lamp. Presently the opening of a latticed shutter is faintly heard, as pale moonlight breaks into the room.

THE DEATH OF A DISCIPLE

*Even if one were to live for three hundred years and be surfeited with
pleasure, it would, in comparison to the joys of the eternity that awaits
us, be naught but a passing dream.*

(from a Keichō-era translation of *Guia do Peccador*)[1]

*Those who follow the path of virtue will know the wondrous taste of
holy doctrine.*

(from a Keichō-era translation of *Imitatio Christi* by Thomas à Kempis)

I

Long ago there was a boy by the name of Lorenzo, who lived in the
Ecclesia of Santa Lucia, in the city of Nagasaki. He had been found
prostrate at the entrance to the church one Christmas night, overcome by hunger and exhaustion. The worshippers had gone to his
aid, whereupon, it appears, the padre out of sheer compassion had

resolved to take him under his wing. Yet whenever he was asked about his origins, Lorenzo would parry all questions with a guileless smile and offer only the vaguest of replies: his home, he said, was *Paraiso*, his father *Deus*. From the blue *contas* (rosary beads) encircling his wrist, one could see that his parents were not *gentios*. Thus, both the padre and the *irmãos* (monks), thinking that there was certainly no reason for suspicion, were most hospitable. For all his youth, he was so firm in the faith that the *superiors* (elders) could only marvel, and though neither his place of birth nor parentage was known, the entire community showered him with boundless affection, declaring that he was surely a heavenly guardian appearing in the guise of a child.

Moreover, his features were of a jewel-like purity, and his voice was as gentle as a maiden's. This too no doubt added to the love that he drew.

Among the Japanese monks, there was one called Simeon, who treated Lorenzo as a younger brother, so that whenever they came into or left the church, they were arm in arm. Simeon, the tallest of them all, came from a family of spearmen in service to one of the great lords. He had inherited the preternatural strength of his forebears and on more than several occasions had warded off the slate tiles thrown at the priest by the *gentios*. The friendship between Lorenzo and Simeon might have been likened to a dove enfolded in the wings of a fierce eagle or to a blooming vine entwined round a cedar on the slopes of Lebanon.

More than three years passed, and it was now time for Lorenzo to undergo the coming-of-age ceremony. It was then, however, that a strange rumor was heard. The daughter of the umbrella-maker living in the city not far from the church, it was said, had become intimate with Lorenzo. The father was himself a Christian, and it was his custom to bring the girl to mass with him. There, even during prayers, she could not keep her eyes off Lorenzo, whom she could see holding an incensory in his hand. Moreover, with her hair arranged most beautifully, she would invariably fix her gaze on him whenever she entered or left the church.

This was, of course, seen by the faithful. One reported that as the young woman was passing Lorenzo, she had allowed her foot to rest on his. Another swore to having witnessed the two exchanging love missives.

The padre could not ignore the matter and so one day summoned Lorenzo. "Concerning thee and the umbrella-maker's daughter," he said gently, chewing on his white beard, "I have heard whispered this and that, though surely none of it can be true. What sayest thou to it all?"

Lorenzo could only shake his head sadly and tearfully repeat that no such thing had taken place. The priest had to concede that in view of the lad's age and the piety that he regularly manifested, it was most unlikely that he was telling anything but the truth.

Thus, at least for the moment, his suspicions were dispelled. But the matter did not end so easily in the minds of his flock. The fraternal feelings of Simeon made him all the more concerned. At first the thought of making an open inquiry into such ignominious allegations filled him with shame, and he found himself quite incapable even of looking Lorenzo directly in the face, much less of directly interrogating him. One day, however, in the rear garden of the church, he happened to find lying on the ground an amorous letter written by the girl and addressed to Lorenzo. Thrusting it before him in a felicitous moment when they were alone in a room, Simeon pressed him for an explanation, threatening the boy one minute, cajoling him the next.

Lorenzo could only reply, a blush on his beautiful face: "She appears to have allowed her heart to be drawn to me, but I have merely received her letters and never spoken to her." Yet Simeon, painfully aware of public calumny, continued to interrogate him. To this Lorenzo stared sadly into the other's eyes and declared with an air of reproach: "So even thou wouldst take me to be a teller of lies!" Then like a swallow he rose and abruptly left the room.

Crestfallen at these words and ashamed at the depth of his own suspicions, Simeon was himself about to leave when Lorenzo came bursting back in. Throwing his arms around Simeon's neck, he breathlessly whispered: "I was wrong! Forgive me!" Before Simeon could reply, Lorenzo, perhaps in an effort to hide his tear-stained face, suddenly pushed him away and ran out again. Simeon was left quite mystified, not knowing whether Lorenzo had intended to express remorse for an illicit liaison with the umbrella-maker's daughter or sorrow at having treated his friend with rudeness.

Not long thereafter came the news that the girl was with child. Moreover, she openly told her father that she had been impregnated by none other than Lorenzo of the Ecclesia of Santa Lucia. The old man flew into a rage and lost no time in reporting the full particulars to the padre. Overwhelmed by the accusation, Lorenzo could offer not a word in his own defense. In the course of the day, the priest and the monks met in council and pronounced their sentence: expulsion. The verdict meant that he was driven from the presence of the padre as well, leaving him quite without any means for supporting himself. Even those who out of love for him might otherwise have offered help were obliged to consider that to keep such a sinner in their midst would do dishonor to the *Gloria* of the Lord and so with many a tear agreed to his banishment.

Simeon was, however, the most miserable of all. His sadness at seeing Lorenzo driven away was greatly exceeded by his anger at having been deceived. At the very moment that the hapless lad was leaving the church portals, heading with heavy heart into a fierce winter wind, Simeon clenched his fist and violently struck the side of that beautiful face. It is said that Lorenzo, felled by the powerful blow, slowly rose again, his tear-filled eyes turned toward heaven, as in a trembling voice he murmured a prayer: "Lord, forgive him, for he knows not what he does." Utterly disheartened, Simeon could only stand in the doorway, shaking that same fist at the sky. When the other brothers had made various efforts to calm him, he stood back with arms folded, his face as ominously dark as the sky on the verge of a storm, staring after the dejected Lorenzo, quite as though he might devour him. The westering sun, shimmering in the wintry wind, was setting Nagasaki's horizon aflame, and as the bowed figure of the youth made his way from their midst, it seemed to the parishioners gathered there that for a moment the gentle lad remained transfixed, as though held in the embrace of that giant globe of fire.

The Lorenzo who once within the chancel of Santa Lucia had held the incensory was now reduced to living as a miserable beggar in a pariah's hovel outside the city. Moreover, having been a servant of the Lord, he was despised by the *gentios* as no better than a jackal. We are told that whenever he ventured into town, he was sure to be taunted by heartless children and that more than once he was subjected to blows from swords and canes, tiles and stones. Once when a terrible fever swept through Nagasaki, he spent seven days and seven nights writhing in agony by the side of the road. Yet *Deus* in His infinite mercy not only spared the life of Lorenzo but also bestowed on him His constant blessings, so that even when he was given no alms in rice or coin, he received his daily sustenance from the fruit of the mountains or the fish and clams of the sea. And for his part, Lorenzo did not neglect the morning and evening prayers he had once offered up in Santa Lucia; his rosary beads were likewise always on his wrist.

Moreover, in the stillness of the night he would stealthily leave his outcast's hut and tread the light of the moon to the beloved church and there pray that the Lord Jesus might watch over him.

Yet the worshippers at the Ecclesia resolutely shunned him, and there was no one, not even the priest, who took pity on him. Having expelled him as guilty of the most despicable and shameless behavior, they would not have dreamt that such a youth was possessed of so deep a faith that he would make nightly journeys to the church. Such are the unfathomable ways of Divine Providence, but all this, needless to say, fell so much the harder on Lorenzo

But we must now return to the umbrella-maker's daughter, who gave premature birth to a baby girl not long after Lorenzo's banishment. Even the stubborn old man was unable to look with enmity on the face of his first grandchild and so lavished the same affection as he had on the mother, cradling the infant and giving her dolls and other playthings. Under the circumstances, this might have only been natural, but, strangely enough, Irmão Simeon, that same towering giant who might have felled o Diabo himself, began to come calling whenever he found the time, holding the child in his uncouth arms and allowing a flow of tears to cover his embittered face, as he remembered the delicate and graceful figure of the lad he had once regarded as a brother. As for the young mother, however, she appeared to be vexed to the point of despair that Lorenzo had not shown himself once since being expelled from Santa Lucia and at the same time somehow less than pleased at the visits of Simeon.

No border guardsman, as the proverb tells us, can halt the passage of time. One should imagine how within a twinkling of an eye, a year had come and gone. Then there was in Nagasaki a conflagration that in one night destroyed half of the city. So terrifying was the spectacle that the hair of those who witnessed it stood on end, for they might well have believed that they had heard the trumpet of the Last Judgment thundering across the fiery sky.

To the misfortune of the old umbrella-maker, his house lay downwind of the blaze and was quickly enveloped. The entire family fled in panic, only to realize that the grandchild was nowhere to be seen. They had clearly left her asleep in one of the rooms. The old man scuffed the ground and cursed, while his daughter attempted to rush into the inferno, only to be restrained. The wind grew all the more intense, the flames licking upward as though to engulf the very stars in the heavens. Even the townspeople who had gathered with the intention of battling the fire could do no more than mill about or attempt to calm the frantic mother. But now pushing his way hurriedly through the crowd came Irmão Simeon. A stout warrior who had survived arrow and bullet on the field of battle, he bravely entered the burning house as soon as he understood what had come to pass. Yet the flames proved too much even for him, and after two or three attempts at plunging through smoke, he turned back and hastily retreated. He came to where the grandfather and mother were lingering and said: "This too is in accordance with all that the Divine Will has ordained. To this you must resign yourselves."

At that moment, someone to the side of the old man was heard to cry out: "Lord, help me!" Simeon turned, recognizing the voice with both wonder and certainty. One look at those pitiful, fair features was enough for him to know that this was Lorenzo. His pure, gaunt face glowing red with the fire and his dark hair, now grown beyond his shoulders, fluttering in the wind, the beggar stood in front of the crowd and stared straight ahead at the blazing house. Yet only an instant later, it seemed, he had rushed in amidst those burning pillars, walls, and beams, even as a terrible wind arose to fan the already raging flames. Simeon felt his body covered in sweat, as he made the sign of the cross in the air and cried out, "Lord, save him!" In his mind's eye, he could see once again the beautiful, mournful Lorenzo, standing at the portals of Santa Lucia, bathed in the light of the sun, as it shimmered in the wintry wind.

The Christians gathered there looked on in amazement at Lorenzo's courage, but they seemed unable to forget his past sin. Immediately the sound of wagging tongues was borne through the air over the din of the crowd: "A fine display of paternal love! His shame was too great for him to show his face until now that he must leap into the fire to save his own child!" There was not one among them who did not exchange such words of scorn.

The old man appeared to agree with them. He stared at Lorenzo, and then, as though to conceal the strange agitation in his heart, twisted and turned where he stood, shrieking absurdities. His daughter, now utterly distraught, knelt motionless; covering her face with both hands, she was earnestly praying. The sky rained sparks, as smoke swept over the ground and into her face. Lost to the world, she continued silently in her entreaties.

Now again there was a stirring in the multitude facing the blaze, as Lorenzo, emerging from the inferno, his hair disheveled, appeared as though descending from heaven, the infant in his arms. But suddenly a beam, apparently having been burned asunder, came crashing down with a terrifying roar, sending smoke and flames high into the night sky. All sight of Lorenzo was lost, with nothing remaining but pillars of fire, rising from the earth like branches of coral.

There was no one in the crowd of the faithful, from Simeon to the old umbrella-maker, who was not stunned and confounded by the terror and horror. The young woman uttered a shriek and jumped up, exposing her bare legs, before collapsing again, as though, they say, struck by lightning. Yet whatever the truth may be, it suddenly and wondrously appeared to them, though when they did not know, that the infant, for all the tenuousness of earthly life, was now in her mother's firm embrace.

Oh, there are no words that can do homage to the infinite wisdom and power of *Deus*! Lorenzo had, with all his force, thrown the child forward as the burning beam fell, so that she had rolled, quite unharmed, to the very feet of her mother. The girl threw herself prostrate on the ground, her voice choked with tears of joy, while her father, standing erect, raised his arms and in solemn tones spontaneously offered up a hymn of praise to the Lord of Mercy – or rather, I should say, had just begun to do so, when Simeon moved ahead of him and with a single bound threw himself into the surging storm of fire, intent on the rescue of Lorenzo. Now the old man raised his voice again, though now directing an anxious and piteous prayer into the dark firmament. He was not, of course, alone. All of the faithful around them were in unison in their tearful entreaty: "Lord, save them!" And the Son of the *Virgem Maria*, our Savior *Jesu Cristo*, who taketh upon Himself the sufferings and sorrows of us all, at long last heard their prayer. Behold! Lorenzo, horribly burned, now emerged again from the fire and smoke in the protective arms of Simeon.

This was not, however, to be the end of the night's wondrous and terrible events. The faithful hastened to carry Lorenzo, who was struggling for breath, to the doors of the church, which was mercifully upwind of the fire. There they laid him down to rest.

As the padre came out to meet them, the umbrella-maker's daughter, who had been clutching the infant to her breast even as her tears continued to flow, suddenly knelt at his feet and before the entire assembly made a most unexpected *confissão*: "This child is not of Lorenzo's seed. In truth, she was conceived through my sinful liaison with the son of the *gentios* next door."

The earnestness of her trembling voice and her glistening, tear-filled eyes would alone have dispelled any suspicion as to the veracity of her confession. The crowd around them could only gasp in astonishment, oblivious to the firestorm that filled the sky.

She ceased her weeping and continued:

"I pined and yearned for Lorenzo, but so fervent was he in his faith that he quite rebuffed me. I sought to tell him of the resentment that filled my heart by falsely claiming that the child in my womb was his. Yet such was his nobility of spirit that rather than despising me for my great sin, he has this night put his own life in peril by entering the flames of this veritable *Inferno* to save my daughter. His merciful and benevolent deed would seem to me to be truly like the return of our Lord *Jesu Cristo*. But knowing the grave and terrible wrongs I have committed, I could have no reason for grudge if my body were now instantly torn to pieces by *o Diabo* himself."

No sooner had she completed her confession than she threw herself again on the ground and sobbed. From the surrounding faithful, now two or three deep, burst a wave of voices: *"Mártir! Mártir!"*

And what else might he have been called? Neither the padre to whom he had looked up to as a father nor the brother who had been Simeon had known what lay in his heart. Yet had he not out of pity for a sinner most admirably followed in the steps of our Lord *Jesu Cristo*, even allowing himself to be degraded to mendicancy?

As he listened to the girl's words, Lorenzo could do no more than nod his head twice or thrice. His hair burned, his skin scorched, he was unable to move his hands and feet and so close to the end of his strength as to be unable to speak. The old umbrella-maker and Simeon, heart-stricken as they heard the daughter's confession, crouched by his side and did what little they could for him. As he drew ever-shorter breaths, it was clear that he was not far from death. All that remained unchanged was the hue of his starry eyes, gazing into the distant heavens.

With his back to the portals of Santa Lucia and his white beard blowing in the fierce night wind, the padre listened to the confession and then solemnly declared: "Happy are the repentant. What human hand would dare inflict punishment on anyone so blessed? Henceforth be bound to God's commandments and serenely await the Day of Judgment. Ah, Lorenzo, seeking to serve the Lord by following in His footsteps . . . Rare is such virtue among all the Christians of this land – especially for a lad so young . . ."

Yet what was this? The priest suddenly fell silent and stared intently, indeed reverentially, at Lorenzo there at his feet, as though he had seen the light of *Paraiso*. The trembling of his hands too suggested that here was nothing of the ordinary, and now tears were flooding his withered cheeks.

Behold! Simeon! And you, old maker of umbrellas! As the exquisitely beautiful boy lay silently before the portals of Santa Lucia, illuminated by the reflection of the flames, redder still than the blood of our Lord, the holes in his burned upper garment revealed two pure, pearl-like breasts. Even in his fire-seared face, there was an unmistakable and now undisguised tenderness and sweetness. Ah! Lorenzo was a woman, a woman!

See now the faithful, their backs to the fierce flames, forming a fencelike circle round her! This Lorenzo, once charged with lasciviousness and banished from Santa Lucia, was as lovely a girl of this land as the umbrella-maker's daughter!

At that awe-filled moment, they say, it was as though the voice of God could be heard from beyond the starry heavens. Like heads of grain before the wind, one, then another, and finally the entire flock bowed their heads and knelt before Lorenzo. The roar of the towering flames, reverberating through the sky, was the only sound to be heard – except now for a sobbing voice, that of the umbrella-maker's daughter perhaps or of Irmão Simeon, the elder brother. Presently amidst the desolation was also the trembling voice of the padre, his hand raised high over Lorenzo, as he intoned a solemn, mournful chant. When he had finished, he called out to her, but she now looked up into the still dark night sky and then beyond to the glory of Paradise. With a peaceful smile upon her lips, she breathed her last . . .

I have heard it said that this is all that is known about her life. But what of it? That which is most precious in a human life is indeed found in such an irreplaceable moment of ecstasy. To hurl a single wave into a void of depravity, as dark as a nocturnal sea, and capture in the foam the light of a not-yet-risen moon . . . It is such a life that is worth living. If so, is it not in knowing the end of Lorenzo's life that one knows it all?

2

Among my books is one published by the Jesuits of Nagasaki; despite its title, *Legenda Aurea*, it is not strictly the collection of "golden legends" known in the West. Rather it contains, along with the words and deeds of Occidental apostles and saints, a record of valiant and dedicated Japanese Christians, apparently intended to further the cause of evangelization.

Printed on *mino* paper, the two volumes are written in a mixture of cursive-style characters and the *hiragana* syllabary. The letters are so faint as to cause one to doubt whether they were, in fact, printed. On the front leaf of the first volume, the Latin title is written horizontally; below it, two vertical lines in Chinese characters note: "Imprinted in the first days of the third month in the Year of Grace 1596, the Second Year of the Keichō era." On each side of the date is the image of an angel blowing a trumpet; these are technically quite crude but are nonetheless possessed of a certain charm. The front leaf of the second volume is the same, though the printing date is given as the middle of the fifth month.

The volumes each contain approximately sixty pages; the "golden legends" contained in the first are eight, those of the second, ten. Each also begins with a preface by an anonymous writer, followed by a table of contents that includes words written in Roman letters.

The style of the prefaces is hardly polished, and intermittently the reader even encounters expressions that suggest literal translation from a European language. Even a cursory examination raises the suspicion that they were indeed written by an Occidental priest.

This story is an adaptation of Chapter Two in the second volume. In all probability, it is the faithful rendition of events that took place at a church in Nagasaki, but of the great fire it describes there is no other record, not even in the *Chronicles of Port Nagasaki*. Thus, it is quite impossible to assign a precise date.

The exigencies of publication have obliged me to embellish the text here and there. I trust that in so doing I have not marred the simple elegance of the original.

O'ER A WITHERED MOOR

Summoning Jōsō and Kyorai, he said to them: "Last night, as I lay sleepless, I suddenly thought of this and had Donshū write it down. Each one of you should read it."

> *Ill on a journey,*
> *Wandering in fevered dreams*
> *O'er a withered moor.*[1]
>
> HANAYA'S DIARY

It was the seventh year of the Genroku era, on the twelfth day of the tenth month. The merchants of Ōsaka had awakened to the fleeting hues of a rosy dawn, fretfully seeing in this a sign, as they gazed far beyond the tiled roofs of the city, that yesterday's rain would return. Happily, however, not even the tops of the leafless willow trees were obscured by rain, so that now it was a pale early winter's day, cloudy but calm. Even the water of the river, flowing absentmindedly between the rows of houses, was somehow lusterless, and the discarded leek leaves floating on its surface seemed – or was this merely an impression? – to be a tepid green. The passersby along its banks, some hooded, others shod in split-toed leather socks, likewise appeared, without exception, to be quite lost to the world, oblivious to the bitter wind that blew. The color of the curtains hanging outside of the shops, the carriages going to and fro, the distant sound of a *shamisen* playing for a puppet theater – all conspired to guard the pallor and tranquillity of this wintry afternoon, not so much as disturbing the urban dust on the decorative knobs of the bridge posts.

It was there, at this same time, in the rear annex of Hanaya Nizaemon's residence in Midōmae-Minami-kyūtarō-machi, that the revered *haikai* master Matsuo Tōsei of the Banana Plant Hermitage, then in his fifty-first year, was quietly drawing his last breaths, "like the slowly fading warmth of buried embers." Tending to him were disciples from the four corners of the land. As for the time, the Hour of the Monkey[2] may have half elapsed.

The sliding doors in the middle had been removed to form a single immense room; from a stick of burning incense placed at the bedside rose a wisp of smoke, casting a thin, bone-chilling shadow on the bright, new paper of the door, beyond which lay the veranda, the garden, and the all-embracing winter. Bashō lay serenely with his head toward the door. Prominent among those around him was his physician, Mokusetsu, frowning as he held a hand under the bedclothes to check his patient's sluggish pulse. Sitting hunched behind him was the unmistakable figure of the master's old servant Jirōbei, who had come with him from Iga. For some time he had been reciting in a low, unceasing voice the holy invocation of the Amida Buddha.

Next to Mokusetsu sat another whom all would recognize: Shinshi Kikaku, massive and obese, his breast generously inflating his square-sleeved pongee half coat. He was intensely observing their master's condition, as was the dignified Kyorai, wearing a finely patterned, deep-brown, square-shouldered garment. Sitting quietly upright behind Kikaku was Jōsō; the bodhi prayer beads dangling from his wrist conveyed the air of a priest. The place beside him was occupied by Otsushū, whose constant sniffling was no doubt a sign of the unendurable grief that had seized him. Glaring at this spectacle, his cantankerous chin jutting out, was a diminutive monk, arranging and rearranging the sleeves of his old clothes. This was Inenbō, who sat facing Mokusetsu. To his side was the dark-complexioned Shikō, an air of obstinacy about him. The others were apprentices, most maintaining so strict a silence that they scarcely seemed to be breathing. They sat at all sides of his bed, lamenting unceasingly the cruelty of death in separating them from their master. Among them there was one who had thrown himself prostrate into a corner, his body flattened against the straw mats. This was probably Seishū, who was wailing uncontrollably, though the sound was swallowed up in the frigid silence of the room and did not distract from the faint scent of incense that rose from the bedside of the invalid.

A few moments before, in a voice rendered uncertain by phlegm, Bashō had expressed his last wishes and then appeared to fall into a comatose state, his eyes half-open. Only the cheekbones of his terribly emaciated face, marked by slight traces of smallpox, stood out; his lips, swallowed up in wrinkles, were drained of all color. Most pitiful of all was the expression in his eyes, in which floated a vague light, as though they were vainly searching for a distant place far beyond the roof – in cold, infinite space.

> *Ill on a journey,*
> *Wandering in fevered dreams*
> *O'er a withered moor.*

Perhaps drifting dreamlike in that moment of delirium, as in his death verse of several days before, was the vision of a vast desolate field in a moonless twilight. At length Mokusetsu turned toward Jirōbei sitting behind him and murmured:

"Water . . ."

The old servant had already prepared a bowl and a small plumed stick. These he timidly pushed toward his master; then, as though the thought had suddenly occurred to him, he began to move his mouth rapidly in a single-minded recitation of the mantra: "Namu Amida Butsu." Deeply ingrained in the simple soul of Jirōbei, a man reared in the mountains, was the belief that to be reborn in the Pure Land, whether Bashō or any other, one must cling to the mercy of Amitābha.

At the very moment that he called for water, Mokusetsu found himself wondering anxiously, as was his wont, whether he had done all that he could as a physician. Bolstering his courage, he turned to Kikaku beside him and gave a wordless nod. All those gathered around Bashō's bed were immediately seized by the tense premonition that the moment of death was at hand. It is also undeniable that mixed with this taut emotion was a fleeting sense of relief, indeed, something akin to serenity in the thought that the inevitable moment had now arrived.

It was, however, so subtle a sentiment that none was conscious of it. Not even Kikaku, the most realistic of them all, could help shuddering when he happened to catch the eyes of Mokusetsu and see in them a fleeting hint of that same thought. He hastily turned away and took up the plumed stick with an air of unconcern and said to Kyorai beside him: "Allow me to be the first."

He dipped the plume into the water, edged forward on his thick knees, and glanced surreptitiously at the face of the dying master.

Previously he had, to be sure, imagined with what sadness he would one day bid farewell to him, but now that the moment had arrived and he was making the last offering of water,[3] his actual emotions quite betrayed his somewhat theatrical expectations: they were of cold and cloudless indifference. Moreover, to his surprise, the eerie appearance of the moribund Bashō, who quite literally had wasted away until he was no more than skin-covered bones, filled him with such violent revulsion that he nearly turned his face away. Indeed, "violent" is hardly a sufficient expression. It was a most unbearable repugnance, quite invisible to the eye but so strong as to produce in him a physiological reaction, as though from a vile poison. Had this happenstance encounter with the sick body of the master caused him to give vent to his horror of all that is ugly? Or did this emblem of Death's reality emanate as an ominous threat from Nature, upon which he, a hedonistic proponent of Life, was wont above all else to pronounce his curse? . . . Whichever it may have been, Kikaku, with no more than the slightest feeling of sadness, had no sooner moistened the thin, purplish lips with the brush, the face of the dying man filling him with inexpressible loathing, than he grimaced and drew away. In that instant, he felt a vague twinge of conscience, but so intense was his sense of disgust that it appeared to preclude any such moral considerations.

Kikaku was followed by Kyorai, who since Mokusetsu's signal appeared to have lost his composure. True to his reputation as a consistently modest man, he nodded slightly to all assembled as he slid his way to Bashō's side, but as soon as he saw the disease-ravaged face of the old poet stretched out before him, he felt despite himself a strange mixture of satisfaction and remorse. These emotions, as inextricably linked as darkness and light, had indeed been troubling the mind of the timid man over the course of the last four or five days. Learning of Bashō's serious illness, Kyorai had immediately set out by ship from Fushimi and, having rapped on Hanaya Nizaemon's door in the dead of night, watched over his master day in and day out. Moreover, by prevailing upon Shidō to arrange for an assistant, sending someone to Sumiyoshi Shrine to pray for their ailing master, and consulting with Hanaya for the purchase of various personal effects, he had, more than anyone, endeavored zealously and relentlessly to provide whatever was required. Needless to say, he had done all of this quite on his own, never intending to impose a debt of gratitude on anyone.

The intense awareness of having immersed himself in the care of his master had naturally planted within him the seeds of enormous satisfaction. Hardly knowing his own mind in this, he felt rather untroubled in allowing the emotion to warm his carefree heart as he went about his daily tasks.

Had this been otherwise, he might well have conducted himself differently with Shikō, as one evening they kept their vigil under the light of an oil lamp. Rather than holding forth on the subject of filial piety and dwelling endlessly on his desire to serve Bashō as a son would a father, he would have conversed of mundane matters. Though basking in such complacency, he had caught in the spiteful face of Shikō the flicker of a sarcastic smile and now felt his tranquil state of mind dis-turbed. The cause was the dismal realization, as brought home to him by his own self-critical eye, of a hitherto unconscious sense of self-approval. Even as he nursed his master, so gravely ill that there was no knowing what the next day would bring, he was far from anxious or concerned for him; rather he was vainly and smugly observing the pains that he was taking on his behalf. For a man of such honesty, such a revelation would surely have aroused in him terrible pangs of conscience.

Since then, in whatever he sought to undertake, he had naturally felt constricted, trapped between the conflicting emotions of pride and contrition. Of the former, he became all the more aware whenever he glimpsed, if only by chance, the hint of a smirk in Shikō's eyes, a frequent and ever more painful reminder of his lowliness.

Thus the days had passed, and now here he was at the master's bedside, taking his turn to offer him these last drops of water. That this man, so morally upright and, at the same time, so strangely overwrought, should have lost complete control in the face of such a contradiction was a cause for pity but hardly surprise. As he grasped the feathered stick and with its wetted white point caressed the lips of Bashō, his body oddly stiffened, and his hand trembled unceasingly with the abnormal agitation that had seized him. Fortunately, it was just then that his eyelashes were flooded with pearl-like tears, so that all of Bashō's disciples gathered there, even including the caustic Shikō, could no doubt grasp that his outward appearance reflected a profound sadness.

The shoulders of his kimono rising again, Kyorai now timidly resumed his place, and the plumed stick passed to the hand of Jōsō, who sat directly behind him. This ever-faithful disciple murmured a chant with respectfully lowered eyes as he dampened the lips of the master, his solemn demeanor doubtlessly noticed by all. But now amidst the solemnity there was heard from a corner of the room an eerie peel of laughter – or at least so it seemed. It could well have been taken to be the sound of a chortle coming from the intestinal depths and, though held back by the throat and lips, issuing in bursts from the nostrils under the irrepressible pressure of a droll event or comment. Needless to say, from that assembly came no such sound. It was merely that Seishū, his eyes already dim with tears, was at last unable, despite heroic efforts, to hold back a great cry of lament; it gushed forth as though his very heart had broken. It was, of course, the expression of sorrow at its most extreme. Among the disciples there must have been many who remembered their master's celebrated verse:

Shake, O grave mound, shake,
For the sound of my wailing
Is the autumn wind.[4]

Though he too was choked with dark grief, Otsushū could not but feel unease at what seemed amidst it all to be an excessive display or, at the very least, to put it more cautiously, a certain lack of self-restraint. Yet such may well have been no more than a purely rational judgment, for now, whatever his reason might say, his heart was suddenly moved by Seishū's lamentation, and his eyes were filled with tears. His discomfort at the other's outburst – and, in turn, shame at his own – remained unchanged. But still he gave way to the full flood of emotion. His hands resting on his knees, he sobbed in spite of himself. In this, he was not alone: the very air of that hitherto cold and grimly silent room quivered, as in near unison even those disciples who had sat demurely at the foot of Bashō's bed broke out in fitful sniffling.

Amidst all these mournful voices, Jōsō, his bodhi prayer beads still dangling from his wrist, quietly resumed his place. Sitting directly across from Kikaku and Kyorai was Shikō, who now took his turn. But Tōkabō, known as a cynic, did not appear to suffer in the least from the sort of distraught nerves that would cause him, induced by the sentimentality all around him, to shed vain tears. As he unceremoniously moistened the lips of the master, there was on his swarthy face the same familiar expression: a mélange of mockery and a strange haughtiness. Yet it is, of course, indisputable that even he was filled with a measure of emotion.

Cutting to the quick,
("Here I leave my bones to bleach . . .")
The harsh autumn wind.[5]

Four or five days before, the master had said: "I had long thought that I would die stretched out on the grass, with earth for my headrest. I could not be happier than to see the hope for a peaceful end here fulfilled on this splendid bed." This he had oft repeated as an expression of his gratitude, though whether he was now lying on a withered moor or in the rear annex of Hanaya Nizaemon's residence was of no significant difference.

In fact, up until three or four days before, the very person now moistening the lips of the dying man had worried that his master had not yet composed his last verse; just the day before he had contemplated how he might compile a posthumous book of his *hokku*. Now today, just a few minutes before, he had been intently observing the old man as he rapidly slipped into the arms of death, seeking anything in that process that might be of poetic interest. Indeed, to advance one step further in cynicism, one might even suppose that behind his watchful gaze was the hope of finding inspiration for at least one line in an account he would later write of these last days and hours. Even as he was ministering to him in these final moments, his mind was obsessed with the renown he would win among other schools of poetry, the consequences for the disciples, favorable or otherwise, and all that he might reasonably expect to gain himself.

None of this had the remotest bearing on the imminent death of his master, whose fate was now faithfully fulfilling what he had so often predicted in his verses, for truly he was now being left as a bleached corpse in a vast and desolate moor of humanity. His own disciples were not lamenting the death of their master but rather their own loss at his passing. They were not bewailing the piteous demise of their guide in the wilderness but rather their own abandonment here in the twilight.

Yet, as we humans are by nature coldhearted, of what use is it to offer moral reprobation? Lost in such world-weary thoughts, even as he exalted in his capacity to indulge in them, Shikō wetted the lips of his master and returned the plumed stick to the water bowl. Then glancing about at the weeping faces of his fellow disciples in apparent derision, he slowly and calmly returned to his place. For the good-natured Kyorai, Shikō's cold demeanor had from the beginning only renewed his anxieties; for his part, Kikaku returned the look with an oddly awkward expression, apparently irritated by the air of brazen disdain that was Tōkabō's wont.

Shikō was followed by Inenbō. As his diminutive figure crawled along the straw mats, trailing the hems of his black robe behind him, it was clear that the moment of Bashō's passing was at hand. His face was all the more drained of blood, and, as though he had grown forgetful, there were long moments when no breath escaped his moistened lips. Then, as if he had suddenly remembered, his larynx would begin to move with renewed force, a feeble stream of air again emerging. Twice or thrice from deep within his throat came the rumbling sound of phlegm; his respiration meanwhile grew fainter.

Applying the white end of the plumed stick to those same lips, Inenbō was suddenly seized by a fearful thought quite unrelated to the sadness of parting from his master: *Was he not destined to follow his master into death?* Though verging on the utterly irrational, the emotion, once felt, was therefore all the more impossible to subdue.

Inenbō was by nature among those who respond to any mention of death with morbid panic. From long ago, he had only to think of his own mortality, even when on pleasurable sojourns, to find his entire body drenched in sweat from the dire terror of it all. Thus, hearing of the demise of anyone else provided him with the reassurance that it was indeed the passing of someone other than himself. Yet at the same time he had been assailed by the anxiety-inducing plausibility of the opposite proposition: what if, after all, he were to be the one so summoned?

Bashō was for him no exception. At the beginning, before it became apparent that already he lay at death's door, when in the late autumn sky the sun was shining brightly on the sliding paper doors and the pure scent of narcissus – brought by Sonojo – was wafting through the air, all of his disciples gathered there had composed verses to amuse him. And so Inenbō's spirits had wandered from pole to pole, as though twixt day and night.

Yet the end inexorably grew nearer. There was the unforgettable day of early winter showers, when Bashō appeared unable even to eat the pears of which he was so fond. Seeing this, Mokusetsu had worriedly tilted his head to one side. With this, Inenbō's serenity steadily gave way to fear and then to the looming shadow of dark, cold terror, as he imagined that his own hour would soon be upon him.

So firmly was he in the grip of that fear that even as he sat at Bashō's side and painstakingly wetted his lips, he seemed unable to bring himself to look directly into his face. When for an instant he appeared to make the effort, a death rattle emanated from the master's throat, blocked by phlegm, shattering what courage Inenbō had managed to muster. "You may be the one to follow . . . ," came a nagging, prescient voice in his ear, and as the small figure went crouching back to his place, an ever-darker frown grew on his face. Seeking to avoid the eyes of others, he lowered his head, though sometimes raising his eyes for a surreptitious glance.[6]

Next from among those around Bashō's bed came Otsushū, Seishū, Shidō, and Mokusetsu, each in their turn. But now each breath was more constricted and less frequent than the last, his throat no longer moving. His entire appearance – the small, now waxlike, pockmarked face, his lusterless eyes gazing fixedly into distant space, and the sparse, silver-white beard that covered his chin – was now frozen by the ice that is the human heart; already he appeared to be lost in dreamlike contemplation of that Realm of Eternal Tranquillity and Light to which he would presently be journeying.

Behind Kyorai sat Jōsō, the faithful student of Zen, his head bowed in silence; even as his boundless sorrow deepened with each sign of weakening in Bashō's breathing, his heart was gently filled by a boundless sense of peace. His sorrow required no explanation, but this feeling of serenity was strangely like the feeling of cheer that comes when the cold light of dawn slowly penetrates the shadows of night. Moment by moment it was purging his mind of idle thoughts, so that in the end his sadness was one purified of all tears and heartache.

Was he rejoicing in his master's transcendence of the illusory distinction between life and death, his attainment of Nirvana in the Realm of Treasures? No, that was not the reason that he could affirm even to himself. Then . . . Ah, who could have been so foolish as to vacillate in vain, to dare to deceive himself as to the truth? Jōsō's serenity sprang from the joy of liberation, of being freed from the shackles with which the sheer force of Bashō's personality had long bound him, of feeling his drearily oppressed soul allowed at last to exercise its own inherent strength.

As he rubbed his prayer beads, filled with joy both rapturous and sad, his eyes no longer seemed to see any of his companions, engulfed in tears. A faint smile on his lips, he reverently paid homage to the dying Bashō.

Thus, it was that Matsuo Tōsei of the Banana Plant Hermitage, the great and incomparable master of *haikai*, then and now, suddenly expired, surrounded by disciples "lost to boundless grief."

THE GARDEN

1

The garden belonged to an ancient family, Nakamura by name, whose inn had once served traveling lords in a post-station town along the Central Mountain Road. For the first decade after the Meiji Restoration, it remained much as it had been. In the gourd-shaped pond lay limpid water, and atop a miniature hill drooped the branches of pine trees. The two pavilions, the House of the Resting Crane and the Bower of the Purified Heart, had also endured. Into the pond, from a cliff at the far end of the garden, cascaded swirling white water. Among the golden kerias – their expanse growing year by year – stood a stone lantern to which Princess Kazu is said to have given a name on her journey through the region.

There was nonetheless the undeniable intimation of impending ruin. Particularly at the beginning of spring, when the upper branches of the trees within and beyond the garden suddenly sprouted new buds, one could sense all the more intensely that lurking behind this picturesque artifact was a menacing and savage power.

The retired head of the family was a gruff old man who spent untroubled days in the main house, which looked out on the garden. With his elderly wife, who suffered from an ulcerated scalp, he would sit at the heated table, playing *go* or flower cards. Sometimes, however, after losing to her five or six times in succession, he would fly into a rage.

To his eldest he had relinquished his rights as householder. This son was married to a cousin and lived with her in a cramped annex connected by an elevated corridor. He had taken the nom de plume of Bunshitsu and was of so petulant a disposition that even his own father, to say nothing of his frail wife and younger brothers, was eager to avoid his displeasure.

One visitor to the inn in those days was the mendicant poet Seigetsu, who in his wanderings would turn up from time to time. Strangely enough, he was the only guest welcomed by the elder son, who served him drink and encouraged him to compose. Among the linked verses they have left for posterity is:

> *The scent of flowers*
> *Lingering in the mountains –*
> *The nightingale's[1] song; (Seigetsu)*
> *Here and there – here and there*
> *A waterfall's glimmerings (Bunshitsu)*

Of the two younger brothers, the first had been adopted into the family of a relative, a grain merchant; the other worked for a large sake brewer in a village four or five leagues away. As though by tacit agreement, they rarely returned to their parental home. The youngest was inconvenienced by the distance but was also disinclined by long-standing ill feeling between himself and the current householder. The sibling between them was leading a dissolute life and was hardly seen even in the home of his adoptive parents.

Within two or three years, the garden had gone further to seed. Duckweed had begun to appear on the surface of the pond, and withered trees mingled with the shrubbery. During a terribly dry summer, the old man suddenly died of a cerebral hemorrhage. Four or five days before, he had been drinking *shōchū* when he saw on the other side of the pond the form of a court noble, dressed in white, going in and out of the bower. At least it should be said that he had seen such a phantom in the daylight.

At the end of the next spring, the second son absconded with money from his adoptive parents and ran off with a tavern maid. In the autumn, the wife of the eldest gave premature birth to a baby boy.

After the death of his father, this son had moved into the main house to live with his mother. The annex was rented to the local schoolmaster, who having embraced the utilitarianism of Fukuzawa Yukichi, succeeded over the course of time in persuading the owner to plant fruit trees in the garden. Now when the spring came, there were among the familiar pine and willow trees the richly colored blossoms of peach, apricot, and plum. As he strolled with the eldest son through the new orchard, he would remark: "One could host splendid blossom-viewing parties here, thereby killing two birds with one stone." The artificial hill, the pond, and the pavilions merely looked the more forlorn, as though, so to speak, man had lent a hand to nature in the ruin of the garden.

Moreover, in the autumn, a fire, such as had not been seen in many a year, broke out on the hill in the back. Suddenly and completely, the waterfall was no more. Then, with the first snowfall, the householder fell ill. The diagnosis of the physician was consumption or, as it is called today, tuberculosis. Whether lying in bed or up and about, he was more irascible than ever. At New Year's, when his second brother came to offer his best wishes, he concluded a heated argument with him by throwing a hand-warmer in his direction. The intended target took his leave and never saw the other again, not even on his deathbed over a year later. Lying under the mosquito net in the nocturnal care of his wife, the elder brother had said just before breathing his last: "The frogs are quacking. What's become of Seigetsu?" But the poet had long ago ceased coming round to beg, perhaps having wearied of what there was to see.

The third son waited until the year of mourning was over and then married the grain merchant's youngest daughter. Taking advantage of the schoolmaster's transfer to another post, the new couple moved into the annex. Into their abode came black-lacquer wardrobes and red-and-white cotton decorations.

But now the widow of the first son fell ill, diagnosed with the same disease as that of her late husband. She had spat out blood, so that now their one and only child, Ren'ichi, having already been separated from his father, was taken away from her and made to sleep with his grandmother. Every night she wrapped a kerchief round her head, but the smell of her head sores nonetheless attracted the rats, and when on occasion she forgot the kerchief, she was bitten.

At the end of that year, the wife of the first son died as quietly as the dimming of an oil lamp. On the day after her funeral, the House of the Resting Crane, below the artificial hill, collapsed under the weight of snow from a heavy storm.

When spring returned, the garden seemed to all appearances, except for the thatched roof of the bower near the turbid pond, little more than a budding thicket.

2

One snow-cloud-covered evening, ten years after his elopement, the second son returned to his father's house, or rather to what was now in reality the house of his younger brother. The prodigal was received with neither open displeasure nor particular joy; it was as though nothing at all had occurred.

He spent the days thereafter in the main house, stretched out in the room with the Buddhist altar. There, suffering from a foul disease, he huddled at the warmed table. In the altar stood the mortuary tablets of his father and elder brother. But he had closed the cabinet doors to avoid the sight of them and, for that matter, rarely glimpsed his mother, younger brother, and sister-in-law except at mealtimes. The only occasional visitor to his room was his orphaned nephew. For him he would draw pictures of mountains and ships on the boy's paper slate. There too the lyrics of an old song would sometimes turn up in a faltering hand:

> *"Mukōjima is now in bloom.*
> *Come out, come out, O teahouse maid."*

Again it was spring. Amidst the overgrown grass and shrubbery of the garden, meager peach and apricot blossoms bloomed. The Bower of the Purified Heart was still reflected in the dull water of the pond, but the second son remained as ever, shut up alone in the altar room, for the most part dreaming the day away.

One day he heard the faint sound of a *shamisen* and simultaneously fragments of a song:

> *"Of Matsumoto, Lord Yoshie*
> *With cannon armed,*
> *Went out to battle at Suwa . . ."*

He raised his head from where he lay and listened. It was without doubt from his mother in the sitting room that the music was coming. "In dazzling attire, the valiant warrior, set proudly forth that day . . ." She was singing, it seemed, to her grandson; the ballad was of a style popular two or three decades before, one that her high-spirited husband might well have learned from a courtesan.

> "At Toyohashi, his fate was sealed,
> By hostile cannonball cut down;
> As dew on the grass,
> His precious life vanished,
> His name passed on from age to age . . ."

His face covered by an unkempt beard, the second son listened, a strange light appearing in his eyes.

Several days later, the youngest son discovered his elder brother digging at the foot of the hill, now overgrown with butterbur. He was panting for breath, wielding his hoe uncertainly. It was a somewhat comical sight, though there was also an earnest intensity in his efforts.

"What are you doing, elder brother?" asked the third son, a cigarette in his mouth, as he came up behind him.

"Me?" he replied, looking up as though dazzled by the light. "I thought I'd make a small crick here."

"A crick? Whatever for?"

"I'd like to make the garden what it once was."

The youngest of the brothers smiled and asked nothing further.

Every day, hoe in hand, the second son labored zealously on his creek. Illness had so weakened him that he had no easy time of it. Vulnerable to fatigue, he was also unaccustomed to such work and thus prone to the disabilities that come with blistered hands and broken fingernails. Sometimes he would throw down the hoe and lie down as though dead, the flowers and leaves all about him obscured in the summer haze that filled the garden. After a few minutes of rest, he would nonetheless struggle up to his feet and doggedly resume his hoeing.

But even with the passing days, there was little noticeable change. Weeds still filled the pond, and in the shrubbery the brushwood was putting out branches. Particularly when the fruit trees had shed their blossoms, the garden looked more desolate than ever. Moreover, no one among the other members of the family, young or old, had any sympathetic interest in the second son's endeavors. The third son had caught speculation fever, his head filled with the fluctuating prices of rice and silk stocks. His wife felt a womanly revulsion toward her brother-in-law's illness, while the mother worried that all his puttering about would only cause him to overexert himself. Turning his back on both nature and human society, he stubbornly carried on, incrementally reforming the garden.

One morning he went out after the rain had lifted and found Ren'ichi arranging stones at the edge of the stream, overgrown with the drooping butterbur. "Ojisan!" he happily exclaimed, looking up at his uncle. "Starting today, I'll give you a hand!"

For the first time there was a bright smile on the man's face. "And so you shall," he said.

Thereafter, Ren'ichi no longer went out to play; instead he became a steadfast assistant to his uncle. Resting in the shade of a tree, the second son would entertain his nephew with tales of the world beyond his ken: of the sea, of Tōkyō, of the railway. As he munched on green plums, Ren'ichi would listen intently, as though mesmerized.

There was no rainy season that year. Despite the fierce sunlight and the suffocating vapors of the overheated plants, the aging invalid and the boy persevered, digging out and clearing the pond, cutting down the scrub, and gradually moving on to other tasks. Yet though they might manage to overcome the external obstacles, those within remained immovable. The second son had before his eyes the phantom of the garden as it once had been, but in regard to the details, the arrangement of the trees or the course of the paths, his memory quite failed him. Sometimes in the midst of his work, he would suddenly stop, lost in thought, leaning for support on his hoe and gazing about.

"What is it?" Ren'ichi would invariably ask, giving him a look of concern.

Drifting about, drenched in sweat, the other could only mumble in confusion to himself: "Now what was it like before? This maple couldn't've been here . . ." There was nothing Ren'ichi could do but crush ants with his muddied hands.

There was more to the interior obstacles than this. At the height of the summer, the second son, perhaps a victim of his own unceasing labor, began to grow ever more befuddled. He repeatedly undid his own work, filling in the pond he had once dredged, replanting pine trees he had just uprooted. It particularly angered Ren'ichi to see him make stakes for the pond by cutting down the willows along the embankment.

"But we just planted those trees!" he protested, glaring at his uncle.

"Yes, I suppose you're right," came the reply. "I don't understand anything at all anymore." He stared sadly at the pond, blazing in the noonday sun.

With the coming of autumn, however, the garden could again be distinguished, if only dimly, amidst the mass of weeds and scrub. Of course, anyone who had known it as it once had been, would have seen that the House of the Resting Crane was no more and that the waterfall had ceased to flow. Moreover, that was the least of it: the elegant beauty that the renowned designer of the garden had bestowed upon it had all but utterly vanished.

And yet it was still what one would call a garden. The water of the pond was again clear, reflecting the round miniature hill, and in front of the Bower of the Purified Heart the pine trees once more spread forth their branches in languid majesty.

At the very moment of the restoration, however, the second son was forced to take to bed, burning with fever day after day, his body wracked with pain. "It's all because you've gone beyond your strength!" lamented his mother repeatedly, sitting at his bedside.

Her son was nonetheless content. There remained, of course, many places in the garden to which he might have liked to attend, but now there was naught to be done about it. It had in any case been all worth the effort, and for that he was at peace. A decade of suffering had taught him resignation, and such had become his salvation.

It was unbeknownst to all that he slipped away, just as the season was drawing to an end. Ren'ichi ran shrieking over the elevated corridor into the annex when he found him. Their faces filled with dismay, the members of the family immediately gathered around the deceased. The youngest son turned to his mother and said: "Look. He seems to be smiling." With her eyes fixed on the large Buddhist altar and away from the body of her brother-in-law, his wife exclaimed: "Oh, the panel doors are open today!"

After his uncle's funeral, Ren'ichi often sat alone in the Bower of the Purified Heart, invariably gazing forlornly at the water and the trees of the deepening autumn . . .

3

It had been the garden of a venerable clan, the Nakamuras' inn having served the great feudal lords. Within ten years it had all gone to ruin.

The house was torn down, and on the site a railway station was built, with a small restaurant in front.

Of the Nakamura family, no one remained. The mother had, of course, long since made her place among the dead. Having failed in business, the third son had reportedly gone off to Ōsaka.

Trains daily pulled into the station and departed. The young stationmaster sat at a large desk. Pausing in his already leisurely routine, he would look out at the blue mountains or chat with his subordinates from the region. Yet in all their talk was never a mention of the Nakamuras. Indeed, it never occurred to anyone that here, in the very place where they now found themselves, had once stood a miniature hill and pavilions.

In the meantime, Ren'ichi had made his way to Akasaka in Tōkyō and was studying in an institute for European art. As he stood in front of his easel, there was nothing in the atelier – neither the light that came in through the roof window, nor the smell of the paint, nor the model, her hair in a split-peach bun – that might have reminded him of home. And yet as he moved his brush over the canvas, he sometimes saw in his inner mind the sad face of an old man, who, smiling again, was surely speaking to him now that he too was weary from uninterrupted work: "When you were still a child, you helped me, so let me help you now."

Ren'ichi lives in poverty, toiling every day on his oil paintings. Of his uncle, the youngest son, there is nary a word.

THE LIFE OF A FOOL

To Masao Kume: *June 20, 1927*

I leave entirely in your hands the questions of whether, when, and where to publish this manuscript. You know most of those who appear in it, but should it see the public light, I would ask you not to provide an index. Strangely enough, though I am presently living in the unhappiest of happy circumstances, I regret nothing. My great sorrow is only for those who have suffered the bad husband, the bad son, and the bad parent that I have been. And so I bid you farewell. Here I have not sought – at least not consciously – to defend myself.

Finally, I am entrusting this manuscript to you because I think you know me better than anyone else. With my feigned urbanity peeled away, please laugh at my foolishness.

Akutagawa Ryūnosuke

1. The Era

He was twenty years old and on the second floor of a bookstore, having climbed the Western-style ladder set against a tier containing new works. Here were Maupassant, Baudelaire, Strindberg, Ibsen, Shaw, and Tolstoy . . .

Though the end of the day was looming, he went on avidly reading the lettering of the backs. On display was less a collection of books than the embodiment of *la fin de siècle*: Nietzsche, Verlaine, the Goncourt brothers, Dostoyevsky, Hauptmann, Flaubert . . .

Resisting the darkness, he recited their names, but quite on their own they were sinking in the melancholic gloom. Finally, his stamina exhausted, he started to descend the ladder when an unshaded electric bulb just above was suddenly illuminated. He stood still, looking down on the customers and clerks passing between the rows of books. They looked strangely small – and so shabby as well.

"A single line of Baudelaire is worth more than all of life."

From his perch, he lingered for a moment, still staring down at those below.

2. His Mother

The lunatics were all dressed in the same gray uniforms. That gave the large room an all the more depressing appearance. One of them sat at the organ and fervently went on playing a hymn. At the same time, in the exact middle of the room, another was dancing or, more precisely, was hopping about.

He was observing this scene in the company of a ruddy-faced physician. His own mother of ten years before was in no way different from these inmates. In no way at all . . . He sensed that even the odor was the same.

"Shall we go then?"

The doctor led the way through the corridor to another room. In the corner were huge jars filled with alcohol, in which a number of brains were submerged. On one of these he saw something white, looking quite as though it had been dabbed with egg albumen. As he stood talking with the doctor, he thought again about his mother.

"The owner of this brain was an engineer at X Electric Company. He always thought of himself as an enormous, black-luster dynamo."

To avoid the doctor's eyes, he stared out the glass window. Outside there was only a brick wall, on top of which bottle shards had been embedded. Thin patches of moss lent a vaguely white appearance to the façade.

3. The House

He rose and slept in a room on the second floor of a suburban house. The instability of the ground made for a strange tilt.

In this room on the second floor he would sometimes quarrel with his mother's elder sister, his foster parents sometimes interceding. He nonetheless had an unrivaled affection for his aunt. Never married, she was at the time close to sixty, while he was still twenty.

There on the second floor of that suburban house, he often pondered how it is that those who love one another can engage in mutual torment, even as the tilt of the house gave him a feeling of unease and foreboding . . .

4. Tōkyō

The Sumida River was a dull, leaden gray. He was gazing out of a window on a small steamboat at the cherry trees of Mukōjima. The blossoms, now at their peak, were no less dispiriting to his eyes than had they been rows of rags. Yet in those blossoms – renowned since Edo times – he had come to see himself.

5. Ego

He sat at a table in a café with one who had preceded him at the university.[1] Smoking one cigarette after another, he barely spoke, listening intently.

"I spent half the day in a taxi."

"Did you have matters to attend to?"

Resting his chin in his hand, the other replied in a quite offhand manner:

"Oh, no, I merely wished to enjoy the ride."

These words opened a window in his mind to an unknown world – the world of *self* so akin to that of the gods. He felt pain – and, at the same time, joy.

The café was quite small, but under a portrait of Pan was a gum tree in a red pot, its thick, fleshy leaves drooping.

6. Illness

The wind was blowing steadily from the sea as he opened an English dictionary and searched the entries with his fingertip:

Talaria: winged shoes or sandals

Tale: a story

Talipot: A palm tree native to the East Indies, attaining a height of fifty to one hundred feet, its leaves used for umbrellas, fans, and hats, blooming once in seventy years . . .

In his mind he could clearly picture the flowers of the palms. He felt a tickling in his throat he had never known before. He found himself spitting into the dictionary. Was it sputum? No. He contemplated the brevity of life and once again imagined the palm flowers, high aloft the trees, far across the ocean.

7. Paintings

Suddenly – indeed suddenly . . . He was standing in front of a bookstore, looking at a collection of Van Gogh paintings, when he suddenly understood what a painting is. They were, of course, a photographic edition, but from them he felt Nature springing forth in all her splendor.

His passion for the paintings renewed and altered his vision. He began to dwell on the sway and bend of branches and the sensual plumpness of female cheeks.

At the end of a rainy afternoon in autumn, he was walking through a suburban railway underpass. Beneath an embankment on the other side stood a horse-drawn wagon. As he passed it, he felt the presence of someone who had walked the same path. Someone? He had no need to ask himself twice. In his twenty-three-year-old mind he saw a Dutchman with an amputated ear, a long pipe in his mouth, looking out with a penetrating gaze at the bleak landscape . . .

8. Sparks

Drenched by the rain, he walked the asphalt street. It was raining rather heavily. In the pervasive dampness, he noticed the rubbery smell of his mackintosh.

From an overhead trolley cable in front of him came a burst of violet sparks. He felt strangely moved. In his coat pocket he had tucked away a manuscript intended for a literary coterie. As he went on through the rain, he looked up again at the cable behind him: it was sparkling as ever.

He had taken a survey of life and found nothing in particular that he wanted or desired. But now those violet sparks . . . To seize those stupendous sparks exploding in space, he would happily have forfeited his life.

9. Cadavers

On a big toe of each cadaver hung an identifying tag, including name and age. A friend of his was bent over, skillfully wielding a scalpel as he began to peel away the facial skin of one. Underneath lay a beautiful layer of yellow fat.

He looked carefully at the cadaver: he needed background for a short story set in the Heian period. He was, however, made uneasy by the smell – suggesting rotting apricots – that emanated from the body. With knitted eyebrows, his friend calmly carried on his work.

"We've recently had quite a shortage," his friend remarked.

To this he had a ready answer: *If I were faced with that problem, I suppose I'd resort to murder – without any sort of animosity,* he thought.

Needless to say, he kept this comment to himself.

10. Sensei

Sitting under a large oak, he was reading one of Sensei's books. Not a leaf was stirring in the autumn light. In distant space, a crystal balance scale was maintaining perfect equilibrium. This was the scene he saw in his mind's eye as he read . . .

11. Dawn

The day gradually dawned. At a corner of a street, he looked out on a vast market. The crowds and their vehicles were bathed in rose light. He lit a cigarette and calmly strolled on through. A scrawny black dog suddenly began barking at him, but he was neither surprised nor dismayed; indeed, he felt some affection for the dog.

In the middle of the market was a plane tree, spreading its branches all around. He stood at the base of the trunk and looked up through those branches at the distant sky, in which a star was twinkling directly above his head.

He was in his twenty-fifth year. It had been three months since he had made the acquaintance of his mentor.

12. Military Port

The interior of the submarine was dimly lit. Crouched down among the machines on all sides, he peered through a small telescope. He could see reflected in the bright light the military port.

"There you'll be able to see the *Kongō*," an officer told him. Looking at the reduced image of the battle cruiser through the square lens, he was somehow reminded of Dutch parsley, its scent lingering even when mounted on a portion of *thirty-sen* beefsteak.

13. Sensei's Death

In the wind that followed a lull in the rain, he was walking the platform of a new railway station. It was not yet dawn. On the other side, a few workers were chanting robustly as they swung their picks up and down in unison.

Both their song and his sentiments were scattered by the wind. Leaving his cigarette unlit, he felt an anguish bordering on joy. "Sensei critically ill" read the telegram that he had thrust into his pocket.

The 6 AM Tōkyō-bound train came curving round the pine-covered slope and pulled in, trailing a wisp of smoke.

14. Marriage

"You know, we can't have you *already* wasting money," he complained to his wife the day after their wedding. It was less his complaint than one his maternal aunt had ordered him to deliver on her behalf. His wife had, of course, apologized not only to him but also to the aunt – as they sat in front of the pot of jonquils she had bought for him . . .

15. They

They led a tranquil life in the shade of a broad-leafed banana tree, for their house was situated in a coastal town a good hour away by train from Tōkyō.

16. Pillow

He read a book by Anatole France, his head propped up by a pillow of skepticism exuding a rosy fragrance; the presence in that same pillow of a centaur quite escaped his notice.

17. A Butterfly

A butterfly fluttered in the seaweed-scented breeze. For an instant, he felt its wings touch his parched lips. Even many years later, the powder on those wings that brushed his lips still glistened.

18. The Moon

On the stairs of a hotel, he met her, quite by accident. Even in the daytime, her face seemed bathed in moonlight. As his gaze followed her (they were not in the least acquainted), he experienced a sadness he had not seen before . . .

19. Artificial Wings

He shifted from Anatole France to the eighteenth-century philosophers, though skipping over Rousseau, perhaps because in one respect, being prone to be carried away by passion, he resembled him. Leaning toward another side of himself, the coldly rational, he went to Candide's philosopher.

He was twenty-nine years old, and already all was gloom. Yet in this way Voltaire provided him, such as he was, with artificial wings.

He spread those wings and rose easily into the air, the joys and sorrows of human life, flooded with the light of reason, now sinking below his gaze. Unimpeded on his course toward the sun, he rained down his smiles and smirks on the miserable towns below, as though having forgotten the Greek of long ago who, with his own artificial wings scorched by Helios, went plunging into the sea and drowned . . .

20. Shackles

Having joined a newspaper company, he found himself and his wife sharing a house with his foster parents. He entrusted himself to a contract he had signed. It was written on a yellow piece of paper. Yet on rereading it, he realized that all duties and obligations rested with him, none with the company.

21. The Daughter of a Lunatic

Two rickshaws were running along a deserted country road on an overcast day, heading, it was clear from the briny breeze, toward the sea. He was sitting in the one behind, wondering what had induced him to embark on this rendezvous in which he had utterly no interest. It was certainly not love that had brought him here. If it was not love . . . To avoid responding to that question, he could not help thinking that at least they were on the same footing.

Riding in the rickshaw ahead of him was the daughter of a lunatic. Jealousy had driven her younger sister to suicide.

There is no longer any alternative.

Toward this girl, this lunatic's daughter, driven by base animal instincts, he felt a certain abhorrence.

The rickshaws were now passing along a cemetery that smelled of the sea. Dark gravestones stood beyond the brushwood fence covered with oyster shells. Through the gravestones he gazed out on the faintly glittering waves. Suddenly he felt contempt for her husband, unable to win her heart.

22. A Painter

It was a magazine illustration, an India-ink drawing of a rooster, striking in its individuality. He asked a friend about the artist.

A week later the artist paid him a visit. It was one of the most memorable events of his life. In the painter he discovered a poem that no one knew and in so doing his own soul, which likewise he never had known.

On a chilly autumn evening, an ear of maize reminded him instantly of the artist. Armed with its rough leaves, the tall plant spread its thin, nervelike roots over the soil; in its revelation of vulnerability, it was, of course, none other than his own self-portrait. Yet the discovery only dispirited him.

It is already too late. Yet if the die is cast . . .

23. She

Standing in front of a public square as dusk was falling . . . Feeling somewhat feverish, he started to cross it, the electric lights in the multistoried buildings twinkling against a faintly silver sky.

He stopped along the way, resolved to wait for her arrival. Five minutes later she was coming toward him, looking somehow haggard. As soon as she saw his face, she smiled and said: "I'm tired." They walked side by side through the darkening square – for the first time together. He sensed that to be with her, he would abandon everything.

They were riding in a taxi when she gazed earnestly into his face and asked: "Have you any regrets?"

"I regret nothing," he said firmly.

"Nor I," she replied, pressing his hand. At that moment too, her face appeared to be bathed in moonlight.

24. Birth

Standing in front of the sliding door, he gazed down at the midwife, dressed in her white surgical gown, as she washed the newborn. It grimaced pitifully whenever the soap stung its eyes, crying at the top of its voice. He noticed that the infant had a rodentlike odor and thought in all earnestness:

Why have you too come into this world so full of vain desire and suffering? And why is this your burden of fate: to have the likes of me as a father?

This was the first son that his wife had borne to him.

25. Strindberg

He stood in the doorway of the room and watched some grimy Chinese playing mahjong in the light of the moon, the pomegranates in bloom. Stepping inside again, he sat down at a low-hanging lamp and read Strindberg's *Confessions of a Fool*. Two pages were enough to bring a wry smile to his lips . . . The lies Strindberg was telling in writing letters to the countess, his lover, were hardly different from those he himself was writing.

26. Ancient Times

The faded Buddhas, the gods, the horses, the lotus flowers . . . The weight they bore down on him was all but crushing. He looked up at them and forgot everything, even his own happiness at having shaken free of the lunatic's daughter.

27. Spartan Discipline

He was walking the backstreets with a friend. A canopied rickshaw came racing directly toward them. To his amazement, the passenger was the woman he had seen the previous evening. Even in the full light of day, her face seemed bathed in moonlight. In the presence of his friend, needless to say, they did not exchange greetings . . .

"What a beautiful woman!" his friend exclaimed.

He responded without hesitation, even as he stared straight ahead to the verdant hill at the end of the road.

"Yes, quite a beauty indeed!"

28. Murder

The odor of cow dung drifted across the sunlit countryside. He walked up the slope, wiping away perspiration. The fields on both sides of the road were wafting forth the rich smell of ripened barley.

"Kill! Kill!" He was mumbling the words again and again. Whom should he kill? He knew only too well, as he remembered an utterly contemptible man with short-cropped hair. Suddenly beyond the fields of golden barley the dome of a Roman Catholic church came into view . . .

29. Form

It was an iron sake flask. The fine lines engraved in it had at some point impressed upon him the beauty of *form*.

30. Rain

On the large bed he talked with her about this and that. Beyond the windows of the room it was raining. The crinum blossoms, it appeared, had begun to rot. Just as before, her face seemed to be bathed in the light of the moon, and yet he could not help finding their conversation tedious. Lying on his stomach, he quietly lit a cigarette. It occurred to him that he had been living with her for seven years. He asked himself: *Do I still love her?* For all his habitual self-reflection, he was surprised at the answer: *Yes, I do.*

31. The Great Earthquake

It resembled the odor of overripe apricots. He vaguely sensed it as he walked about the burned-out ruins. It occurred to him that the smell of corpses rotting under a burning sun is not as unpleasant as one might think. Yet as he stood in front of a pond heaped with bodies, he discovered that *gruesome*[2] is not too strong a word. He was particularly moved by the remains of a young girl of twelve or thirteen. He gazed at her and felt something close to envy, as he remembered: *Those whom the gods love die young.* His elder sister and younger half brother had lost their homes to fire. But his sister's husband had been found guilty of false testimony and given a suspended sentence.

Death to one and all! he could not help ruminating to himself, as he stood amidst the ashes.

32. Quarrel

He scuffled with his younger half brother. While the latter doubtlessly felt constrained by his presence, it was equally true he had lost his freedom because of that brother. Their relatives constantly urged the younger: "Learn from the example of your elder brother!" Yet the very advice only served to bind that same elder brother hand and foot. In their struggle, they rolled out onto the veranda. He still remembered that in the garden, under the rain-threatening sky, stood a crape myrtle, its bright-red blossoms in full bloom.

33. Heroes

In the house of Voltaire, he was gazing out from a window at the high mountains. Above the glaciers there was not so much as the shadow of a vulture. A short Russian nonetheless continued persistently up the mountain path.

When night had fallen on the house of Voltaire, he wrote a tendentious poem as he remembered the figure of the Russian on the sloping trail:

> You who more than any other kept the Ten Commandments
> You who more than any other broke them
>
> You who more than any other loved the people
> You who more than any other despised them
>
> You who more than any other burned with idealism
> You who more than any other knew reality
>
> You are the flower-scented electric locomotive
> To which we of Asia have given birth

34. Color

At the age of thirty he discovered that he had a great fondness for an empty plot of land. Scattered about on the moss-covered ground were numerous bricks and tile shards. Yet in his eyes it was a veritable Cézanne.

He happened to remember his passion of seven or eight years before. He then realized that at the time he had been ignorant of color.

35. Pierrot Puppet

He intended to live with such intensity that he would have no regrets at his death. He nonetheless continued to spend his days in diffident deference to his foster parents and his aunt, thereby creating for himself a life divided between light and darkness. One day he saw standing in an Occidental clothing shop a Pierrot puppet and wondered how much like one he was himself. But his unconscious, that is, his second self, had long since included this intuition in a short story.

36. Languor

He was walking with a university student through a field of pampas grass.

"You and your classmates must still possess a lust for life."

"Yes, but surely you do as well . . ."

"As a matter of fact, I do not. All I have is my desire to produce."

That was his honest feeling. Somewhere along the way he had lost interest in life.

"But the creative urge is really the same thing, is it not?"

He gave no reply. Now taking distinct shape over the red spikes of the pampas grass was an active volcano, for which he experienced a feeling close to envy, though he himself did not know why . . .

37. Woman of the North

He met a woman who even in sheer mental prowess was his match. By composing lyrical poems such as *Koshibito*,[3] he narrowly escaped danger. The twinge of regret he felt was as when one removes dazzling snow frozen to a tree trunk.

The sedge hat dancing in the wind
Will fall in time into the road.
What care have I for my good name
When thine alone is dear to me?

38. Vengeance

He sat on the balcony of a hotel surrounded by trees in bud, drawing pictures to amuse a young boy, the only son of the lunatic's daughter, with whom he had broken all ties seven years earlier.

She lit a cigarette and watched them. Despite his despondency, he went on drawing trains and airplanes. Fortunately, the child was not his, though it pained him terribly to be addressed as Ojisan.

When the boy had momentarily left them, she continued to smoke her cigarette, asking him coquettishly:

"Don't you think he resembles you?"

"Not at all. In the first place . . ."

"Well, there is such a thing as 'prenatal influence,' is there not?"

He turned his eyes without replying. Yet in the depths of his heart he could not help feeling a cruel urge to strangle the woman.

39. Mirrors

In the corner of a café he was conversing with a friend. The friend was talking about the recent cold, while munching on a baked apple. He suddenly sensed a contradiction in what was being said.

"You're still single, aren't you?"

"Well, actually, I'm to be married next month."

He fell silent despite himself. Coldly, somehow menacingly, the mirrors attached to the walls reflected multiple images of his face.

40. Dialogue

Why do you attack the present social system?

Because I see the evils born of capitalism.

The evils? I thought you did not distinguish between Good and Evil? Then what about *your* life?

He was engaged in dialogue with an angel – an angel who, incidentally, was wearing a silk hat and would have blushed before no one.

41. Illness

He began to suffer from insomnia and from a loss of stamina as well. Each of various physicians offered multiple diagnoses, all of these including: gastric hyperacidity, gastric atony, dry pleurisy, neurasthenia, chronic conjunctivitis, brain fatigue . . .

But he knew the source of the malady: his shame of himself and his fear of *them* – the society he despised.

One afternoon, the sky darkened with snow clouds, he sat in the corner of a café, a lighted cigar in his mouth, his ear inclined to music coming from a gramophone on the other side of the room. It worked an uncanny effect on his spirits. When the record had come to a stop, he walked over and looked at the label: *The Magic Flute* – Mozart.

Suddenly he understood. Mozart, who had violated the Ten Commandments, had surely suffered – yet perhaps not as *he* had . . . Bowing his head, he quietly returned to his table.

42. The Laughter of the Gods

He was thirty-five years old. Walking through a pine forest, spring sunlight falling on the trees, he recalled the words he had written two or three years before: much to their misfortune, the gods, unlike us mortals, cannot kill themselves . . .

43. Night

Once more dusk was falling. The storming sea relentlessly threw its spray against the twilight shore. Under such a sky he celebrated with his wife a second marriage. In this they felt both joy and sorrow. Together with their three children, they gazed at the lightning flashes in the offing. His wife was holding one of them in her arms, apparently holding back her tears.

"I think I see a ship out there."

"Yes."

"A ship whose mast is split in two."

44. Death

Taking advantage of being alone in his room, he set about to hang himself with a sash tied to the bars of the window. Yet when he put his head in the noose, he was suddenly struck by the fear of death, though he was not afraid of the momentary pain that such would entail. He took out his pocket watch the second time and by way of experiment measured how long it might take for him to be strangled. After a few uncomfortable moments, all became quite muddled. Once beyond that stage, he would surely enter the realm of death. He consulted his watch and saw that his distress had lasted one minute and some twenty seconds. Beyond the window all was pitch-black, but in that darkness could be heard the raucous crowing of a rooster.

45. Divan

A rereading of the *Divan* was giving his spirits a new vitality. This "Oriental Goethe" had previously been unknown to him. Seeing

Goethe standing serenely in the realm of enlightenment, beyond all good and evil, he felt an envy bordering on despair. In his eyes, the poet Goethe was greater than the poet Christ; in his heart bloomed the roses not only of the Acropolis and of Golgotha but also of Arabia. If only he had possessed the strength to follow in his footsteps . . . Even when he had completed his reading of the *Divan* and stilled his terrifying emotion, he could not help feeling all the more keenly his self-loathing at having allowed his life to become that of a Chinese imperial eunuch.

46. Lies

He was suddenly felled face downward by the suicide of his elder sister's husband. He was now further obliged to take care of her and her family. At least to him, his own future seemed as dark as impending nightfall. He viewed his mental ruin with a feeling close to derision, being thoroughly aware of all his vices and weaknesses, even as he continued to read volume after volume. Yet even Rousseau's *Confessions* were filled with heroic falsehoods. And as for *Shinsei*, he had never encountered as wily an old hypocrite as the protagonist of that particular work. Only François Villon was able to touch the depths of his soul. In some of his poems, he discovered "a beautiful male."

The figure of Villon awaiting the gallows haunted him even in his dreams. Numerous times he had attempted to fall to the utter depths of human life, as had Villon, but neither his social circumstances nor his limited physical energy would permit it. He steadily grew weaker, much like the tree that Swift saw long ago – withering at the top.[4]

47. Playing with Fire

She had a radiant face. It was quite as though one were seeing the light of dawn reflected in a thin sheet of ice. He felt affection for her but not love; not one finger of his had ever touched her body.

"You have said that you wish to die, have you not?" she asked.

"Hmm . . . It is not so much that I wish to die as that I am weary of living."

After this exchange, they joined in a suicide pact.

"A platonic suicide, I suppose," she remarked.

"Yes, a double platonic suicide."

He himself could not help being surprised at how calm he was.

48. Death

He did not carry through with the pact. For some reason he felt satisfaction at not having touched her. She sometimes talked with him, acting as if nothing had happened. She also handed over to him her small bottle of cyanide, saying:

"This should make us both feel stronger."

In doing so, she did, in fact, bolster his spirits. Sitting alone in his rattan chair, he gazed at the young leaves of the chinquapins and found that despite himself he would often think of what peace death would bring him.

49. A Stuffed Swan

Mustering his last strength, he set about to write his autobiography, only to find that his amour propre, his skepticism, and his keen awareness of his own self-interest made the task surprisingly difficult. He could not help despising himself, even as he was equally compelled to think that when we peel back the skin we are indeed all the same. The title of Goethe's *Dichtung und Wahrheit* seemed to suggest the essence of autobiography. He also knew perfectly well that not everyone is moved by a literary work. His own writings could only appeal to likeminded individuals who lived lives similar to his own. It was with and for this feeling moving within him that he attempted to write his own brief blend of reverie and reality.

On completing "The Life of a Fool," he happened to pass by a secondhand shop, in which he saw a stuffed swan. It stood with its neck stretched upward, but its yellowed feathers had been eaten away by vermin. Smiling wryly through his tears, he thought about his life. Before him lay only madness or suicide. He walked alone through the streets in the twilight, resolved to await the slow but steady approach of a destiny bent on his obliteration.

50. Prisoner

A friend of his became mentally ill. He had always felt very close to him. He knew better than anyone his loneliness, the loneliness that lay beneath the cheery mask. He visited him several times after his breakdown.

"We are both haunted by demons," his friend remarked, lowering his voice, "the so-called *fin-de-siècle* demons."

He heard that two or three days later, while on his way to a hot-springs resort, the friend had even been eating roses. After his friend's hospitalization he remembered the terra-cotta bust that he had given him. It was of the author of a work that he had loved: *The Inspector General*. He remembered that Gogol too had gone mad and was thus reminded of the power that ruled them all.

He was at the point of exhaustion when once again he heard the laughter of the gods. He had just read the last words of Raymond

Radiguet: "The soldiers of God are coming for me."[5] He tried to resist his own superstition and sentimentality, but he was physically incapable of any sort of struggle.

There could be no doubt: he was being tormented by the *fin-de-siècle* demons. He envied the people of medieval times, who could entrust themselves to the power of God. But belief in God . . . Belief in the love of God was for him utterly impossible – a belief that even Cocteau possessed.

51. Defeat

Even the hand holding his pen began to tremble; he also started to drool. Except when he had taken a 0.8 gram dose of Veronal, his mind was never completely clear, and those moments of relative lucidity lasted no longer than thirty minutes to an hour. He spent his days in spiritual twilight, as though, so to speak, leaning on a thin sword whose blade had been chipped.

THE VILLA OF
THE BLACK CRANE

1

It was a cozily designed dwelling, with an unpretentious gate. As such, it was, to be sure, not unusual for the neighborhood. It was in its plaque – *Genkaku Sanbō* – and the trees in the garden that rose above the height of the wall, that it clearly outshone every other house in elegance.

The master was Horikoshi Genkaku. Though rather well-known as a painter, he had made his fortune in the acquisition of a patent for rubber seals and subsequently in the purchase and sale of properties. The soil of the land he owned on the outskirts of the city had been so poor that not even ginger could be grown, but now all of this had been transformed into a "cultural village,"[1] boasting red- and blue-tiled roofs . . .

Genkaku Sanbō was nonetheless a cozily designed dwelling, with an unpretentious gate. Adding to the sense of refinement were both the straw ropes recently used to protect the pine trees from the snow and the bright-red ardisia berries amidst the withered pine needles carpeting the entrance. There were few passersby along the alleyway that ran by the house. Even the bean-curd peddler, putting down his shoulder pole and tubs in the thoroughfare, would signal his presence with no more than a toot of his trumpet.

"What is the significance of the name?" asked a long-haired student of painting who happened by, carrying an oblong color-box under his arm. His companion, likewise dressed in a gold-buttoned uniform, said in reply:

"Well, I should hardly think a pun on 'severe' or 'straitlaced'!"

The young men laughed lightheartedly as they continued on their way. The path was now again quite deserted, except for a thin blue thread of smoke rising from a Golden Bat cigarette that one of them had left discarded on the frozen lane.

2

Even before becoming Genkaku's adopted son-in-law, Jūkichi had worked for a bank. Thus, on his return home each day, the electric lights were just coming on. For several days now, he had, on entering the gate, immediately detected a strange smell. The source was the bad breath of the old man, who lay in bed afflicted with pulmonary tuberculosis, a rare disease among the elderly. There was nonetheless no reason for the odor to have spread beyond the house. As Jūkichi, a satchel pressed under the arm of his overcoat, made his way along the stepping-stones leading up to the entrance, he could not help worrying about his state of nerves.

Genkaku was situated in an isolated room. When not flat on his back, he would sit up, leaning on a mountain of quilts. Jūkichi would take off his hat and coat and, without fail, put in an appearance to announce his return or to inquire about his father-in-law's condition. Even so, he rarely went beyond the threshold, in part because he feared contagion but also because the odor offended him. Genkaku's greeting in return was no more than a syllable or two, and these he murmured with a voice so weak that it sounded closer to mere breath. Such would sometimes fill Jūkichi with pangs of guilt, but his loathing of going in remained unchanged.

He would then call on his mother-in-law, O-tori, next to the sitting room. She too was bedridden and had been for seven or eight years, well before her husband. Unable to walk, she could not even go by herself to the privy. It was said that Genkaku had married her not only because she was a daughter of the principal counselor to a high lord but also because he had had his heart set on a belle. In this, her eyes retained something of their beauty despite her years. Yet as she sat in her bed, painstakingly darning her white split-toed socks, she bore a more than faint resemblance to a mummy. "Mother, how are you today?" Jūkichi would say as a similarly short salutation before entering the six-mat sitting room.

When his wife, O-suzu, was not there, she would be working in the cramped kitchen with her maid, O-matsu, who came from Shinshū. Needless to say, Jūkichi was much more familiar with both the tidily arranged sitting room and the modernized kitchen than with areas of the house occupied by his parents-in-law.

The second son of a politician who had once served as a provincial governor, he was a brilliant young man, more like his mother, who had been an old-fashioned poetess, than his father, who had always had the aura of *le grand homme* about him. His character could also be discerned from his friendly eyes and delicately narrow chin.

Coming into the sitting room, he would change from Western to Japanese clothes, lounge at the long brazier, smoke a cheap cigar, and playfully tease his only son, Takeo, who had just entered primary school that year. Jūkichi, O-suzu, and Takeo invariably ate together, gathered around their low dining table. Their usual liveliness had recently been partly replaced by a discernible air of formality, the cause of which was the arrival of Kōno, the nurse now taking care of Genkaku. This did not, to be sure, affect in the least Takeo's propensity to engage in childish pranks; indeed, the presence of Kōno-san only aggravated it. Sometimes his mother would glare at him with a frown, but he would respond with no more than a look of utter incomprehension, as he shoveled rice from his bowl into his mouth with an exaggerated flourish. Being a veteran reader of fiction, Jūkichi sensed something "male" in Takeo's exuberance, but though he was not always unperturbed by such behavior, he usually tolerated it with a stoical smile, as he ate in silence.

Nights in the villa were quiet. Takeo, who had to go to school the next morning, would, of course, be asleep by ten, but his parents too generally retired at the same hour. Only Kōno would remain awake, having begun her vigil at about nine, sitting at Genkaku's bedside, her hands at the red-glowing brazier, never once dozing off. Genkaku himself was also sometimes awake, but he only spoke when his hot-water bottle had grown cold or when his compresses were dry. The only sound to be heard in this isolated room came from the rustling bamboo thicket. In the stillness and the cold, Kōno would ponder this and that as she watched over the old man – the state of mind and feelings of the various members of the family, her own future . . .

3

One cloudless afternoon after a snowfall, a woman of twenty-four or -five appeared at the kitchen entrance of the Horikoshi residence, holding a slender boy by the hand. Through the window set in the roof, the bright blue sky could be seen.

Jūkichi was, of course, not at home. O-suzu, who was sitting at her sewing machine, was not entirely surprised but was nonetheless taken aback. She arose and, walking past the long brazier, went to meet the visitor, who, on entering the kitchen, arranged her own footwear and that of the boy,[2] who was clad in a white sweater. Even in this gesture, she was demonstrating considerable deference – and not without reason, for this was O-yoshi, a former maid, whom for the last five or six years Genkaku had openly kept as his mistress somewhere in the outskirts of Tōkyō.

As O-suzu looked at her face, she was astonished to see how quickly O-yoshi had aged. And the evidence was not in her facial features alone. Until four or five years before, her hands had been round and plump. Now they were so slender that the veins were visible. In what she wore as well – the trinket of a ring on her finger – O-suzu could see that her domestic circumstances were indeed wretched.

"My elder brother has instructed me to offer this to the master."

With even greater diffidence, O-yoshi placed in a corner of the kitchen a package wrapped in old newspapers, before entering the sitting room, her knees to the floor. O-matsu had been in the midst of washing, but now, without pausing for a moment, began to cast furtive and disparaging glances at O-yoshi, who wore her hair in a freshly arranged ginkgo-leaf bun. The sight of the package only renewed her frosty expression. It was undeniably true that it gave off an unpleasant odor hardly in keeping with the modernized kitchen or its delicate dishes and bowls. O-yoshi's eyes were not directed toward O-matsu, but she appeared to detect an odd look on the face of O-suzu, for she explained: "This is . . . i-it's garlic." Then turning to the child, who was biting his finger, she said: "Now, Botchan, make a bow."

The boy, whose name was Buntarō, was, of course, the son of O-yoshi by Genkaku. O-suzu was struck with pity for O-yoshi that she should address him as "Botchan,"[3] but common sense also immediately told her that with such a woman this was only to be expected. Feigning unconcern, she offered what tea and cakes she had on hand to the two sitting in a corner of the room, as she spoke of Genkaku's condition and sought to amuse Buntarō.

Having made O-yoshi his mistress, Genkaku had regularly gone to see her once or twice a week, despite the inconvenience of changing trains. At first, O-suzu was revolted by the attitude of her father and would often tell herself that he might act with at least a modicum of consideration for her mother's circumstances. For her part, O-tori seemed quite resigned to it all, though this only added to O-suzu's sorrow for her, so that when her father went off on his visits, she would resort to such transparent lies as "Father has his poetry meeting today." She was not unaware that such artifices were useless, and whenever she saw something close to a sneer on O-tori's face, she regretted her own lack of candor, even as she felt still greater chagrin at her paralytic mother's unwillingness to share her heartache.

Sometimes, having seen her father off, O-suzu would momentarily pause at her sewing machine to think about the household. Even before her father had taken up with O-yoshi, he had not been for her any sort of idealized patriarch, but for a woman as kind and gentle as she was, that was of little concern. She was nonetheless troubled when he began to take more and more paintings, calligraphic works, and antiques to the residence he had set up for his mistress. From the time O-yoshi was still their maid, O-suzu had never thought her to be a wicked person; on the contrary, she appeared to be more timid a woman than most. But her elder brother, a fishmonger somewhere on the edge of Tōkyō, might very well have a scheme or two of his own, and, in fact, he had struck her as a man full of wiles. Sometimes she would entreat Jūkichi to listen to her, as she attempted to confide her concerns to him, but he invariably brushed her aside. "I'm not the one to speak to Father about it," was his reply, thereby obliging her to say no more.

Yet Jūkichi himself would make an occasional remark to his mother-in-law: "I hardly think that even Father regards O-yoshi as capable of appreciating a painting by Luó Pìn." But O-tori would merely look up at her son-in-law and say with wry smile: "Such is Father's nature. He is the sort of person who even asks me: 'What do you think of this inkstone?'"

Such concerns appeared in retrospect to be absurd. That winter Genkaku's illness suddenly took a turn for the worse, so that he was no longer able to visit O-yoshi. With unexpected docility he accepted Jūkichi's proposal to end the arrangement – though, to be more precise, it was O-tori and O-suzu who, in fact, spelled out the conditions.

O-suzu's fears regarding O-yoshi's elder brother likewise proved to be groundless, for he expressed not the least objection to those conditions: She would receive one thousand yen in terminal compensation and a small monthly allowance for the education of Buntarō after she had returned to her parents' house on a beach in Kazusa. He even returned, unbidden, the treasured tea utensils that Genkaku had left with her. O-suzu's favorable feelings toward him now more than overcame her former suspicions.

"Incidentally," he had said, "my sister would be more than happy to assist you in the care of the master, should you find yourselves shorthanded."

Before responding to the proposal, O-suzu had gone for advice to her paralytic mother. There can be no doubt that in this she committed a strategic error, for O-tori's response was to urge her daughter to summon O-yoshi and Buntarō as soon as the very next day. O-suzu tried repeatedly to persuade her mother to change her mind, for she feared that such would throw the entire household into turmoil, to say nothing of the effect on O-tori. But she refused to listen. (Moreover, having acted as an intermediary between her father and O-yoshi's brother, O-suzu found it impossible to issue a blunt rejection.)

"If you had dealt with the matter before telling me, it would be one thing, but I mustn't feel shame in front of O-yoshi."

O-suzu thus resigned herself to accepting the brother's offer. Perhaps this mistake too was a consequence of her ignorance regarding the ways of the world. As it was, when Jūkichi returned from the bank and heard the story from his wife, there appeared between his womanishly gentle eyebrows an expression of displeasure. "The extra help is certainly to be appreciated," he remarked, "but you should have consulted with Father. If he had refused, you would have been freed of any responsibility."

O-suzu, more downhearted than she had ever been, concurred in this opinion. Yet now to consult with the dying Genkaku, who naturally still had a lingering affection for O-yoshi, would clearly have been more impossible . . .

Even as she attended to O-yoshi and her son, O-suzu was recalling all of this regarding the woman, who, without presuming to warm her hands over the long brazier, was now talking, with occasional lulls, of her brother and of Buntarō. She had reverted to the provincial accent with which she had spoken four or five years earlier. On O-suzu it worked a soothing effect, even as she felt a vague uneasiness at the presence of her mother behind the single-layered paper door, whose silence was not broken by so much as a cough.

"So you can stay with us for about a week?"

"Yes, if my lady has no objection."

"But you will need at least a change of clothes, won't you?"

"My brother assures me that he will have such items sent by this evening."

This she said as she reached into the bosom of her kimono for a caramel to give to the bored Buntarō.

"Well then, let us inform my father. He is now much weaker, you know. The ear he has directed toward the draft is chilblained."

Before getting up from the long brazier, O-suzu absentmindedly reset the kettle.

"Mother . . ."

O-tori responded in the viscous voice of one just awakened from sleep.

"Mother, O-yoshi-san is here."

With a sense of relief, O-suzu quickly got up, without looking at O-yoshi's face. Passing through the next room, she again announced the arrival of "O-yoshi-san."

Her mother was lying in bed, her mouth buried in her night-clothes, but she nonetheless looked up and with a twinkle in her eyes exclaimed: "Oh, already here?" O-suzu was palpably aware of O-yoshi's presence behind her, as she made her harried and hurried way to Genkaku's room, moving along the veranda that looked out on the snow-covered garden.

Entering his secluded chamber from the brightness outside, she was struck by how dark it seemed. Genkaku was sitting up, listening as Kōno read to him from the newspaper, but when he saw O-suzu, he immediately called out, "O-yoshi?" It was an intense, hoarse, almost needling voice.

"Yes, she's here, Father," said O-suzu reflexively, standing next to the sliding door. This was followed by a strained silence, before she continued:

"I shall bring her here immediately."

"Mmm . . . Is she alone?"

"No."

Genkaku nodded a wordless acknowledgment.

"Kōno-san, come this way," said O-suzu. Without waiting for the nurse to respond, she left the room, passing with short, rapid steps down the corridor. A wagtail was at that moment perched on a hemp-palm leaf still covered with snow, moving its tail up and down, but O-suzu was preoccupied with a sense of foreboding, as though it had emerged from that isolated, foul-smelling room and were now pursuing her.

4

Now that O-yoshi had come to stay, the ambience of the household became visibly strained. It began with Takeo's bullying of Buntarō. The boy resembled his mother more than his father, sharing with her not only facial features but also timidity. O-suzu was, of course, not without sympathy but nonetheless seemed at times to find him much too submissive.

Kōno took a coldly professional look at this banal domestic drama – or perhaps rather found amusement in it. She had her own dark past with which to contend, having attempted on numerous occasions to ingest cyanide in the aftermath of relations with the head of the household where she was employed or with hospital physicians. As a result, she had developed a morbid pleasure in the sufferings of others.

Since having come to work for the Horikoshis, she had discovered that the paralytic O-tori did not wash her hands after having relieved herself. For a time, being the deeply suspicious woman she was, she thought that O-suzu must be a very clever person indeed: "She some-how brings water to her mother without our knowing it." Within four or five days, however, she realized that the fault lay with the daughter of the house. This gave her a feeling close to satisfaction, and now whenever the occasion called for it, Kōno would provide a washbowl.

"Kōno-san," O-tori exclaimed tearfully, pressing her palms together in gratitude, "it is thanks to you that I can now wash my hands as any normal person does!"

Kōno was nonetheless unmoved by O-tori's joy. Her amusement lay in seeing O-suzu obliged to bring the water herself at least every third time. Again being the kind of person she was, she hardly felt displeased or disturbed by the children's quarrels. When with Genkaku, she feigned sympathy for O-yoshi and her son; in the presence of O-tori, her attitude toward the two was full of spite. It was a slow but effective strategy.

O-yoshi had been in the house for about a week when Takeo and Buntarō quarreled once more. The disagreement had begun over nothing more than the question of which is longer, the tail of a pig or the tail of a cow. The two had been in Takeo's 4.5-mat study room, next to the entrance. Takeo had pushed his slender opponent into a corner, where he pummeled him with kicks and punches. O-yoshi, who had happened to pass by at that moment, held Buntarō in her arms, the boy still too stunned for tears.

"Now Master Takeo," she remonstrated, "you musn't be pickin' on the weak."

These were unusually barbed words for the usually withdrawn O-yoshi. Takeo was taken aback by her severity and fled crying to the sitting room, whereupon O-suzu left whatever work she was doing at her sewing machine and dragged Takeo back to O-yoshi and her son.

"How dare you behave so selfishly! Now tell O-yoshi-san that you are sorry. Get down on the mats and make a proper bow!"

Finding herself in front of the exasperated O-suzu, O-yoshi could only add her own tears to Buntarō's and offer the most abject of apologies. Again it was Kōno the nurse who invariably assumed the role of arbitrator. She physically restrained O-suzu, whose face was red with anger, while imagining with inner contempt the feelings of someone else: Genkaku, who was listening intently to the commotion. Needless to say, she did not betray such thoughts in either her face or her comportment.

Yet it was not only the children's quarrels that caused family unrest. O-tori, who had once seemed to have quite resigned herself to the existence of her husband's mistress, now found the flames of her jealousy rekindled. Of course, she had never once uttered a bitter word to her. (It had been the same five or six years before, when O-yoshi was still living in the maid's room.) Instead, O-tori was inclined to unleash her resentment on the innocent Jūkichi, who naturally refused to take it in the least seriously. O-suzu felt sympathy for him and would sometimes make excuses on behalf of her mother. But he would always rebuff her with a wry smile, saying: "We can't very well have you behaving hysterically as well."

Kōno also took an interest in O-tori's jealousy, which she thoroughly understood, together with the old woman's desire to punish Jūkichi for it. At the same time, she had come to nurture her own feelings of envy toward the married couple. O-suzu was in her eyes the spoiled daughter of the house. As for Jūkichi, he was clearly a man who stood above the crowd, but he was also precisely the sort of male she despised.

Their happiness struck her as undeserved, and so to "remedy" the injustice, her manner toward him took on an air of familiarity. Though such may have been quite meaningless to him, it provided a fine opportunity to annoy O-tori, who, leaving her knees fully exposed, would spitefully taunt him: "Jūkichi, is the daughter of an invalid not enough for you?"

Yet O-suzu did not cast the least suspicion on Jūkichi. Indeed, she seemed to feel a measure of pity for Kōno. This, however, only added to Kōno's resentment and even increased her contempt for the kind-hearted O-suzu. She was pleased to see Jūkichi begin to avoid her and at the same time to show signs of male interest. He had previously been quite unperturbed about undressing in Kōno's presence when he entered the bath located next to the kitchen. Recently, however, he had not allowed himself even once to appear to her in such a state. He was now undoubtedly ashamed of his body, which resembled that of a plucked rooster. Seeing him in this way (his face was also covered with freckles), she secretly sneered at him, asking herself how anyone except O-suzu could possibly fall in love with him.

On a frosty, overcast morning, Kōno was sitting in front of the mirror in her three-mat room at the house entrance, arranging her hair into the straight-back style in which she always wore it. Now at last O-yoshi was to leave the next day for her home in the countryside. While Jūkichi and O-suzu were happy to see her go, O-tori appeared to be all the more irritated.

As she occupied herself with her hair, Kōno could hear O-tori's shrill voice and somehow remembered a story she had once heard from a friend. It seems that a certain woman had, while living in Paris, become acutely homesick. Fortunately, a friend of her husband was about to return to Japan, and so she accompanied him on the same ship. The long ocean voyage did not appear to cause her any particular distress, but as they were approaching the province of Kii, she suddenly became so agitated that she threw herself into the water. The closer she had come to Japan, the more intensely homesick she had become . . . As Kōno slowly wiped her oily hands, she thought about a similar sort of mysterious force that acted on the jealousy of the invalid O-tori – and on her own.

"Mother! What have you done, crawling all the way out here? Mother! Kōno-san, could you please come?"

The voice of O-suzu appeared to come from the outside corridor near Genkaku's room. Hearing it, Kōno looked into the clear mirror and for the first time permitted herself a cold snigger. Then with an air of surprise, she called out in reply: "Yes, I'll be right there!"

<h1 style="text-align:center">5</h1>

Genkaku's condition steadily deteriorated. He also suffered from excruciating sores running from his back to his hips, the consequence of having been bedridden for so many years. To ease his misery, if only slightly, he would occasionally groan. Moreover, his suffering was not only physical. Though O-yoshi's presence provided some consolation, he was also constantly tormented by O-tori's jealousy and the children's quarrels. Yet that was still preferable to the terrifying loneliness he felt in the wake of O-yoshi's departure, forcing him to come to terms with the long years he had lived.

In his present state, it seemed to him that his life had been a wretched one. He had certainly enjoyed comparatively sunny days when he first obtained the rubber-seal patent, whiling away the hours playing cards and drinking. He was nonetheless in a constant state of fretfulness about the envy of his contemporaries, about opportunities for profit that might slip by him. Moreover, in making O-yoshi his mistress, he had had to contend not only with the resultant bickering within his family but also with the constant and heavy burden of finding discreet financial means for her support. Adding all the more to his misery may have been a hidden desire that he had sometimes felt in the last year or two: for all his attraction to young O-yoshi, he had wished that she and her child would simply die.

Wretched? Yet on reflection, I know that I am not the only one in this condition.

Such thoughts would run through his mind in the night, as he remembered in minute detail his relatives, friends, and acquaintances. In the name of "safeguarding constitutional government,"[4] the father of his adopted son-in-law had brought to social ruin many a weaker political opponent. An aging antiquarian, his closest friend, had had intimate relations with the daughter of his first wife. A lawyer had embezzled money from a trust fund. And then there was a seal engraver . . . Yet strangely enough, their sins could not in the least alleviate his suffering. On the contrary, they cast an even darker shadow over his life.

Ah, but this misery too will pass, once the auspicious day comes . . .

This was Genkaku's sole source of comfort. Again to distract himself from the multiple torments that assailed him, both body and soul, he would attempt to revive happy memories. Yet again, he had had a wretched life. If there was a single part that was in the least cheerful, it was in the innocence of his early childhood. Often between waking and dreaming, he would remember the village in the mountain valley of Shinano, where his parents had lived. In particular, he could see the shingle roofs weighed down with stones and the dried mulberry twigs that smelled of silk worms. Yet even these recollections were but fleeting shadows. Sometimes between his groans he would try to chant the *Lotus Sutra*:

Myōon Kanzeon, Bon'on-kaichōon, Shōhi-seken'on[5]

After that, he wanted to hum popular songs of yore, but to sing *Kappore, kappore* after having just extolled Lady Kannon struck him as strangely profane.

Sleep is paradise! Sleep is paradise!

Genkaku wished simply to forget everything through deep and sound sleep, and, in fact, he had Kōno give him not only sedatives but also injections of heroin. Yet even in sleep he did not always find rest. Sometimes in dreams he would meet O-yoshi and Buntarō, and such were for him happy encounters. He also once dreamt that he was talking to a new twenty-point Cherry Banner card; on it was O-yoshi's face of four or five years before. Awakening from such reverie only made him feel all the more miserable. Now the contemplation of sleep began to fill him with an uneasiness bordering on dread.

One afternoon, as the end of the year was approaching, Genkaku was lying on his back when he called to Kōno, who was sitting at his bedside:

"Kōno-san, it's been a long time since I've worn a loincloth. Please have one made of bleached cotton, six *shaku* long."

There was no need to send O-matsu to the clothing shop just to buy bleached cotton.

"I'll put it on myself. Just fold it and leave it here."

He had intended to use the loincloth to hang himself and spent a good half day thinking how he might carry out his plan. Yet being unable even to sit up without help, he could hardly expect to find the opportunity. Moreover, in the face of death, even Genkaku was fearful. Gazing in the dim electric light at a calligraphic scroll in the Ōbaku style hanging in the alcove, he sneered at his own lingering greed for life.

"Kōno-san! Please help me to sit up!"

It was about ten o'clock in the evening.

"I want to take a short nap. You shouldn't refrain from taking a bit of rest yourself."

"No, thank you," replied Kōno curtly, giving him a strange look. "I shall stay awake. It is my duty."

Genkaku sensed that she had seen through his plan. He nodded without saying anything further and pretended to sleep. Kōno sat at her patient's bedside, opened the latest edition of a women's magazine, and appeared to be absorbed in it. Genkaku still had his mind on the loincloth next to his futon, as he watched Kōno through half-closed eyes. He felt a sudden urge to laugh.

"Kōno-san!"

The nurse in turn gave him a startled look. Leaning against the pile of bedclothes, he gave vent to uncontrollable mirth.

"What is it?"

"Never mind. It was nothing."

And yet he continued to laugh, waving his bony right arm.

"A moment ago I was struck by something quite amusing, though I'm not sure what . . . Now help me lie down again."

About an hour later, Genkaku had fallen asleep. In the night, he had a terrifying dream. He was standing in a dense wood, looking into what appeared to be a sitting room, through the gap in the papered doors, whose solid board below the latticed panels was quite tall. In the room lay a child, stark naked. Though still an infant, its face, which was turned toward him, was covered with the wrinkles of old age. Genkaku almost cried out and awoke, covered with sweat . . .

He was alone in the dark room. "Is it still night?" he wondered, but then saw from the table clock that it was nearly noon. For a moment the feeling of relief filled him with cheer, but soon he had reverted to his normal state of gloom. As he lay on his back, he counted his inhalations and exhalations. He felt a vague presence urging him on: "Now is the time!" He silently reached for the loincloth, wrapped it about his head, and pulled hard with both hands.

At that moment, Takeo, a veritable ball of thick winter clothing, stuck his head in the door and then went running as fast as his legs would carry him to the sitting room, hooting with amusement:

"Grandfather's doing something funny!"

6

Approximately a week later, surrounded by members of his family, Genkaku died of tuberculosis. He had a magnificent funeral. (O-tori's paralytic condition precluded her attendance.) Having expressed their condolences to Jūkichi and O-suzu, the mourners burned incense in front of the coffin, which was wrapped in white damask silk. Once outside the gate of the house, most quite forgot about the deceased, but this was clearly not true of his old friends. "The old man must have achieved his life's dream, with a young mistress and a tidy sum of money." Such was the unanimous sentiment of their talk.

The sun was hidden behind the clouds, as a horse-drawn hearse moved through the streets of late December, heading toward the crematorium. Jūkichi rode behind, accompanied by a cousin, a university student, who, perturbed by the swaying of their shabby carriage, exchanged few words with him, concentrating instead on the small volume he was reading, an English translation of Wilhelm Liebknecht's *Erinnerungen eines Soldaten der Revolution*. Having been up all night for the wake, Jūkichi dozed off or stared out the window at the newly constructed houses passing them by. "The entire neighborhood has changed," he muttered listlessly, talking to himself.

Toiling their way through streets mired in mud and slush, the carriages at last reached the crematorium. Yet despite the telephone arrangements he had made, Jūkichi was told that the first-class furnaces were all in use; there were still, however, second-class places available. To the two men, such would have been a matter of indifference, but for O-suzu's sake more than out of consideration for his father-in-law, Jūkichi ardently negotiated with the official on the other side of the half-moon window:

"You see, to be honest, the deceased began to receive medical care

6

only after it was too late, and so at the very least we should like to give him a first-class cremation."

This fabrication proved to be more effective than he had hoped.

"Well then, as the regular first-class furnaces are not available, we shall offer you the special first-class furnace – but without extra charge."

Feeling awkward, Jūkichi repeatedly offered his thanks to the kind-looking elderly man in brass-framed spectacles.

"Oh, no, there's nothing for which you have to thank me."

Having sealed the furnace, Jūkichi and his cousin returned to their shabby carriage. They were on their way through the crematorium gate, when to their surprise they saw O-yoshi standing alone in front of the brick wall. She bowed her head in their direction, and Jūkichi, somewhat disconcerted, started to raise his hat to return the greeting. But already the carriage, listing from side to side, had passed her by, heading down a street lined with leafless poplar trees.

"Isn't that . . . ?" asked his cousin.

"Mmm . . . I wonder whether she was already there when we arrived."

"I think I remember only a few beggars . . . What's to become of her?"

Jūkichi lit a Shikishima and replied as coolly as possible.

"Who's to know?"

His cousin, saying nothing in reply, pictured in his mind a fishing village on the coast of Kazusa and then O-yoshi and her son, who would be living there . . . His face suddenly took on a severe look, and in the sunlight that had now appeared from behind the clouds, he turned once again to his reading of Liebknecht.

COGWHEELS

1. Raincoat

I had been at a resort in the western hinterlands but now found myself in a taxi, a single satchel in hand, speeding toward a railway station along the Tōkaidō Line, on my way to an acquaintance's wedding reception. On both sides of the road, dense, nearly unbroken rows of pine trees were sweeping by, as I pondered my doubtlessly meager chances of catching the Tōkyō-bound train. I was sharing the taxi with the owner of a barbershop. He was cylindrically plump, like a jujube, and sported a short beard. Even as I worried about the time, I engaged in occasional conversation with him.

"Strange things do occur, do they not," he remarked. "Why, I've heard that at the X estate, a ghost appears even during daylight hours."

"Even in daylight hours, you say?" I gave him a perfunctory reply, as I gazed at the distant pine-covered hills bathed in the westering winter sun.

"Mind you, it apparently doesn't show itself when the weather is good. It seems to come out mostly on rainy days."

"On rainy days it may be out for a wet wander."

"Ah, you're joking . . . But they say the ghost wears a raincoat."

With its horn blaring, the taxi pulled up alongside a railway station. I took my leave from the barbershop owner and rushed in, but, just as I feared, the train for Tōkyō had left just two or three minutes before. Sitting alone on a bench in the waiting room, looking blankly outside, was a man in a raincoat. The story I had just heard about a ghost came back to me. I managed a wry smile and resigned myself to waiting for the next train in a café in front of the station.

"Café" . . . a dubious appellation. I took my place in a corner and ordered a cup of chocolate. The table was covered with a white oil-cloth on which broad grids had been drawn in fine blue lines. The four corners were worn, revealing the drab canvas beneath.

The chocolate had the taste of animal glue. As I drank it, I gazed about the deserted room. Pasted on the dusty walls were paper strips, advertising such offerings as rice with chicken and egg, cutlets, local eggs, and omelettes; they reminded me that here along the Tōkaidō Line we were not far from rural life and that it was through barley and cabbage fields that the electric locomotives were passing . . .

My train did not pull in until near nightfall. I was accustomed to traveling second-class, but this time, as it happened, I had settled for third class.

In the already crowded carriage, I was surrounded by school-girls apparently on an excursion, perhaps returning from Ōiso. I lit a cigarette and observed the cheerful flock of virtually ceaseless chatterers.

"Please tell us what *ravu shiin* means," said one of them to a man sitting in front of me; he was apparently accompanying them as a photographer. He attempted an evasive answer, but a girl of fourteen or fifteen persisted in peppering him with questions. I found myself smiling at her manner of speaking, reminding me vaguely of nasal empyema. Next to me was another pupil, aged twelve or thirteen, sitting on the knee of a young schoolmistress. With one hand curled around her neck, she stroked her cheek with the other. Babbling with fellow classmates, she would periodically pause and speak to her:

"Sensei, you are so lovely! What beautiful eyes you have!"

I had the feeling – were I to overlook how they munched on unpeeled apples and removed the paper from their caramels – that these were not schoolgirls but rather full-grown women. A pupil seemingly older than the others happened to step on someone's toe as she was passing me. "Oh, I'm terribly sorry!" she exclaimed. It was precisely her relative maturity that made her the only one among them to typify a schoolgirl. The cigarette still hanging between my lips, I could not help ridiculing the contradictions in my own perceptions.

The electric lights in the train had already been illuminated when at last we pulled into a suburban station. A cold wind was blowing as I stepped out onto the platform. I crossed the overpass, intending to take the electric train, when quite by chance I encountered T, a company man of my acquaintance. As we were waiting, we discussed this and that, including the current recession, of which T naturally knew more than I. On one of his stout fingers he was wearing a splendid turquoise ring that seemed hardly congruent with our topic.

"That's quite something you have on display there!"

"Oh, this? A friend who'd gone off to Harbin on business got me to buy it from him. Now that he can't do business with the cooperatives, he's in quite a bind."

Fortunately, the train that arrived was not as crowded as the one before. We sat down next to each other and continued talking. T had just returned to Tōkyō in the spring from a position he had held in

Paris, and so it was this that dominated our conversation: Madame Caillaux, crab cuisine, the sojourn of an imperial prince . . .[1]

"The situation in France is not as bad as it appears. It's just that the French are stubbornly opposed to paying taxes, so the governments go on falling."

"But the franc has plunged."

"That's what one reads in the newspapers. But what do the newspapers there say about Japan? One would think that we have nothing but massive earthquakes and flood disasters."

Just then a man in a raincoat sat down in front of us. Feeling a bit uneasy at this, I thought about telling T about the ghost, but he was now turning the knob of his cane to the left. Looking straight ahead, he said to me in a low voice:

"The woman over there . . . in the gray woolen shawl . . ."

"Wearing her hair in European style?"

"Uh-huh, with the cloth-wrapped bundle on her lap . . . She was in Karuizawa this summer. She was dressed in quite fashionable Western clothes."

Nevertheless, to anyone's eye she would doubtlessly have appeared to be shabbily dressed. As I talked to T, I furtively looked at her. Something between her eyebrows suggested the expression of madness. Moreover, protruding from her bundle was a piece of sponge that somehow resembled a leopard.

"They say she was dancing in Karuizawa with a young American. How very – what should I say? – *moderne*!"

When I took my leave from T, the man in the raincoat was no longer there. I got off the train and walked to a hotel, satchel in hand. Nearly the entire way there were large buildings on both sides; I suddenly remembered the pine forest I had passed. At the same time, I saw coming into view objects quite strange. Strange? That is to say constantly turning, semitransparent cogwheels. More than once I had already had this experience, the number of such gears steadily increasing until they half blocked my field of vision. This did not last long. Soon they were gone, but then my head would begin to ache. Such was the invariable pattern. The ophthalmologist had repeatedly ordered me to give up cigarettes as a means for ridding myself of these optical illusions (were they?), but I had suffered such since when I was in my teens, well before I took up smoking. *It's started again!* I thought to myself, covering my right eye to test my left, which showed no sign of the objects. But behind my other eyelid, there were many still turning. As I saw the buildings on my right disappearing one by one, I quickened my pace.

The cogwheels were gone by the time I entered the hotel lobby, but my head still ached. I checked my coat and hat at the desk and took the opportunity to reserve a room. I then called a magazine editor to discuss a question of payment.

The wedding reception appeared to be already well underway. I sat down at the end of a table and began moving my knife and fork. There were more than fifty guests, sitting perpendicular to the bride and groom, our tables forming a white, rectangular U. They were all, of course, in the best of spirits. For my part, I became increasingly melancholy as I sat under the bright electric lights. In the hope of fleeing my oppressive state of mind, I turned to the gentleman sitting beside me and engaged him in conversation. He was an old man, with a white beard that made him look quite like a lion. I knew him to be a renowned scholar of the Chinese classics, to which our conversation consequently turned.

"The *qílín* is really a unicorn, you know. And the *fènghuáng* is the phoenix."

The scholar seemed to take interest in these comments of mine, but as I was talking quite mechanically, I found myself steadily yielding to a pathologically destructive impulse. I said that the sage kings Yáo and Shùn were, of course, strictly legendary personages and that the author of the *Spring and Autumn Annals* had lived long after his purported time, the work having surely been compiled in the Han Dynasty.

At this, the scholar's face took on an expression of undisguised displeasure; avoiding my gaze, he cut off remarks with a tigerish roar:

"If Yáo and Shùn did not exist, then we can only conclude that Confucius lied. But it is unimaginable that a great sage should lie."

I did not reply, of course. Again, knife and fork in hand, I turned to the meat on my plate. At the edge of it, I saw a small maggot gently wriggling, making me think of the English word *worm*. Like *qílín* and *fēnghuáng*, it could only refer to a mythical animal. I put down my utensils and gazed at the glass into which champagne was being poured.

When the banquet was finally over, I walked to the room I had reserved – down a deserted corridor that gave me the feeling of being in a prison rather than in a hotel. Fortunately, however, at least my headache had faded.

Along with my satchel, my hat and overcoat had been brought to the room. I looked at the latter, hanging on the wall, and had the impression of seeing myself standing there. I hastily threw it into the clothes closet in a corner of the room. I then went to the mirror; staring at my reflection, I could see my facial bones beneath the skin. Suddenly the vivid image of a maggot floated up into the mind of that man there, myself, standing in front of the mirror.

I opened the door, went out into the corridor, and set off aimlessly. At the far end, where the corridor turned toward the lobby, I suddenly saw a tall electric lamp-stand covered with a green shade, the light brightly reflected in the glass door. This gave a momentary feeling of peace. I sat down in a chair in front of it and thought of many things. Yet I was not meant to rest there for even five minutes: someone had with extraordinary carelessness tossed a raincoat onto the back of the adjacent sofa.

But why a raincoat in this cold weather? Brooding on the matter, I walked back down the corridor. At the other end was a personnel room. There was no one to be seen, but I could hear faint voices and a reply to something that was said in English: "All right."

"All right"? I found myself straining to catch the exact meaning of this exchange. "Ōru-raito"? "Ōru-raito"? What in the world could be "Ōru-raito"?

In my room there would, of course, be utter stillness. Yet the thought of opening the door gave me a strange sense of loathing. After a moment's hesitation, I went in. Trying not to look in the mirror, I sat down at the desk in an easy chair covered in blue Moroccan leather that looked quite like lizard skin. I opened my satchel and took out writing paper, intending to continue work on a short story. But the pen I had dipped in ink would not move, and when it finally did, it could only go on writing the same words over and over again: *"All right . . . All right, sir . . . All right . . ."*

Suddenly there was a sound next to my bed; it was the telephone. I bolted up in surprise and put the receiver to my ear.

"Yes? Who's calling?"

"I . . . I . . ."

It was my elder sister's daughter.

"What's wrong? What's happened?"

"Something dreadful . . . And so . . . It's dreadful . . . I've also just called Auntie . . ."

"Something dreadful?"

"Yes, so please come quickly. Quickly!"

The line immediately went dead. I replaced the receiver and reflexively pressed the button to call for a bellboy. At the same time, I was fully aware that my hand was trembling. There was no immediate response. I felt more distress than irritation, as again and again I pressed the button. But now I finally understood the words that destiny had spoken to me: *All right, all right.*

That afternoon my sister's husband had been struck and killed by a train in the open countryside, not far from Tōkyō. The body had been found dressed unseasonably in a raincoat. And now I was here in this hotel room, continuing to work on that same short story. In the wee hours, there was no sound in the corridor, though sometimes I could hear from outside the door the sound of wings. Perhaps someone somewhere was keeping birds.

2. Vengeance

I awakened in my hotel room at about eight. When I tried to get out of bed, I could only find one of my slippers. For two years now I had been constantly plagued by such fears, remembering, moreover, the one-sandaled prince of Greek mythology.

I called for a bellboy and asked him to look for the missing slipper. A dubious expression on his face, he went about searching the small room.

"It's here," he reported, "in the bathroom."

"How could it have gone there?"

"I suppose it could have been a rat . . ."

After he left, I drank some coffee without cream and resumed my work. The square, tuff-framed window looked out on the snow-covered garden. Each time I set down my pen, my gaze would be lost in the snow, which, spread out under a budding winter daphne, was besmirched by the soot of the city. It was somehow a painful sight. While smoking a cigarette, my pen again motionless, I let my mind wander over this and that. I thought of my wife, my children, and especially my sister's husband . . .

Just before committing suicide, he had been suspected of arson. The charge was hardly surprising in light of the fact that prior to the destruction of his house in a blaze, he had insured it for twice its value. He had also been given a suspended sentence for perjury. Yet a greater cause for my anxiety than his suicide was the awareness that whenever I returned to Tōkyō I was sure to see a fire. Once from a train window I had seen passing hills aflame; another time I was in a taxi (with my wife and children) when I saw one in the area around Tokiwabashi. Even well before my brother-in-law's house had burned down, I thus had more than adequate reason for knowing myself to be possessed of pyric premonitions.

"Our house may burn down sometime this year."

"Such ill-omened talk! It would be a catastrophe . . . We are so poorly insured . . ."

My wife and I had had such an exchange, but it was not our house that had burned . . . In an attempt to rid my mind of such obsessions, I picked up my pen once more and began to move it across the page, but I was at pains even to complete a single line. I finally stood up from the desk and lay down on the bed to read Tolstoy's *Polikoushka*. The novella's protagonist has a complex personality: a blend of vanity, morbidity, and ambition. Yet with but a few revisions, this tragicomedy struck me as a caricature of my own life. I had the eerie feeling that through this story I was hearing fate sardonically laugh at my own plight. Not an hour had passed before I abruptly sat up in bed and in the same motion threw the book with all my strength against the curtains in the corner of the room.

"Damn it all!"

At that moment I saw a large rat scampering diagonally from under the curtain to the bathroom. I bounded after it. Opening the door, I searched everywhere, but there was no sign of it, not even under the white tub. With a sudden sense of horror, I hurriedly threw off my slippers, donned my shoes, and ran out into the deserted corridor.

It was as dispiriting a prison as it had been the day before. With drooping head, I walked up and down the stairs and then found myself in the culinary quarters, which were surprisingly bright and cheery. On one side, several stoves were burning. I felt the cold look of several white-capped cooks as I passed on through and simultaneously had the sensation of having fallen into hell. At the moment, a prayer rose spontaneously to my lips: "Chastise me, Lord, but spare me Thy wrath, lest I should come to naught . . ."[2]

I left the hotel. The blue sky was shining brightly on thawing snow and slush, as I plodded toward my sister's house. The trees in the park along the way, their branches and foliage, were all black; like human beings, they each had both a front and a back. The realization brought more than uneasiness; I felt something closer to dread. Remembering the spirits in Dante's *Inferno* transformed into trees, I decided to walk on that side of the streetcar tracks on which there was an almost unbroken line of buildings.[3]

Yet even then I found I could not walk one hundred meters in peace and tranquillity:

"Excuse me . . . ," came a timid voice.

It was a young man of about twenty-two or twenty-three. He was wearing a school uniform with gold buttons. I saw a mole on the left side of his nose. He had taken off his cap. I stared at him without speaking.

"I believe I have the honor of addressing . . ."

"Yes . . ."

"Ah, I somehow thought so . . ."

"Have you some business with me?"

"No, I merely wanted to speak to you and say that I am one of your faithful readers."

I raised my hat by way of acknowledgment and immediately set off.

"Sensei! Sensei!"

At the time, this had become for me a most unpleasant term. I thought myself guilty of all manner of crimes; yet, when the occasion arose, I would be addressed as "Sensei" all the same. I could not help sensing an element of disparagement – but what was it?

My affirmation of materialism forced me to deny any sort of mysticism. Several months before, I had written in a small coterie magazine: "I have no artistic conscience; I have no conscience whatsoever. I have only nerves."

With her three children, my elder sister had taken refuge in a makeshift hut at the back of an alley, the interior walls papered brown. It was colder inside than outside; stretching our hands toward the brazier, we talked about this and that.

My brawny brother-in-law, who instinctively despised me all the more for my scrawniness, had openly denounced my writings as immoral. I in turn treated him with icy contempt; not once did we have a candid or cordial conversation.

Yet as I talked with my sister, I came to the realization that he too had been leading a hellish existence. In fact, I was told that he had seen a ghost on a sleeping car. Lighting a cigarette, I nonetheless endeavored to restrict my remarks to matters financial.

"Under the circumstances, I intend to sell everything."

"Yes, you're right. You could probably get something for the typewriter."

"And then there are the paintings."

"Do you want to sell the portrait of him? . . . Even *that* one?"

I looked at the unframed conté sketch on the wall and sensed that this was no time for lighthearted chatter. The train had turned him, even his face, into no more than a lump of flesh, the only recognizable feature, it was said, being his mustache. The entire story in itself was, of course, undoubtedly loathsome. Yet the portrait was a perfect rendition of his every feature – except for his mustache, which, strangely enough, struck me as blurred. Thinking that the problem was the balance of the light, I tried to look at it from different angles.

"What are you doing?"

"Nothing . . . The portrait . . . Something around the mouth . . ."

My sister turned her head and then, as though quite unaware, remarked:

"The mustache seems a bit faded, doesn't it?"

What I had seen was not an illusion. But if not, then . . . ? I decided to leave, without accepting my sister's invitation to stay for lunch.

"But surely you can stay a bit longer!"

"Perhaps I can come again tomorrow . . . Today I have an errand in Aoyama."

"Aoyama? You are still feeling unwell?"

"I'm constantly taking medicine. The sleeping pills alone are more than enough trouble. Veronal, neuronal, trional, numal . . ."

Half an hour later I found myself entering a tall building and taking the elevator to the third-floor restaurant. I pushed on the glass door and, when it did not open, saw a lacquered sign announcing that on this day the restaurant was regularly closed. Feeling increasingly out of sorts, I gazed through the door at the arrangements of apples and bananas on the tables. I turned to go.

Two men, apparently company employees, were engaged in lively conversation as I left; they brushed my shoulder as they came through the entrance. I thought I heard one of them say: ". . . terribly irritating."

I lingered on the pavement and then looked for a passing taxi. But such were rare, and the few that I saw were invariably yellow. (For some reason, yellow taxis make it a habit of involving me in accidents.) I was finally able to wave down an auspiciously green vehicle, determined after all to make my way to the psychiatric hospital near the cemetery in Aoyama.

"Terribly irritating . . . Tantalizing . . . Tantalus . . . Inferno."

Tantalus was, in fact, myself, gazing through the glass door at the fruits on the restaurant table. I stared at the back of the driver, cursing the Dantesque vision of hell now twice brought before my eyes.

As I brooded, I thought of all that is no more than lies covered with multicolored enamel, concealing from me the true horror of human existence: politics, economics, art, science . . . A worsening shortness of breath drove me to roll down the window, but from the feeling that my heart was being squeezed I had no relief.

My green taxi had now finally brought me to Jingūmae, where, turning into an alleyway, one would come to a certain psychiatric hospital. Yet today I somehow could not remember the location. I had the driver follow the streetcar line up and down several times and then resigned myself to getting out and walking.

I was able at last to find the alleyway. I walked along, sidestepping the many muddy potholes, and then at some point went in the wrong direction, finding myself in front of the Aoyama Funeral Pavilion.

Since the funeral of Natsume Sensei, I had not so much as passed by the gate. Then too, some ten years before, I was unhappy. But at least I had been at peace. I gazed at the gravel spread out inside and remembered the banana plant in his house, the Villa Sōseki. Irresistibly I felt that my life too had come to an end and it was no accident that destiny had brought me here – to this place and at this time, a decade later.

Leaving the hospital, I took a taxi to return to the hotel. As I was stepping out in front of the entrance, I saw a man in a raincoat engaged in a quarrel with what seemed to be a bellboy. No, instead it was an automobile attendant, dressed in green. I took this to be somehow a bad omen and, deciding not to go in, hastily turned around.

The day was waning as I came to Ginza-dōri. The shops lining both sides of the street and the dizzying bustle of people only worsened my sense of gloom. It was particularly distressing to see them passing blithely to and fro, as though oblivious to any concept of sin. I walked steadily onward, heading north, in a mélange of electrical illumination and fading sunlight.

Along the way, my eye was caught by a bookshop with piles of magazines on display. I went in and, having looked absentmindedly at the contents of several tiers, pulled out from one of the shelves a volume: *Girishia-shinwa*. In this yellow-covered book of Greek mythological tales, intended for children, the first words I happened to read sent me instantly reeling: "Even Zeus, the grandest of the gods, is no match for the goddesses of vengeance."

I left the shop and again made my way through the crowds, stooping as I went, as though sensing behind me those same Furies in relentless pursuit.

3. Night

On the second floor of Maruzen, I found in a tier of books an edition of August Strindberg's *Legends* and perused it, two or three pages at a time. The experiences described there did not vary significantly from my own; moreover, the cover was yellow. I returned the book to the shelf and now pulled out almost at random a thick volume. In one of the illustrations, there were cogwheels with eyes and noses no different from those of us, of human beings. (A German had compiled these sketches, drawn by mental patients.) In the midst of my depression, I felt my spirits revolting. In desperation, like a gambling addict, I began to leaf through book after book. Yet wherever I looked, there was invariably a sentence or an illustration that concealed more than a piercing needle or two. All of them? Even when I picked up *Madame Bovary*, which I had read and reread countless times, I found that in the final analysis I was myself but another bourgeois Monsieur Bovary.

I was almost the last customer there on the second floor, as the sun began to set. Wandering between the electrically illuminated tiers of books, I stopped in front of the religion section and perused a volume with a green cover. One of the chapters listed in the table of contents was entitled: "The Four Most Dreadful Foes: Doubt, Fear, Hubris, and Sensual Appetites." No sooner had I seen these words than I sensed all the more strongly my inner revolt. For me, at least, these "foes" were nothing other than a matter of sensibility and reason. All the more unbearable was now the awareness that traditional ways of thinking contributed as much to my unhappiness as did modernity.

Yet as I held the book in my hand, I suddenly thought of the pen name I had once used: Juryō Yoshi, borrowed from the story told in *Hán Fēizǐ* of the lad who, before he had learned to walk like the people of Hándān, forgot how to walk in the manner of his own people in Shòulíng and thus went crawling home like a meandering reptile. Now I am surely seen in the eyes of all as that same Juryō Yoshi. Yet at least I had assumed the pen name before falling into hell . . . Endeavoring to drive away the demons that haunted me by putting this tier of books behind me, I walked to a poster exhibit directly ahead of me. One showed a knight, apparently St. George, slaying a winged dragon. Beneath the helmet I could see his half-exposed, grimacing face; it closely resembled that of an enemy of mine. Again I remembered *Hán Fēizǐ* and the story of the master dragon-slayer. Without moving on to the exhibition room, I descended the broad staircase.

Night had already fallen as I walked along Nihonbashi-dōri, still brooding about the proverbial slayer of dragons – surely a fitting inscription for my own inkstone. That very object had been given to me by a young man of business. Having failed in various undertakings, he had gone bankrupt at the end of the previous year.

I looked up to the towering heavens to remind myself of how tiny is the earth amidst the light of countless stars – as, by consequence, am I myself. But after a day of clear weather, the night sky was covered with clouds. I suddenly felt a vaguely hostile presence and decided to take refuge in a café on the other side of the streetcar tracks.

It was indeed a refuge. The rose-pink walls offered some sort of peace and comfort; I happily collapsed at a table in the rear. As luck would have it, there were only two or three other customers. I sipped my cocoa and puffed on my usual cigarette, sending bluish smoke up against the pale red wall. The harmony of the gentle colors was likewise cheering. A few moments later, however, I saw to my left a portrait of Napoleon and my anxiety was back with me all too soon. Napoleon as a student had written on the last page of his geography notebook: *"Sainte Hélène . . . petite île."* It may have been, as we say, a coincidence, though the fact remains that it inspired fear in Napoleon himself.

Even as I continued staring at him, I thought about the works I had written. The first to float into my mind were the aphorisms included in *Shuju no Kotoba* – in particular, "Life is more hellish than hell." And then, the protagonist of *Jigokuhen*, the painter Yoshihide, and his fate, and then . . . I puffed on my cigarette as I glanced about the café, trying to escape from such memories. I had sought asylum here a mere five minutes before, but in that brief time the café had quite altered its appearance. Particularly disturbing were the imitation mahogany tables and chairs and their utter lack of harmony with the color of the walls. Fearing that I would fall once again into anguish known only to myself, I threw down a silver coin and hastily started to leave.

"Hello, sir? That will be twenty *sen* . . ."

I had put down a copper coin. Feeling deeply humiliated, I made my way along the street, abruptly remembering the home I had once had in the middle of a distant pine forest – not the suburban house of my adoptive parents but rather the one I rented just for myself and my family. I had been living in that sort of arrangement some ten years before, until certain circumstances led me rashly to take up residence again with my parents. It was also then that I became a slave, a tyrant, a powerless egotist . . .

It was not until about ten o'clock that I returned to the hotel. I was so weary from my long walk that I lacked even the strength to go to my room. I threw myself into the chair in front of the fireplace full of burning logs. I thought about the novel that I had intended to write. It was to be an episodic work of some thirty chapters in chronological order, progressing from Empress Suiko to Emperor Meiji, with the ordinary people of each age in the fore. As I gazed at the dancing sparks ascending, I found myself thinking of a bronze statue in front of the Imperial Palace and the armored figure sitting grandly astride his horse,[4] the very embodiment of loyalty. And yet his enemies . . .

"No, no, it cannot be true!"

I came slipping back down from the distant past to the immediate present, as I was fortuitously met at that moment by an upperclassman from university days, a sculptor. He was, as ever, dressed in velvet and was sporting a short goatee. I rose from my chair and shook his hand. (This was not my custom but rather his – the result of half a lifetime spent in Paris and Berlin.) His hand had a strangely reptilian dampness.

"Are you staying here?"

"Yes."

"On business?"

"Yes, on business, among other things . . ."

He stared at me with what seemed to be a quasi-investigative expression in his eye.

"What about continuing this conversation in my room?" I issued the invitation as a challenge. (Though lacking in courage, I have the unfortunate habit of leaping at an opportunity to provoke.)

He replied with a smile: "Where is it, this room of yours?"

We walked shoulder to shoulder, as though the best of friends, passing through a group of softly speaking foreigners. Entering my room, he sat down with his back to the mirror and began talking about this and that – or at least of this or that *woman*, for such was his principal topic.

I was without doubt among those whose sins would send them to hell, but this sort of lascivious gossip only drove me further into depression. Momentarily assuming the role of a Puritan, I began deriding those women.

"Look at S's lips. How many men do you suppose she has kissed to give them that appearance?"

I suddenly fell silent and looked at the back of his head in the reflection of the mirror. He had a yellow plaster bandage below one of his ears.

"How many men she has kissed?"

"That's the sort of person she strikes me as being."

He smiled and nodded, and I felt him looking at me carefully as though to learn some secret buried within me. And yet we continued to dwell on women. I felt less loathing for him than shame at my own cowardice, and this only deepened my sense of utter gloom.

When at last he had left, I lay on my bed and started reading *An'ya Kōro*. One by one, I could keenly feel the struggles in which the protagonist was engaged within his own mind. The realization that, by comparison, I was an utter fool brought tears to my eyes, and these gave me a feeling of peace, though only momentarily. My right eye was now again seeing semitransparent cogwheels. As before, they steadily multiplied as they turned. Fearing that my headache would return, I put the book down next to the pillow and took 0.8 grams of Veronal, resolving in any case to sleep soundly.

I dreamt, however, that I was looking at a swimming pool, where children, boys and girls, were splashing above the water and diving below. I left the pool and walked into the pine forest on the other side. Someone called out to me from behind: "Otōsan!" Half turning around, I saw my wife standing in front of the pool and was immediately struck by a painful feeling of regret.

"Otōsan, don't you want a towel?"

"No. Watch the children."

I continued walking, but at some point my path turned into a platform – at a country railway station, it seemed – with a long hedge. There was a university student (H), together with an older woman. When they saw me, they approached and began talking at the same time.

"What a terrible fire!"

"I barely escaped myself," said H.

I thought I had seen the woman before. I also felt a kind of euphoric excitement in talking to her. Now the train pulled in quietly next to the platform amidst a cloud of smoke. I was the only one to get on; I walked through the corridors of the sleeping compartments; inside, white sheets hung from the berths. On one was the reclining figure of a naked woman, much like a mummy, looking toward me. It was once again the goddess of vengeance – that daughter of a lunatic.

I woke up and, without thinking, immediately sprang out of bed. The room was still bright with the electric lights, but from somewhere I heard the sound of wings and the squeaking of a rat. I opened the door, went out into the corridor, and hurried to the fireplace. I sat down in a chair and gazed at the tenuous flames. A hotel attendant dressed in white came to add more wood.

"What time is it?" I asked.

"About three-thirty, sir," he replied.

Even so, there was a woman who sat reading in a corner at the opposite end of the lobby. I took her to be an American and could see even from across the room that she was wearing a green dress.

Feeling that I had been rescued, I resolved to remain where I was to await the dawn – like an old man who, having gained a respite from years of a tormenting illness, now placidly waits for death . . .

4. Not Yet?

In my hotel room, I managed at last to complete the short story I had been writing and prepared to send it to a certain magazine. The remuneration I would receive would not, of course, pay for a week's lodging expenses. I nevertheless felt satisfied at having finished the project and wanted now to visit a bookstore in the Ginza for an intellectual stimulant.

Perhaps it was the fluctuating winter sun on the asphalt that gave the crumpled scraps of discarded paper the appearance of roses. I felt buoyed by a sense of benevolence as I entered the bookstore, which likewise seemed neater and tidier than usual. The only troubling presence was a girl in spectacles talking to a clerk. Remembering the roselike paper scraps that I had seen on my way, I purchased a collection of conversations with Anatole France and the collected correspondence of Prosper Mérimée.

I went into a café with my two books, took a seat at a table in the back, and waited for my coffee to come. A woman and a boy were sitting across the way – mother and son to all appearances. The son could have been my younger self, so strong was the resemblance. The two talked intimately, face-to-face, quite as lovers might. Indeed as I observed them, I had the feeling that at least he was well aware of providing consolation for her, even of a sexual nature. Such exemplified for me the sheer power of human affinities, something of which I too had some knowledge, providing yet another example of a certain will to transform this vale of tears into a veritable hell.

Nevertheless, fearing that I would fall into yet another round of anguish, I happily took the coffee brought to me at that moment and began reading Mérimée's letters. As with his novels, they are full of brilliant and biting aphorisms. Reading them gave steely reinforcement to my disposition. (It has been a weakness of mine to be so easily susceptible to such influences.) After the coffee, feeling "ready for whatever comes," I left the café.

As I passed along the streets, I looked into the various shop windows. A picture-framer had hung up a portrait of Beethoven, his bristling mane giving him the air of true genius. I could not help finding it quite comical . . .

On my way, I ran into an old friend from secondary school; a professor of applied chemistry, he was carrying a large folding satchel and had a bloodshot eye.

"What's wrong with your eye?"

"Oh, it's just conjunctivitis."

I remembered that for the last fourteen or fifteen years, I have developed the same sort of eye infection whenever I discover that I have an affinity for someone. But I said nothing about that to him. Slapping me on the shoulder, he began to tell me about our mutual friends and then, without pausing in his chatter, led me into a café.

"It's been a long time. I haven't seen you since the dedication of the Shu Shunsui monument."

He was sitting across a marble table from me, having lit a cigar.

"Yes, not since Shu Shun . . ."

For some reason I stumbled over the pronunciation, and this was troubling, all the more so, as this was the Japanese form of the name. But my old school chum went on talking as though quite unaware – of K, the novelist, of the bulldog he had just purchased, of a poison gas known as Lewisite . . .

"You don't seem to be writing anymore. I read *Tenkibo*. It's auto-biographical, isn't it?"

"Yes, it is."

"I found it a bit pathological. How is your health at the moment?"

"I'm still getting by with a constant supply of medicine."

"I understand. I too am suffering from insomnia."

"'I too'? Why do you say 'I too'?"

"Isn't that what you said yourself? Insomnia's a serious matter, you know!"

There was a trace of a smile in his left, bloodshot eye. Before replying, I had sensed that I would have difficulty in pronouncing the final syllable of the technical term.

"How could the son of a lunatic be expected to sleep?"

Within ten minutes I was again walking the street. The crumpled papers scattered on the asphalt were now sometimes taking on the appearance of human faces. A bob-haired woman was coming toward me. From a distance, she appeared to be quite beautiful, but as she passed, I could see a face that was lined, wrinkled, and indeed ugly. She also appeared to be pregnant. I instinctively turned my face away and turned into a broad side street. A few moments later I began to feel hemorrhoidal pain. For me, the only remedy was a *Sitzbad*. A *Sitzbad* . . . Beethoven too had resorted to such . . .

My nostrils were immediately assailed by the smell of the sulfur used in the therapy, though there was, of course, nothing of the sort to be seen on the street. Turning my mind again to the paper-scrap roses, I endeavored to walk with steady steps.

An hour later I had shut myself away in my room, sitting at the desk at work on a new story. My pen raced across the paper at a speed that quite astounded me. After two or three hours, however, it stopped, as though held in check by an invisible presence. Having no other recourse, I stood up and paced the room. It was at such moments that my delusions of grandeur were most striking. Caught up in savage joy, I could only think that I had neither parents nor wife and children, that there was only the life now emanating from my pen.

Four or five minutes passed, and now I had to turn to the telephone. I spoke into the receiver again and again, but all I could hear in response was a vague mumbling, endlessly repeated, that nonetheless doubtlessly had the sound of *mohru*. I finally moved away from the telephone and again paced the room, still haunted by the word.

"*Mohru* – Mole . . ."

The English word for the burrowing rodent. The association was hardly a pleasant one, but then two or three seconds later, I respelled it as *mort, la mort*. The French word for "death" instantly filled me with anxiety. Death had pursued my sister's husband and was now pursuing me. And yet in spite of my fear I found myself feeling strangely amused and even smiled. Why? I had no idea.

I stood in front of the mirror, something I had not done for a long time, and directly looked at myself. My reflection too was, of course, smiling. Staring at my own image, I remembered a second self, the *Doppelgänger*, as one is wont to call such in German, that I had, most fortunately, never encountered. On the other hand, the wife of K, who had become an actor in American films, had seen my double in a theater corridor. (I still remember my perplexity when she apologized to me for not having greeted "me" on that occasion.) So had a one-legged translator, now deceased, in a Ginza tobacconist's shop.

Perhaps it was not I who was death's prey but rather my double. But even if I were . . . Turning my back to the mirror, I returned to my writing desk in front of the window. The square, tuff-framed window looked out on withered grass and a pond. As I gazed at the garden, I thought about all the notebooks and uncompleted theater pieces that had gone up in smoke in that distant pine forest. Picking up my pen, I resumed work on the story.

5. Red Lights

Sunlight had begun to torment me. I was truly living the life of a mole, assiduously continuing to write, the window curtains closed and the electric lights burning even during the day. When I was too weary to go on, I read Taine's *Histoire de la littérature anglaise* and perused his lives of the poets . . . They had all suffered misfortune . . . Even the giants of the Elizabethan age . . . even the era's great scholar, Ben Jonson, having suffered nervous exhaustion, found himself imagining the Roman and Carthaginian armies going into battle on his big toe. I could not help feeling a cruel, spite-filled joy at their misfortunes.

One night when a strong east wind was blowing (which I took to be a good omen), I left the hotel from the basement and went out on the street, resolved to visit an old man of my acquaintance. He lived in an attic of a building housing a Bible publisher, where he worked as the lone caretaker. There he devoted himself to prayer and reading. Sitting under a cross, our hands stretched out toward the brazier, we conversed: Why had my mother gone insane? Why had my father failed in business? Why was I being punished? . . . He knew these secrets and would always listen to me, a strangely solemn smile on his face. Sometimes he would draw in a few short words a caricature of human life. I could not help feeling respect for this hermit in the attic. Yet as we talked, I discovered that he too was capable of being moved by human affinities.

"The daughter of the nurseryman is a beautiful girl, with a sweet disposition . . . She is very kind to me."

"How old is she?"

"Eighteen this year."

Perhaps for him it was a kind of paternal love. But I inevitably caught in his eyes a sign of passion. On the yellowed skin of the apple he offered me I saw the shape of a unicorn. (On occasion I would discover mythological animals in wood grains and finely fissured teacups.) The unicorn was indeed the *qílín*. Remembering that an unfriendly critic had once characterized me as "the *qílín's* offspring of the 1910s," I realized that even here in this attic, under the cross, I had no safe haven.

"How have you been these days?"

"As ever, at the edge of my nerves."

"For that, no medicine will help you. Have you no desire to become a believer?"

"As if the likes of me could manage that . . ."

"It's not in the least difficult. You need only to believe in God, in Christ His Son, and in the signs and wonders that He performed."

"Well, what I *can* believe in is the devil."

"Then why not believe in God? If you believe in shadows, you must necessarily believe in light."

"There are shadows without light, are there not?"

"Shadows without light?"

I could only fall silent. He walked in shadows no less than did I. Yet he believed in a light beyond. It was, to be sure, the only point of difference between us, but it was, at least for me, an impassable gulf nonetheless.

"But the light necessarily exists. Evidence can be seen in the miracles, which occur again and again even in our own times . . ."

"Miracles that are the work of the devil . . ."

"Why do you dwell on the devil?"

I felt tempted to tell him everything I had experienced in the last year or two, but I was afraid that he might tell my wife and children, that I might follow my mother's footsteps into a psychiatric hospital.

"What do you have over there?" I asked.

The vigorous old man turned toward his ancient bookshelves, with something of a Pan-like look on his face.

"The complete works of Dostoyevsky. Have you read *Crime and Punishment?*"

I had, of course, avidly read four or five volumes of Dostoyevsky's works a decade before. But I was struck by his incidental mention – or was it? – of *Crime and Punishment*. I borrowed his copy and returned to my hotel. The streets, with their electric lights and crowds of people, were as unpleasant as ever. Any chance encounters with acquaintances would be particularly unbearable, and so, like a thief, I carefully chose the darker paths.

But then a few moments later, I began to have stomach pains, for which the only remedy was a shot of whiskey. I found a bar, pushed on the door, and started to go in. The narrow confines were enveloped in cigarette smoke. A group of young people, apparently artists, were drinking, and in the very middle was a woman, her hair covering her ears in keeping with the latest Occidental fashion. She was energetically playing the mandolin.

Feeling instantly at a loss, I turned and left. Now, however, I found that my shadow was swaying from left to right, and that, ominously enough, I was being bathed in red light. I stopped in my tracks, but my shadow went on vacillating. I hesitantly looked around and saw at last a colored glass lantern hanging from the eaves of the bar and swinging slowly in the strong wind . . .

It was to a subterranean restaurant that I next made my way. I went to the bar and ordered whiskey.

"Whiskey? I'm afraid that Black and White is all there is."

I poured the whiskey into the soda and began sipping it in silence. Next to me sat two men in their late twenties or early thirties, journalists, I assumed. They were speaking in low voices – and in French. With my entire body, I could feel the focus of their eyes on my back, indeed as though they were sending out electric waves. They clearly seemed to know my name and were clearly talking about me.

"Bien . . .très mauvais . . . pourquoi? . . ."

"Pourquoi? . . . le diable est mort! . . ."

"Oui, oui . . . d'enfer . . ."

I put down a silver coin, my last, and fled the cavern. The night wind was gusting through the streets, soothing my nerves, as my stomach pains eased. I remembered Raskolnikov and felt the desire to confess all. And yet that could bring only tragedy, not just to me and to my family but also to others. Moreover, the sincerity of that desire was dubious. If my nerves could become as steady as that of a normal person . . . But for that I would have to flee somewhere: Madrid, Rio de Janeiro, Samarkand . . .

I was suddenly jolted by a small white advertising sign hanging down from the eaves of a shop: a winged automobile tire trademark. I remembered the story of the ancient Greek who, though able to fly by means of artificial wings, allowed them to be burned by the sun and so plunged into the sea and drowned . . . To Madrid, to Rio de Janeiro, to Samarkand . . . I had to laugh at such fantasies – and at the same time remind myself of Orestes being pursued by the Furies.

I followed the dark street along the canal. I found myself recalling the suburban house of my adopted parents. It was clear that they were spending their days waiting for me to return, as were perhaps my wife and children . . . But I feared the force that would inevitably bind me if I were, in fact, to do so.

Moored in the choppy water was a barge from whose hold a faint light was leaking. A family surely lived there, men and women hating one another out of love . . . But now, though still feeling the intoxicating effect of the whiskey, I summoned once more my combative strength and headed back to the hotel.

I sat again at the desk and continued reading Mérimée's correspondence, which eventually revived me. When I learned that late in life he converted to Protestantism, I instantly felt that his mask had fallen away, that I was seeing his true face. Like us, he had walked in the darkness. In the darkness? Shiga's *An'ya Kōro* was being transformed for me into a terrifying work. In an attempt to forget my depression, I began to read Anatole France's conversations, but this modern Pan too, I could see, had borne a cross . . .

An hour later, a bellboy brought me a bundle of mail. Among the items was a letter from a publisher in Leipzig, asking me to write an essay on the modern Japanese woman. Why did he specifically want *me* for the project? The letter, written in English, included a handwritten postscript: "A simple black-and-white depiction, in the style of a Japanese painting, with no color, would also suit our purposes." The words reminded me of the whiskey brand. I tore the letter to shreds. I opened another envelope, the one closest to hand, and read the enclosed missive, written on yellow stationery. It was from an unknown youth. I had not read more than two or three lines when I saw something that could only set me on edge: a reference to *Jigokuhen*.

I opened a third envelope, containing a message from a nephew. Now at last came a sigh of relief, as I read of domestic problems. But then I came to the line at the end and felt bowled over: "I am sending you a new edition of the poetry collection *Shakkō*."

I heard taunting laughter in my ears – *Shakkō!* – and fled the room. There was no one in the corridor. Propping myself up with a hand against the wall, I managed to get to the lobby, where I sat down in a chair and thought that I should at least light a cigarette. Oddly enough, it was an Air Ship. (Since coming to the hotel, I had made it a habit of smoking only Star.) The two artificial wings appeared again before my eyes. I called over a bellboy and sent him to purchase two packs of Star, but as luck would have it, according to his report, there were none left.

"We still have Air Ship, sir . . ."

I shook my head and looked around the spacious lobby. At the far end were four or five foreigners sitting around a table. It seemed that one of them – a woman in a red dress – was sometimes glancing in my direction, while speaking in a low voice.

"Mrs. Townshead . . ."

An unseen presence was whispering *Misesu-Taunzuheddo* in my ear, a name I had, of course, never heard before. And even if it were indeed to be the name of the woman sitting over there . . . I got up from the chair and returned to my room, terrified at the thought that I was going mad.

It had been my intention to make an immediate call to the psychiatric hospital. But to have myself admitted as a patient there would be tantamount to dying. After agonizing hesitation, I tried to distract myself from my fears by reading *Crime and Punishment*. Randomly choosing a page, I found, however, that it was a passage from *The Brothers Karamazov*. Thinking I had confused the books, I looked at the cover, but there was no doubt about the title. I could see that it was to this binding error at the publishing house and to this very page that the finger of fate was pointing. Yet even as I was driven to continue reading, I had not finished a single page before my entire body began to tremble, for here was the passage that describes Ivan being tormented by the Devil. Ivan, Strindberg, Maupassant, and now I, here in this room . . .

My only salvation was sleep. But I had not a single packet of sleeping medicine left. The thought of more miserable insomnia was unbearable, but summoning up a desperate sort of courage, I had coffee brought and resolved to go on writing as frantically as any madman.

Two, five, seven, ten pages . . . The manuscript was burgeoning before my eyes. I was filling the world of my fictional work with supernatural animals, and one of them was a self-portrait. But now fatigue was gradually clouding my mind. At last I got up from the desk and lay flat on my back in bed. I may have slept for forty or fifty minutes when I thought I heard words being whispered in my ear and immediately bolted up:

"Le diable est mort."

Beyond the tuff-framed window, a pale, cold dawn was breaking. I was standing directly against the door, looking at the empty room, when I saw something in the mottled pattern of steam condensed on the window by the frigid air outside. It was an autumn-yellow pine forest facing the sea. I approached, my heart pounding. Though I realized that it was but a mirage, created by the garden's withered grass and the pond, it evoked a longing akin to *mal du pays*.

I waited until nine and then called the magazine office to settle a question of payment. Putting everything on the desk into my satchel, books and manuscripts, I resolved to return home.

6. Airplane

I had taken a taxi from a railway station on the Tōkaidō Line and headed for a summer resort in the western hinterlands. Despite the cold, the driver was oddly dressed in an old raincoat. To avoid thinking about the eerie coincidence, I fixed my gaze away from him and on the passing scenery. Behind the row of low-lying pines – perhaps on what had been the post-station road – I saw a funeral procession. There were neither white-paper nor dragon lanterns, but both before and behind the palanquin were artificial lotuses, gold and silver, gently swaying . . .

Having at last arrived home, I spent several rather peaceful days there, benefiting both from the company of my wife and children and from the efficacy of barbiturates. From my domain on the second floor, I could look out on the pine forest and faintly glimpse the sea beyond. I had decided to work at my desk only in the mornings, the cooing of the pigeons in my ears. There were other birds, pigeons and crows, as well as sparrows, which came flying down onto the veranda.

This too gave me pleasure. *The happy sparrow enters the temple,* I would remember the phrase each time, pen in hand.

On a warm, cloudy afternoon, I had gone to a sundries shop to buy ink, but the only color on display was sepia, a tint that invariably unsettled me more than any other. Having no alternative, I left the shop and wandered aimlessly along the mostly deserted streets. Coming toward me from the opposite direction was a foreigner, fortyish and apparently myopic, swaggering along by himself. He was the Swede who lived nearby, a man suffering from paranoia. His name was Strindberg. As we passed, I felt a physical jolt.

The street was no more than three hundred meters long, but in the time it took me to walk it, a dog, its face black on one side and white on the other, passed me four times. I turned down a side street, thinking of Black and White, and then remembered that Strindberg's tie was likewise black and white. I could not imagine this a mere coincidence. And if it were not . . . I had the feeling that only my head was moving along; I stopped for a moment in the middle of the pavement. Behind the wire fence along the street lay a discarded glass bowl faintly radiating the colors of the rainbow. There appeared to be along the sides at the bottom a winglike pattern. Sparrows now came fluttering down from the top of the pines, but when they came close to the bowl, they all took flight, as though by common accord, rising again into the sky . . .

I arrived at my wife's family home and sat in a rattan chair – in the garden, next to the veranda. Inside a wire netting situated in a corner at the other end, leghorn chickens were quietly walking about. A black dog lay at my feet. Even as I painfully endeavored to resolve questions comprehensible to no one, I chatted with my wife's mother and younger brother in a strictly superficial tone of sobriety.

"Ah, coming here . . . It is so quiet!"

"Yes, as compared to Tōkyō . . ."

"Is it sometimes noisy here too?"

"Well, after all, we still inhabit the same human world!"

My mother-in-law said this with a laugh. In fact, even this refuge from the summer heat was indisputably situated within that "human world." I knew all too well just how many crimes and tragedies had taken place here within the last year: the physician who had attempted to subject a patient to slow poisoning; the old woman who had set fire to the house of an adopted couple; the lawyer who had sought to deprive his younger sister of her assets . . . The mere sight of their homes was for me none other than a vision of the hell that lies at the heart of human existence.

"You have a local madman, don't you?"

"Do you mean young H?" asked my mother-in-law. "He's not insane; he's merely become imbecilic."

"*Dementia praecox*, as they say. Whenever I see him, I feel horror. I saw him recently bowing – for whatever reason – in front of the statue of Batō Kannon.

"'Horror' you say? You need to be of stronger disposition."

"Well, my brother-in-law is of much stronger than the likes of me."

He was sitting up in his bed, his face unshaven, entering into the conversation with his usual sense of reserve.

"But in strength there is also weakness," I replied.

"Well, well, whatever are we to say to *that*?"

I looked at my mother-in-law as she said this and could not help a wry smile. My brother-in-law too smiled, and continued to speak as though in a trance, gazing at the distant pine forest beyond the hedge. (The young convalescent sometimes seemed to me to be a pure, disembodied spirit.)

"Oddly enough, it is just when we think we have cast off our mere humanity that our all too human desires become all the more intense . . ."

"A man thought virtuous may also be a man of vice."

"No, an opposition more striking than that between good and evil . . ."

"Well then, the child found in the adult."

"That's not it either. I cannot express the idea clearly . . . Perhaps it is like two electric poles. They are antipodes that form a whole."

At that moment we were startled by the rumbling of an airplane. Without thinking, I glanced at the sky and saw the machine as it barely cleared the tops of the pine trees. It was an unusual mono-plane, with yellow wings. The chickens and the dog, alarmed at the sound, ran about in all directions, the dog in particular, its tail between its legs, baying and barking, before crawling beneath the veranda.

"Won't the airplane crash?"

"No . . . By the way, do you know what 'flying sickness' is?"

Instead of responding with a verbal "no," I shook my head, as I lit a cigarette.

"It seems," he explained, "that those who fly such airplanes become so accustomed to breathing the air at high altitudes that gradually they find themselves unable to tolerate ordinary terrestrial air . . ."

I had put the house of my wife's mother behind me and now walked through the pine forest. Not a branch was stirring, as I went on, steadily falling into depression. Why had the airplane flown above my head rather than elsewhere? Why was only the Air Ship brand of cigarette on sale at the hotel? Tormented by such questions, I wandered the least trodden paths.

Beyond a low dune lay the sea, covered by a gray sheet of fog. Atop the dune was the frame of a children's swing, with neither seat nor ropes. I looked at it and immediately thought of a gallows. And indeed several crows were perched on it. They stared at me, with no sign of flight. The one in the middle, its beak pointed to the sky, cawed – I am certain – four times.

I had been walking along an embankment of withered grass and sand but now turned down a narrow street lined with villas. On the right, I expected to see, despite the tall pines in front of it, a whitish, two-storied wooden structure of Occidental style. (A close friend had called it "The House of Spring.") But when I came to where it was supposed to be, there was only a bathtub, sitting on the cement foundation. *Fire!* was my immediate thought. I walked on, averting my eyes. A man on a bicycle was coming directly toward me. He was wearing a burnt umber fowling cap and had a strangely fixed expression, his body bent over the handlebars. I sensed that the face resembled that of my elder sister's husband and so took another small side street before we came eye to eye. But there I encountered, right in the middle of the road, lying belly up, the decaying body of a mole.

In the knowledge that something was stalking me, I felt renewed anxiety with each step I took. One by one, semitransparent cogwheels were beginning to block my vision. I walked stiff-necked, fearing that my last hour might well be nigh. The cogwheels were turning ever more rapidly, even as their number was increasing. At the same time, I was seeing the intertwining branches to my right as if through finely cut glass. I felt the palpitations of my heart growing more intense. Again and again I tried to stop along the way, but even that was no easy task, as I felt myself being pushed forward . . .

Thirty minutes later I was home again, lying on my back upstairs, my eyes tightly closed, as I endeavored to endure my throbbing headache. Behind my eyelids I began to see a wing, its silver feathers enfolded like fish scales. The image was clearly printed on my retinas. I opened my eyes and looked up to the ceiling, and having ascertained that, of course, nothing of the kind could be there, I closed them again, only to find the silver wing still there in the dark. I suddenly remembered that I had seen a wing on the radiator cap of a taxi I had recently taken . . .

I thought I heard hurried footsteps coming up the stairs and then clattering back down again. I knew them to be those of my wife. Startled, I got up and went down into the semidarkness of the sitting room directly below the stairs. She was lying prostrate, taking short, shallow breaths, it seemed, her shoulders constantly shaking.

"What is it?"

"Oh, nothing, my dear." she replied. Raising her head and giving me a forced smile, she continued. "It was really nothing at all – only that I had the feeling that you were about to die . . ."

This was the most terrifying experience of my life . . . I have no strength to go on writing. To go on living in this frame of mind would be unspeakable torment. Oh, if only someone would gently and kindly strangle me in my sleep.

NOTES

Mandarins (*Mikan*)

The Japanese *mikan* (*Citrus unshui*) is a small, easy-to-peel citrus fruit. Enormous quantities of *mikan* are eaten in Japan, particularly during the winter months. Also known as the Satsuma orange or mandarin, it has been variously translated as "mandarin orange" and "tangerine"; strictly speaking, it is neither. So representative is it of Japanese daily life, at least when in season, that English-speaking residents of Japan have come to refer to Tōkyō as the Big Mikan.

Akutagawa published this story in the May 1919 edition of *Shinchō* [New Tide], two months after resigning from his position as an English teacher at the Naval Engineering School in Yokosuka, four months after the opening of the Paris Peace Conference, to which the story alludes. The electrically powered trains that today travel to and from this coastal city in hilly southeastern Kanagawa Prefecture still pass through tunnels.

At the Seashore (*Umi no Hotori*)

Although the story was published in September 1925 (*Chūō-kōron, The Central Review*), well after the beginning of Akutagawa's struggles with mental illness and depression, it is set in the years of the writer's happier youth, with scarcely a trace of the gloomily misanthropic musings so apparent elsewhere. Here we catch a glimpse of seemingly carefree, relatively privileged, but hardly affluent, youths, balancing literary ambition with awareness of economic realities, boastfully, aggressively "male" toward one another, awkward in the presence of females, who, quite literally, swim away from them, apparently quite immune to the stinging jellyfish.

The setting of the story is Chiba Prefecture, occupying the entire Bōsō Peninsula across the bay from Tōkyō-Yokohama. In American terms, Chiba might be seen as standing in relation to Tōkyō as New Jersey does to New York City. Today, the communities that lie immediately to the east of the Edo River, including Chiba City, are culturally almost entirely indistinguishable from the capital. Yet journeying farther east, north, or south brings one at least to a landscape, if not to a way of life, that is no longer metropolitan. Needless to say, this would have been all the more so in Akutagawa's day.

Until the end of the Edo period, the Bōsō Peninsula was divided into three provinces: roughly, Shimōsa to the north, Awa to the south, and Kazusa between them. It is the last of these that appears in Akutagawa's autobiographical story: In the late summer of 1916, he and his friend Kume Masao (1891–1952), himself a novelist-to-be, lodged in Ichinomiya, on the eastern coast of Kazusa. In his description of the attraction felt by "M" (Kume) for the girl in the scarlet bathing suit, Akutagawa may well have been thinking of his friend's unrequited love for the daughter of Natsume Sōseki, their common mentor, who was to die in December of that same year. (The cigarette description at the beginning of the story appears to echo a passage in Sōseki's last – and unfinished – novel, *Meian*, tr. *Light and Darkness*). It was also in their seaside cottage that Akutagawa wrote his first love letter to his future wife, Tsukamoto Fumi.

1   The Sino-Japanese term in the original (*enzen*) suggests the beguiling smile of a woman.

2   'Sensual face'; in Japanese universities, German was the second most commonly studied foreign language after English.

3   A better-known cicada (*semi*) hs come to be associated in Japanese culture with the summer, while the evening cicada (*higurashi*) remains a symbol of early autumn. The literal meaning is "day-darkening."

An Evening Conversation (*Issekiwa*)

Though the geisha is a perennially – and perhaps excessively – popular topic in Occidental descriptions and discussions of Japan, "An Evening Conversation," which appeared in the July 1922 edition of *Sandee* [Sunday] *Mainichi*, is less about the female entertainer Koen, 'Little Penny,' (and even less about the plight of such women in Akutagawa's time) than about what Dr. Wada calls *tsūjin* ('sophisticates, men of the world'). The story follows in a long Japanese literary tradition of rambling conversations among males concerning life, love, and art. In a famous passage in the *The Tale of Genji*, four young aristocrats while away a rainy summer's night in the Imperial Palace, waxing philosophical as they comment on their various amorous adventures. Like Wakatsuki, the consummate *tsūjin*, they put great store on the proper artistic training of their ideal lovers.

With its flashes of humor and cheerful rather than melancholic irony, the story may seem somewhat atypical of Akutagawa, and indeed it has been suggested that it was intended as a parody of *Ame-shōshō* (1922, tr. *Quiet Rain*, 1964) by Nagai Kafū (1879–1959), whose work lovingly focuses on the demimonde.

Wakatsuki may be seen as embodying social and cultural contradictions very much on the mind of the author. On the one hand, he is the sort of "modern man" who wears a jumper. (In the original, Akutagawa adds an exotic air by rendering the word *chanpa* with the same characters as those for the ancient Southeast Asian kingdom, Champa. Though *janpā*, 'jumper,' is a familiar word today, the garment would have been unknown to the great majority of Dr. Wada's contemporaries.) On the other hand, Watasuki lives in an artistic milieu that could just as well have been that of the Edo period. Mentioned in this story are Ike no Taiga (1723–76), an Edo-period artist and calligrapher, and Katō Chikage (1735–1808), an Edo-period scholar and poet. Mushanokōji Saneatsu (1885–1976) was a writer and artist who at the time Akutagawa wrote the story had recently founded a utopian village à la Tolstoy.

1 "Seigai's Collected Poems"; *Seigai* literally means "blue lid."

The Handkerchief (*Hankechi*)

The Japanese have long been known for ruminating on who they are and where they are going – especially in relation to Western culture. Even if the notion of reviving *bushidō* ('the way of the warrior') is now (almost entirely) out of fashion, the concerns of Professor Hasegawa would make him feel quite at home among today's Japan's earnest, if self-absorbed, intellectuals. *Plus ça change . . .*

As would have been obvious to many of Akutagawa's contemporaries, when the story was published in October 1916 (*Chūō-kōron*), Professor Hasegawa is based on Nitobe Inazō (1862–1933). Born in northern Japan, he first studied agricultural economics in Hokkaidō and then, following his conversion to Christianity, entered Tōkyō Imperial University to study English literature. He spent a total of six years abroad, in the United States and Germany, earning several doctorates and publishing books in several languages. Like Professor Hasegawa, he married an American woman and perceived himself as a "bridge" between Japan and the West. At Tōkyō Imperial University, he became a professor of colonial policy before leaving with his wife for the United States, where in 1899 he published *Bushidō: The Soul of Japan*, a widely read, if controversial, book. In 1918, he attended the Versailles Peace Conference and later served as the undersecretary general of the League of Nations.

Akutagawa's portrait of Professor Hasegawa may, on the whole, seem unsympathetic. Westerners familiar with Japan may also squirm at the repeated references to the Gifu lantern, seeing in it a symbol of naïve and sentimental exoticism. Yet the story is arguably not intended as a satire on individuals but rather as a meditation on abstract intellectualism and facile multiculturalism.

1   German *Manier* (Swedish manér) is in the original, transcribed in Japanese as *maniiru*. The earliest translations of Strindberg were into German and English.

2   *Shonanoka*: the day of the death being included in the calculation.

3   German *Mätzchen* 'nonsense, hokum' is apparently the translation of the

Swedish *choser* 'affectations'. Akutagawa uses the Japanese word *kusami* 'bad odor, affectation', glossing it phonetically as *mettsuhen*.

An Enlightened Husband (*Kaika no Otto*)

In the original title, *Kaika no Otto* (February 1919, *Chūgai* [Home and Abroad]), the Sino-Japanese term *kaika* 'opening, enlightenment, progress' forms part of a Meiji-era slogan: *bunmei-kaika* 'civilization and enlightenment'. Akutagawa, who had just become an adult when that era ended in 1912, looks back on it with a characteristic mixture of nostalgia and irony, the question posed by Viscount Honda at the end of the story being very much his own. At the same time, the setting reflects Akutagawa's enduring love for the capital's eastern region, his childhood home, in particular the Sumida River, which he first celebrated in *Ōkawa no Mizu* ('The Waters of the Great River'), published in 1914, when the writer was still a university student.

From the Meiji era until 1947, Japan had a peerage system, whereby aristocratic titles were conferred first on former samurai and later on successful entrepreneurs and distinquished civil servants. Viscount Honda also appears in Akutagawa's *Kaika no Satsujin* [A Civilized Murder] (July 1918, *Chūō-kōron*).

Both in form and mood, "An Enlightened Husband" may remind readers of Natsume Sōseki's *Kokoro*, published only five years before, in 1914. There too most of the story is taken up by a secondary narration, telling of love and shattered ideals. Yet while the beautiful woman portrayed in Sōseki's novel is almost implausibly innocent, the women in Akutagawa's short story have an aura of evil about them.

1   In the original, the term is *gonsai* ('apparent provisional wife'); this became a commonly used euphemism in the Meiji era as Japanese society adopted "modern ways," albeit fitfully. Miura's choice of words is the unadorned *mekake* ('concubine').

2   The word in the original is *kōtō*, lit. 'high grade', a Sino-Japanese compound that came to be used to express concepts ranging from higher education to higher species. Like *kaika* ('enlightened'), Akutagawa uses

it with irony. By the time of this story, *kōtō* had also come to appear in *Tokubetsu-kōtō-keisatsu,* "Special Higher Police."

3 The Kabuki play by Kawatake Mokuami (1816–93) was written in 1879, shortly after the trial and execution (the last legal decapitation) of Takahashi O-den, a notorious young murderess. The play serves to extol the new civil code, including ideal male-female roles hardly consistent with the couple being described by Viscount Honda.

4 *Kan-tsū,* a punishable offense for women until 1947.

Autumn (*Aki*)

"Autumn" first appeared in the April 1, 1920, edition of *Chūō-kōron* (*The Central Review*). The beginning of the story may lead the reader to expect a sad but familiar tale of quintessentially "Japanese" self-sacrifice and the crushing of a woman's budding literary talent by a brutish, philistine husband. The actual content, however, proves to be richer and subtler – and indeed ultimately ambiguous.

Akutagawa's grim description of the Tōkyō suburb where Teruko and her husband live may be seen as consistent with her apparent unhappiness, yet it also clearly reflects the writer's own view of residential expansion, a development that was only accelerated by the Great Kantō Earthquake of 1923.

1 The renowned swordsman Miyamoto Musashi (1584–1645) developed the two-sword fencing style. *Gorin no Sho* (*The Book of the Five Rings*), attributed to him, became something of a cult classic in the English-speaking world during the 1980s.

2 Rather than Rémy de Gourmont (1858–1915), the French symbolist poet and critic, the source is more likely the English illustrator Aubrey Beardsley (1872–98).

3 *Jūsan'ya,* the thirteenth day of the ninth month according to the lunar calendar, a traditional moon-viewing evening. (*Jūsan'ya* is the title of a novel by Higuchi Ichiyō [1872–96] about an unhappy marriage.)

4 The price of rice rose in 1914 with the outbreak of the First World War. Newspaper coverage of the rice riots of 1918 led to press censorship.

Winter (*Fuyu*)

Though "Winter" is fictional, Akutagawa was clearly thinking of his elder sister's husband, Nishikawa Yutaka, when he completed this story in June 1927, a month before his death. Both the theme and ambience are familiar: unhappy family relations set against the background of a cold and gray society. They may also remind us, particularly in the description of the prison visit, of another writer: Franz Kafka, whose posthumous work *Der Prozess* (*The Trial*) had been published just two years before.

The narrator visits his incarcerated relative, to whom he refers as his cousin, more precisely, we may surmise, his cousin-in-law. (There are speech-level differences in the original that suggest he is not a blood relative.) He then travels to his home on the western edge of Tōkyō, in "uptown" Yamanote, which, particularly after the Great Kantō Earthquake, was becoming culturally dominant. His general hints at the social contrasts in wealth and status are reinforced by his remarks about the vicissitudes of fortune relating to his cousin.

The oppressiveness of a highly conformist society is reflected in the reference to the youth organization (*seinendan*) of which T is a leader. Such groups were already taking on a nationalistic, militarist character, and though the story is set in the waning years of "Taishō Democracy," Akutagawa would have been well aware that at the end of that period, in 1925, all *seinendan* had come under government control in a federation known as the Dai Nippon Rengō Seinendan. That same year had seen the passage of the Peace Preservation Law, intended to introduce thought control and suppress dissent.

The nature of the charges against the narrator's cousin-in-law is never specified, but whatever they are, Akutagawa does not need to explain to his readers the dire social consequences of T's arrest or the significance of the narrator's question to his cousin: "The neighborhood doesn't know yet?"

Ichigaya is located to the northwest of the Imperial Palace in central Tōkyō. Though the inmates of the now long-since-vanished prison were for the most part the not-yet-convicted, it was also there that prominent radicals were hanged for high treason.

The ending of the story seems to echo Akutagawa's account in "Cog-wheels" of his visit to his sister following the suicide of Nishikawa Yutaka. Another autobiographical element is the fact that Akutagawa, like the narrator, was at one time a journalist, though his contributions were that of a writer, not a news reporter.

1   In the original, this literally means 'varieties of people' but perhaps refers specifically to *The Charactres* by Theophrastus (372–287 BC).
2   "Long live Master T!"

Fortune (Un)

The title of the original is a Sino-Japanese word that may be variously rendered into English as 'fate', 'fortune', or 'luck'. Published in January 1917 (*Bunshō-sekai*), the story is among those Akutagawa adapted from the folk-tale collection *Konjaku Monogatari* [Tales of Times Now Past]. The setting is the imperial capital in the late Heian period. As in Akutagawa's famous *Rashōmon*, inspired by the same folktale collection, there is an aura of decay. Just as the great city gate has fallen into ruin and become a refuge for outlaws, so has the Yasaka pagoda been taken over by a thief and his apparent confederate, an elderly nun.

In *Konjaku Monogatari*, all thirty-nine stories in Volume 16 center upon the wondrous workings of the bodhisattva Kannon (Kanzeon), known in India as Avalokiteçvara, in China as Guānyīn, and sometimes in the English-speaking world as the goddess of mercy. KJM 16:33 is consistent with the other tales of piety. A poor woman takes a pilgrimage to Kiyomizu-dera ('temple of clear water') to pray to Kannon, where she is told in a vision to comply with the commands of a man she is to meet. He takes her to the nearby Yasaka pagoda of Hōkanji and, in the morning, offers her both marriage and gifts of valuable cloth. He then departs, leaving her with strict instructions to remain. When she discovers his treasure horde, she concludes that he must be a thief. Waiting until the old nun attending to her has gone for water, she makes her escape, taking the gifts with her. She makes her way to a friend's house and spies the thief in the hands of the authorities. Having profited from the sale of the cloth, she is able to marry and live in comfort.

In Akutagawa's otherwise faithful adaptation, the waters are muddied by the moral uncertainty concerning the old nun's death and the religious agnosticism implicit in the old potter's role as narrator. The banter between the two men strikes a note of ironic – and irreverent – humor entirely lacking in KJM.

1 An *aozamurai* (or *aozaburai*), lit. 'blue retainer', a low-ranking attendant.
2 Foxes were regarded as quasi-supernatural creatures, capable of assuming the form of humans and of bewitching them. There are many stories concerning them in Japanese folklore.
3 The bush warbler (*ettia diphone*), *uguisu* in Japanese, known for its beautiful song, is regarded as a symbol of joy and good fortune.
4 One of Kyōto's landmarks. The formal name for the temple is Hōkanji, of which only the oft-destroyed and rebuilt pagoda remains.

Kesa and Moritō (*Kesa to Moritō*)

Published in April 1918 (*Chūō-kōron*), the story is based on an incident recorded in *Genpei-seisuiki* [*The Rise and Fall of the Genji and Heike*]. First compiled in the late thirteenth or early fourteenth century, this work is an account of the colossal struggle between the Minamoto and Taira, culminating in the final defeat of the latter in 1185.

Late Heian-period Japan saw the rise of such warrior clans and their usurpation in all but name of imperial authority. The characters in the story are Kesa, a court lady married to Minamoto no Wataru, and Endō Moritō, a guard in the palace of the retired emperor.

In the original version, Kesa's mother, Moritō's aunt, has lived in the northeast, in the Minamoto enclave of Koromogawa, hence the name by which she is called. She returns to the the Heian capital, where she resides in straitened circumstances with her beautiful daughter. At the age of fourteen, Kesa is wed to Wataru. Three years later, at the dedication of a bridge, Moritō catches a furtive glimpse of her through the bamboo screen of her carriage and is infatuated. Moritō rebukes his aunt for not having given Kesa to him and even threatens to kill her.

Kesa, as suggested by her name, referring to a Buddhist monk's modest surplice, is a paragon of fidelity and self-sacrifice. In order to save her mother, Kesa yields to her cousin and then, fearful for her husband's life as well, pretends to contrive with Moritō to kill him. Wetting her long hair and tying it up into a knot to make herself resemble a man, she lies in Wataru's bed; Moritō stealthily enters and, intending to cut off his rival's head, slays instead his beloved. When he realizes what he has done, he is mad with grief and remorse. He wanders about with Kesa's head until, renouncing the world, he becomes a Buddhist ascetic.

Moritō is known to history by his priestly name, Mongaku. Later a sometime associate of Minamoto no Yoritomo, the first Kamakura shogun, he is thought to have died in the early thirteenth century.

The story of Kesa's fate has been dramatized many times, notably in Kinugasa Teinosuke's 1953 film *Jigokumon* (*Gate of Hell*). The female role is played by Kyō Machiko, who also appears in Kurosawa's *Rashōmon*.

Japanese Buddhism is replete with tales of black-hearted sinners who, seeing at last the evil of their ways, embark on the arduous path to sainthood. In his retelling of this story, Akutagawa not only alters details but also narrows the focus. Clearly, he is more interested in damnation than redemption, as he probes the complex motives not only of Moritō but also of Kesa – none of which is touched upon in the original version. Here Kesa is driven to adultery not by sacrificial love for others but rather by despair, vanity, and strangely ambivalent feelings toward Moritō. Her mother becomes, in Akutagawa's version, an incidental aunt. The tale thus offers an ironic twist on the star-crossed lover motif, a familiar theme in Japanese lore.

The language, no less than the psychology, is modern, the story containing lexical concepts introduced only after the beginning of the Meiji era. The Sino-Japanese word *ai* 'love', for example, which Akutagawa uses with striking frequency, traditionally referred primarily to affection, attachment, or (in Buddhist terminology) carnal lust. Occurring once in Moritō's soliloquy is the compound *ren'ai*, a Meiji-period coinage referring to romantic love. Moritō and Kesa's musings about their true feelings and motives are thus couched in terms that are clearly and deliberately anachronistic.

In *Romeo and Juliet*, external miscommunication contributes to tragedy. In "Kesa and Moritō," intense introspection on the part of each character is juxtaposed with a disastrous misunderstanding of the other's thoughts and intentions. In that respect, the story may be seen as a forerunner of "In the Grove" and radical point-of-viewism.

Death of a Disciple (*Hōkyōnin no Shi*)

In the late sixteenth century, Nagasaki, the setting of Akutagawa's story, the fortunes of the Christian community were dramatically shifting. In February of the following year, twenty-six believers, seventeen Japanese and nine missionaries were crucified in Nagasaki. It was only in 1873, less than twenty years before the birth of Akutagawa, that the Meiji government finally lifted its anti-Christian edicts. Akutagawa had a strong interest in the predominant faith of the West, as is reflected in many of his stories, even if his view of religion in general was ambivalent.

Despite Akutagawa's pseudo-documentary postscript, including his reference to the eighteenth-century *Chronicles of Port Nagasaki [Nagasaki-minato-gusa]*, "The Death of a Disciple" is clearly fiction. (Though, for example, the thirteenth-century *Legenda Aurea* is clearly a real work, there is no edition to which descriptions of Japanese Christians have been added.) In fact, it may not be too much to say that the motifs here, albeit placed in the historical context of Japan's "Christian century," reflect the influence of those early medieval Japanese folktales that inspired some of the writer's most famous stories. The saintly figure of Lorenzo would be quite at home in the Buddhist tales of *Konjaku Monogatari*. Indeed, he is first described even by the Christians of Nagasaki as a *tendō*, a strictly Buddhist term, referring to fierce guardian deities disguised as boys. Akutagawa's comments at the end of the narration may be seen as an imitation (or parody) of the moralizing didacticism with which those stories inevitably conclude. The word translated into English as 'depravity' – *bonnō* – is itself the rendition of a Sanskrit Buddhist term: *klesa*.

In particular, the surprise ending points to a mélange of traditions. In the minds of the story's first readers, Lorenzo would surely have evoked a non-Christian figure with a nonetheless specifically Christian association: Kannon. A well-known subterfuge of the "hidden Christians" during the centuries of persecution was to use images of this enormously popular bodhisattva (cf. "Fortune") to represent the Virgin Mary. Kannon, as it happens, was originally male, becoming female along the journey to Japan from India via China. In a story that was surely known to Akutagawa, she is born Miào-Shàn, the daughter of a rich king in Sumatra, who seeks to thwart her in her desire to become a Buddhist nun, even to the point of setting fire to the temple in which she resides. She miraculously puts out the flames but in the end is put to death.

For this story, published in September 1918 (*Mita Bungaku* [Mita Literature]), Akutagawa adopts a form of late medieval Japanese appropriate to the period. Along with Greco-Latin *ecclesia*, there is also a generous sprinkling of Portuguese borrowings. Nearly all have a specifically Christian reference, e.g. *zencho* (from *gentio*) 'Gentile', and so, unlike such everyday terms as *pan* 'bread' (from *pão*) and *kappa* 'raincoat' (from *capa*), were as archaic or obsolete in Akutagawa's day as they are today. In the Japanese title of the short story, the word for 'disciple' (*hōkyōnin*), lit. 'one who serves the Church / the faith', has likewise long since fallen out of ordinary use.

1   This Japanese version of *Guia do Peccador* (*Guide for the Sinner*) was apparently published in 1599. The Keichō era extended from 1596 to 1615.

O'er a Withered Moor (*Karenoshō*)

Bashō 'banana plant' is the sobriquet adopted by the poet born Matsuo Kinsaku in 1644. In the West, he is doubtlessly the best-known composer of the seventeen-syllable verse form (5-7-5) that has subsequently come to be called haiku. Also widely read, both in Japanese and in translation, is his travel diary of 1689, *Oku no Hosomichi* (*The Narrow Road to the Deep North*).

A native of Ueno, Iga Province (now Mie Prefecture), in central Japan, Bashō had been living in Edo for some eight years when in 1680 he moved to a hut on the outskirts of the city. Hitherto known by the nom de plume of Tōsei 'peach blue', he renamed himself for the banana plant that a student had given him. In the spring of 1680 or 1681, accompanied by his disciple Enomoto Kikaku, he composed his most famous, oft-cited, structurally ambiguous, and therefore barely translatable poem. About it, written when the melancholic Bashō had begun to practice Zen, enough ink has been spilled to fill more than a pond:

> Furu-ike ya / kawazu tobi-komu / mizu no oto
> An old pond: the sound of a frog jumping into the water

In the autumn of 1684, Bashō began the first of his journeys, first traveling from Edo to Ueno, then to Nara, Ogaki, and Kyōto. The following year, having returned to Edo, he published *Nozarashi no kikō* (tr. *Records of a Weather-beaten Skeleton*), from which the last verse cited by Akutagawa is drawn. Having recently lost his mother, Bashō, already forty and never in very good health, was conscious of his own mortality.

Toward the end of his journey of 1689, as he passed southward through Kanazawa on the Sea of Japan, he sought to meet a fellow poet, Isshō, whom he only knew from correspondence. On learning that he had died at the end of the previous year, Bashō visited his grave, composing another renowned verse, the second of the three cited by Akutagawa.

Bashō resided in Kyōto for two years before returning once more to Edo. Then in the summer of 1694 he set off again for the west but fell ill with dysentery in Ōsaka and died. The date according to the modern calendar is November 28, 1694. His death verse, cited at the beginning of Akutagawa's story, is nearly as familiar to Japanese as that of the pond, the frog, and the sound of the water.

Though still a revered figure in Akutagawa's time, Bashō had also come under attack by the poet and critic Masaoka Tsunenori (1867–1902), known by his pen name, Shiki. He in turn was a close friend of Akutagawa's mentor, the renowned novelist Natsume Sōseki, whose premature death in 1916 at the age of forty-nine clearly contributed to the background of "O'er a Withered Moor," published in October 1918 (*Shinshōsetsu* [New Fiction]). The story should thus be read not as hagiography but rather as the writer's own intensely personal meditation.

The story makes mention of *haikai* and *hokku*. The former refers both to what would now be called haiku and to *haikai no renga* 'linked verse', the latter to the initial stanza (5-7-5) of such. As this had long been used as a poem in itself, Shiki advocated the use of a distinct term, hence haiku, which has been generalized in Japan and internationalized abroad.

1 *Tabi ni yande / yume wa kareno wo / kake-meguru.*
2 Sometime between four and five in the afternoon.
3 The Buddhist custom of wetting the lips of the dying (or sometimes of the deceased) survives to the present day. A "plumed stick" (*hane-yōji*) was used both for administering medicine and, by married women, for applying tooth-blackener.
4 *Tsuka mo ugoke / waga naku koe wa / aki no kaze.*
5 *Nozarashi wo / kokoro ni kaze no / shimu mi kana.*
6 In reality, Inenbō outlived his master by nearly fifteen years.

The Garden (*Niwa*)

In Edo-period Japan, there were five main highways, converging in Nihon-bashi, near what is now the Imperial Palace in Tōkyō. The busiest and best-known of these was the Tōkaidō (East Sea Road), celebrated in Andō Hiroshige's woodblock prints. All were administered by the central government, whose strict and precise regulations covered everything from road maintenance to traveler accommodations. The great lords of the provinces, obliged by the shogunate to spend alternate years in the capital, journeyed to and fro with large retinues, spending their nights at the best and most prestigious inns of the post-station towns: the *honjin* ('headquarters').

In the original, Akutagawa identifies the Nakamuras' inn as one of the *honjin*, and while he does not directly name the highway, numerous clues point to Nakasendō ('Central Mountain Road'), whose semicircular route passed through what are now Saitama, Gunma, Nagano, and Shiga prefectures. First, there is the mention of Princess Kazu (1846–77), who in 1862 was betrothed to Shōgun Iemochi and sent from the old imperial capital to Edo, now Tōkyō, on a long and difficult journey along the Nakasendō, accompanied by a party of ten thousand. Then there is the mention of the mendicant poet Seigetsu, an actual historical figure. Moreover, the elements of dialogue that appear in the story are all consistent with dialects spoken in the mountainous Chūbu region, specifically what is now Nagano Prefecture. The small stream that the second son sets out to dig is, for example, called a *senge*, a local word. The song that the grandmother sings likewise refers to events that took place in this same region.

Akutagawa, who first published this story in July 1922 (*Chūō-kōron*), is writing of the great transitional era two decades before his own birth, the decline of the garden – and the fall of the Nakamura family – emblemizing the passing of Old Japan. The perspective of the writer, himself very much part of the modern era, blends a sense of sad inevitability with the subtle irony that is a consistent characteristic of his work.

The vain and irascible first son may be seen as representing the last of the old order, his younger brothers being unable either to sustain it or to adapt to the new. With the death of the eldest, the third son returns to assume his duties but apparently can do no more than fantasize about making easy money. In the entrepreneurial flurry of the early Meiji period, rice speculation was very much a reality. (In 1872, exactly a half century before the publication of this story, a modern silk-reeling mill had been established in Tomioka, Gunma, a town lying on a secondary route connected to the Nakasendō.)

The ballad sung by the old woman refers a battle in November 1864, between, on the one hand, the Suwa and Matsumoto clans, defenders of the shogunate, and, on the other, pro-imperial rebels from Mito in eastern Japan. Akutagawa's notes suggest that it was his own adoptive father who passed on the song, having learned it from a courtesan he had engaged while traveling.

In describing the dissolute second son, Akutagawa uses the Sino-Japanese term *hōtō*, in his own time already familiar to his readers as the loan-translation of a word used in a well-known New Testament parable. It is perhaps not too much to suppose that here too Akutagawa is being ironic, for the prodigal, having, it is later suggested, squandered his absconded portion on harlots and even contracted syphilis, returns not to a loving father but to a younger brother, who, rather than forgiving, is simply indifferent.

1 Variously translated as 'cuckoo' and 'nightingale,' the *hototogisu* makes a frequent appearance in Japanese verse. It is said to sing until it coughs up blood and has thus often been used as a symbol for tuberculosis.

The Life of a Fool (*Aru Ahō no Isshō*)

In the original title, the word *ahō*, 'fool, simpleton, idiot,' originates in Western dialects. As a term of abuse (and sometimes affection), it competes with the more commonly heard *baka*, though the latter has the more restricted meaning of 'stupid'.

Whatever self-deprecation there is in Akutagawa's use of the word, he is also putting himself in the grand tradition of socially alienated, morally flawed, but nonetheless prophetic "fools" – specifically, no doubt, of Strindberg, whose *Confessions of a Fool* (*En dåres försvarstal* [1887], lit. 'A Madman's Defense') is mentioned in the text. Though Akutagawa does not, for all his many other literary allusions, refer to Shakespeare, the English-speaking reader may also recall the words of Jaques in *As You Like It*: "Oh that I were a fool! I am ambitious for a motley coat . . . Invest me in my motley; give me leave to speak my mind, and I will through and through cleanse the foul body of the infected world."

Though Akutagawa explicitly identifies himself with Icarus, there appears to be a more consistent, albeit implicit, suggestion of Baudelaire's famous albatross, the gracefully soaring bird, which, when land-bound, becomes terribly awkward, its name in Japanese being, appropriately enough, *ahō-dori*, lit. 'fool-bird'. The mention of "flying sickness" in "Cogwheels" suggests much the same idea.

"The Life of a Fool," published in October 1927 (*Kaizō* [Reconstruction]), three months after Akutagawa's death, is not without its painful excesses. Surely a single line of Baudelaire is not "worth more than all of life," and even the vain Goethe might have blushed at being compared (favorably) to Christ. Yet, together with "Cogwheels," likewise published posthumously, we may read it both for its poignant flashes of brilliance and as a chronicle, both lyrical and grim (*Dichtung und Wahrheit*), of the author's relentless journey into night.

1   A reference to the novelist Tanizaki Jun'ichirō (1886–1965), with whom Akutagawa often collaborated. Together with other writers, they met in June 1917, at Café Maison Ōtori-no-su in Nihonbashi. In conformity to Japanese thinking, Akutagawa regarded Tanizaki as an "upperclassman" (*senpai*), as he had also attended Tōkyō Imperial University. Tanizaki had, however, interrupted his studies two years before Akutagawa began his own.

2   In the original, the term used derives from Classical Chinese, meaning literally 'acid nostrils'.

3   *Koshibito* refers to a person from northeastern Japan. Akutagawa composed (in classical form) the collection of twenty-five love poems by that title as a means of resisting the temptation to become involved with the poetess and translator Katayama Hiroko, an older woman married to a banker originally from Niigata, a prefecture in the northeast.

4   Though Villon was sentenced to be hanged in 1462, at the age of 31, he was reprieved in early 1463; his subsequent life is unknown . . . The poet Edward Young reported that on a walk through Dublin, Jonathan Swift saw an elm tree with a withered crown and (prophetically) remarked: "I shall be like that tree; I shall die at the top."

5   The words attributed to the young writer Radiguet (1903–1923) before his death of typhoid fever, are, in fact: "Dans trois jours je vais être fusillé par les soldats de Dieu" ('In three days I shall be shot by the soldiers of God.')

The Villa of the Black Crane (*Genkaku-sanbō*)

In the central character of this story, published in January–February 1927 (*Chūō-kōron*), when his own health was failing, Akutagawa undoubtedly sees something of himself, though the story is otherwise hardly autobiographical. The biting irony with which it concludes might be seen as social commentary, particularly regarding the status of women. Yet Akutagawa is an observer, not a revolutionary, the writer of elegies, not manifestos. If Jūkichi's cousin is reading Wilhelm Liebknecht, the father of the Sparticist Karl Liebknecht, Jūkichi himself is merely staring out the window, wearily noting the changing urban landscape and, with it, the passing of his father-in-law's era.

Genkaku is written with the Chinese characters meaning 'black crane', but there is much homophony in Japanese, so that though the inquiring student surely knows this, he asks why Genkaku has chosen the name as his *nom d'artiste*. Written with other characters, *genkaku* can variously mean not only 'strict' but also 'hallucination'.

The death of the artist Genkaku suggests parallels to that of the admittedly nobler but nonetheless forlorn poet Bashō in "O'er a Withered Moor." More distantly, the description of a selfish old man contemplating his miserable life and impending death in an isolated room surrounded by a family he has somehow contrived to alienate may be heard echoing in François Mauriac's (1932) *Le Noeud de Vipères (The Vipers' Tangle)*. The difference, of course, is that while Mauriac's Louis ultimately experiences grace, the despairing Genkaku chants familiar words from the twenty-fifth chapter of the *Lotus Sutra* and then thinks of a decidedly profane folk song and dance. When we last see him, he is quite unintentionally amusing his grandson with a failed attempt to strangle himself by means of his own loincloth. The reader is grimly reminded of Akutagawa's own experiment, as recorded in "The Life of a Fool."

1   *Bunka-mura*: the word *bunka* 'culture' was a highly fashionable term of embellishment and thus came to be applied to newly constructed suburban settlements.

2   Shoes left at the entrance are normally turned outwards to facilitate departure. The task would normally be that of the host or a servant. The fact that the woman performs it herself indicates her sense of inferiority – or her residual status as a domestic.

3   A mother would normally not address her own son as "Botchan" ('young

master'); O-yoshi is presumably doing so as a sign of deference toward the child's father and his family.

4 This was the slogan of the political parties that sought to challenge the power of the bureaucratic elites. In 1913, they forced the resignation of the prime minister and in 1918 saw one of their own brought to power.

5 Translated by Burton Watson as: "Wonderful sound, Perceiver of the World's Sounds, Brahma's sound, the sea tide sound – they surpass those sounds of the world."

Cogwheels (*Haguruma*)

The first section of this story appeared under the title of *Rēn-kōto* ('Raincoat') in the June 1927 edition of *Daichōwa* ('Great Harmony'). All six sections were published in *Bungei-shunjū* in October of the same year; the posthumous title was *Haguruma*, lit. 'toothed wheel(s)'.

The image easily suggests Charlie Chaplin's vision of *Modern Times* (1936), the hapless human individual caught in inhuman, industrial machinery, but, anachronism aside, the reader soon realizes that Akutagawa's themes are, as ever, far more personal and psychological than social.

As with the previous story, there is autobiographical detail that is not so much lost in translation as obscured by time; there is also, of course, the issue – especially given the writer's state of mind – of the boundary between fact and fiction. Moreover, Akutagawa, the voracious reader, was not a meticulous scholar. The story about the lad who went home "meandering like a reptile" is indeed from ancient China, but Akutagawa has his sources confused, for the folktale is found in *Autumn Floods* by the Daoist Zhuāngzǐ (fourth Century BCE), not in *Hán Fēizǐ* by the third century BCE legalist philosopher Hán Fēi. And the atheist Prosper Mérimée did not, in fact, convert to Protestantism but merely arranged for a Protestant burial to spare his friends scandal.

Not surprisingly, Akutagawa drops hints that are more apparent to Japanese than to non-Japanese readers. When he refers to dragons, he plays on his own name, the *ryū* ('dragon') of Ryūnosuke; black and white are funeral colors. "White" occurs so often in the story that even the "white, rectangular U" at the wedding reception becomes, at least in retrospect, a morbid symbol. The Sino-Japanese word for 'four' (*shi*) is homophonous with that for 'death', resulting in a superstition shared by other East Asian peoples.

1   In March 1914, Henriette Caillaux, wife of Joseph Caillaux, the former prime minister and at the time the minister of finance, shot and killed the editor of *Le Figaro*. She was acquitted, and by the time of this story, her husband was again in the throes of directing financial policy . . . The member of the Japanese imperial family to whom reference is made is probably Prince Higashikuni (1887–1990), who had studied at the Ecole Supérieure de Guerre in Paris from 1920 to 1926. Having become accustomed to *la dolce vita*, he had to be ordered home by the Imperial Household Ministry.

2   Clearly taken from Jeremiah 10:24, cf. Psalms 6 and 38.

3   In Canto XIII of *The Inferno*, Virgil guides Dante to the Seventh Ring of Hell, in which they encounter gnarled, black trees, inhabited, he learns, by the souls of those who have done themselves harm, squandering their wealth or committing suicide.

4   The statue is of Kusunoki Masashige, the warrior chieftain who in obedience to the reckless orders of exiled Emperor Go-Daigo went off in 1336 to certain death in battle with the turncoat Ashikaga Takauji, founder of the Muromachi shogunate. Kusunoki was idealized by both Edo period Neo-Confucianists and modern nationalists as a symbol of loyalty.

ADDITIONAL TERMINOLOGY

dhārāni: A long chant, recited in Chinese-transcribed Sanskrit, as pronounced in Japanese, intended, among other things, to ward off evil.

fènghuáng (Chinese): Whatever the cross-cultural roots of the *qílín* (Sino-Japanese *kirin*) and the *fènghuáng* (Sino-Japanese *hōō*), the narrator's bold and improbable suggestion in "Cogwheels" that they are of Occidental origin is clearly intended to provoke. Similarly, though Yáo and Shùn are thought to exemplify the wisdom of nonhereditary rule, a distinctly un-Japanese idea, Confucianism was part of Japan's eclectic ideology, so that the narrator is again baiting the scholar by denying the historical existence of the philosopher-kings.

ginkgo-leaf style (Japanese *ichō-gaeshi*): Originally the hairstyle of unmarried women of the samurai class, it came to be common among women of various ages and classes after the beginning of the Meiji era, including apprentice geishas.

haikai: Refers both to what would now be called haiku and to *haikai no renga* 'linked verse'.

haori: A jacket worn over a kimono.

hokku: An initial stanza, consisting of 5-7-5 syllables, sometimes functioning as a verse on its own.

kana: Referring to the two sets Japanese syllabic letters, *hiragana* and *katakana*, deriving originally from simplified Chinese characters.

koto: A thirteen-stringed plucked zither.

-kun: A somewhat less polite honorific name suffix than "-san," typically used in reference to young men.

marumage: A married woman's hairstyle, with a bun at the top. It was going out of fashion even in Akutagawa's time.

Meisen: A famous silk fabric produced in Tochigi Prefecture and characterized by its glossy sheen.

nagauta: Kabuki dance music, lit. 'long song'.

o-: An honorific prefix; until recent times, it was still used before women's names, as in "The Villa of the Black Crane."

ojisan: Lit. 'uncle', though often used fictively, particularly as a vocative.

okusan: A polite term for wife, it is sometimes used vocatively.

otōsan: 'Father', as a polite term of reference or address, sometimes used by wives when speaking to or about their husbands.

qílín: The birth of sages, notably Confucius, is said to be heralded by the *qílín*. (Also see *fènghuáng*.)

sen: One-hundredth of a yen, valued at the time at fifty cents.

sensei: Derived from Chinese (lit. 'prior-born'), the term is used most commonly to address and refer to teachers and physicians, but also, more generally, attorneys, politicians, and writers. It can be used sarcastically and, as such, is regarded with ambivalence, particularly by frequent addressees. Akutagawa nonetheless refers in his writings to his mentor Natsume Sōseki as "Sensei."

shaku: A measure of length, ca. 14.4 inches.

shamisen: A three-stringed plucked lute.

shōchū: Sometimes described as "Japanese gin," it is a distilled liquor made variously from rice, barley, and sweet potatoes.

suikan: An upper garment, washed without starch and left to dry, came to be part of the uniform dress of low-ranking attendants, though the thief in "Fortune" is also noted as wearing one at the time of his capture.

tatami: A straw mat covered with a soft reed surface. A six-mat room measures approximately 18 square feet.

ukiyoé (lit. 'pictures of the floating world'): This genre of woodblock print, a symbol of the Edo period, was already dying in the Meiji era.

yukata: An unlined summer kimono, typically made of cotton.

NAMES

Abbot Toba (or Toba Sōjō, 1053–1140): Best known for his association with the Heian-period satirical depiction of frolicking animals, he is no longer believed to have been the author of this or any other work credited to him.

Fukuzawa Yukichi (1835–1901): Born into a low-ranking samurai family, Fukuzawa became a highly influential educator and writer, founding what is now Keiō University. His image appears on the Japanese ten-thousand-yen note.

Gozeta Hōbai: A play on the names Goseda Hōryū (1827–92) and Goseda Yoshimatsu (1855–1915). Hōryū was a student of the Italian painter Antonio Fontanesi; Yoshimatsu, his son, studied in France and was known in particular as a portrait artist.

Hé Rú Zhāng (1838–91): China's first modern ambassador to Japan (1876–79).

Hiroshige (1797–1858): The *nom d'artiste* of Andō Tokutarō, most famous for his *Fifty-three Stations of the Tokaido Road*.

Ichikawa Sadanji I (1842–1904): One of the three great Kabuki actors of the Meiji era.

Inoue Seigetsu (1822–87): The wandering poet was much extolled by Akutagawa. He is buried in the City of Ina in Nagano Prefecture.

Iwai Hanshirō VIII (1829–82): A famous *onnagata*, a Kabuki female impersonator.

Kikugorō V (1844–1903): Regarded as one of the two greatest Kabuki actors of the period, he first appeared in Western garb in the 1880s.

Mushanokōji Saneatsu (1885–1976): A painter as well as an important literary figure; a co-founder of Shirakaba ('White Birch'), a literary school intended to offer an alternative to naturalism.

Shu Shunsui (1600–82): Japanese form of Zhū Shùnshuǐ, who fled Manchu rule in China to settle in Japan, where he made an important contribution to the understanding of Neo-Confucianism. The monument was erected in 1912 at the elite Tōkyō First Higher School, where Akutagawa was a pupil.

Sonojo (1649–1723): A female disciple of Bashō.

Taiso Yoshitoshi (1838–92): Known for his realistic, indeed shocking, woodblock prints; became a newspaper illustrator in the Meiji era.

Tōkabō: Also Watanabe no Kuro, Kagami Shikō. Still in his late twenties when Bashō died, he had only recently become a disciple. He later wrote *Oi–Nikki* (*Knapsack Diary*), one of the accounts of Bashō's death.

PLACES

Asakusa: Located on the west bank of the Sumidagawa not far from where Akutagawa grew up, it is a symbol of *shitamachi*, the low-lying eastern area of Tōkyō known both for the temple Sensōji (Asakusa Kannon) and for its entertainment area, including the Rokku area.

Hagidera (lit. 'bush-clover temple'): An alternate name for Ryūganji, located in eastern Tōkyō, across the Sumida River from Miura's mansion.

Keijō: The Korean capital (Seoul) as it was known during Japanese rule (1910–1945).

Oumayabashi: The bridge crosses the Sumidagawa just below Kumakata, once the site of the entrance to Asakusa Temple.

Shubi-no-matsu: In Edo times, men would take boats through a canal of the Sumida River to Machiyama and there proceed to Shin-Yoshiwara, the licensed quarter. The tree in question ('pine tree of beginnings and endings') was a point of rendezvous going to and fro.

Suijin: In the forested area ('the grove of the water god') of Mukōjima Shrine, on the eastern side of the Sumida River.

HISTORICAL AND LITERARY REFERENCES

An'ya Kōro: A Dark Nights Passing is as heavily autobiographical novel by Shiga Naoya (1883–1971).

Divan: *West-Östlicher Divan*, written between 1814 and 1819, reflects both Goethe's Orientalism and his ambivalence toward Christianity.

Divine Age: *Kamiyo*, a term dating back to the early eighth-century *Chronicles of Japan* (*Nihon-shoki*), which begins with a mythological account of the nation's origins.

Jigokuhen: "Hell Screen," Akutagawa's heavily adapted story from a Heian-period collection of tales (*Uji-shūi Monogatari*) about a brilliant but monstrous painter.

Jinpūren Rebellion: The "League of the Divine Wind" (also *Shinpūren*) was formed in 1872 by former samurai in Kumamoto, Kyūshū. Deprivation of their right to wear swords triggered a short-lived rebellion in 1876, leading to other insurrections in southern Japan.

Nansō-Satomi-Hakkenden: *Chronicle of the Eight Dogs of Nansō Satomi*. The epic by Takizaki Bakin (1767–1848) is set in the fifteenth century. After being defeated in a rebellion, the warrior family Satomi puts down roots in Kazusa (Nansō). The eight "dogs" (with each bearing '-inu', 'canine', as a name suffix) are the warriors who lead the successful restoration of the clan.

Shakkō: *Red Lights* by Saitō Mokichi, Akutagawa's friend, physician, and the provider of the Veronal with which Akutagawa killed himself.

Shinsei: *New Life* by the writer Shimazaki Tōson (1872–1943), who confessed to having seduced and impregnated his own niece Komako before running off to France to escape the consequences.

Shuju no Kotoba: *Words of a Dwarf*, serialized between 1923 and 1927 in *Bungei-shunjū*.

Tenkibo: *Death Register*, published in 1926. The autobiographical sketch mentions, among other things, the mental illness of Akutagawa's mother, hence the comment that ends the conversation.

TRANSLATOR'S AFTERWORD

"The district in which I was born," wrote Akutagawa Ryūnosuke in 1912, "lies near the banks of the Great River." Still in secondary school when he composed a youthfully exuberant encomium to the lower reaches of the Sumidagawa, flowing through the heart of Japan's capital and into the bay, he was already composing autobiographical fiction. In fact, the author was born in Akaishi, on the western side of the river, not far from Tsukiji. His boyhood home was Mukōjima, situated on the eastern bank, across from Asakusa, and known for its geisha and teahouses. The date of his birth was March 1, 1892.

As is clear from the stories, Akutagawa was a voracious and eclectic reader. Since boyhood, he had been particularly fond of the classical folktale collection *Konjaku Monogatari* [Tales of Times Now Past]. While still a student, he wrote several ironic and psychologically insightful adaptations of these (cf. "Fortune"). If judged solely by titles, the most famous of these is *Rashōmon*, published in 1915, though in actual content, it is *Yabu no Naka* [In a Grove] (1922), which centers on a crime of rape and murder (or suicide) related from multiple perspectives. It is this story that forms the basis of Kurosawa Akira's renowned 1950 film *Rashōmon*. Though the film's title is only peripherally related to Akutagawa's tale of the same name, it has nonetheless become the source of *rashomonesque*, an epithet for the theme of subjectivism.

In his later years, Akutagawa suffered greatly from physical and psychological ailments, the latter aggravated by his fear of hereditary insanity. On July 24, 1927, a Bible beside his bed, Akutagawa took an overdose of Veronal. Included in letters left for his wife and friends is the oft-cited, cryptic explanation: "a vague sort of anxiety about my future" (*boku no shōrai ni tai-suru tada bon'yari to shita fuan*). The event was cause for a huge media sensation, and these words in particular were seized upon by pundits as somehow symbolic of the times and portentous for Japan.

It is not difficult to imagine that Akutagawa himself would have found it all both amusing and exasperating. In 1935, a literary prize in his honor was established at the suggestion of his friend and fellow writer, Kikuchi Kan (1888–1948), by the magazine *Bungei-Shunjū*. In the West, Akutagawa's name, though hardly unknown, is most likely to be associated with those stories containing macabre or supernatural elements, with the theme of *Rashōmon*, or simply with Japan's oft-noted history of literary suicides. His more famous works have been translated and retranslated, with considerable variation in literary skill, leaving Akutagawa to suffer less from obscurity than from typecasting. The present collection, containing several stories made available to the English-speaking audience for the first time, is intended to contribute to a richer understanding and appreciation of this, one of Japan's early modern literary giants.

The original texts are taken from the *Akutagawa-zenshū* [The Complete Works of Akutagawa Ryūnosuke], Volumes 1–4, published by Chikuma-shobō, Tōkyō, 1964 [1970]. Japanese names are given in East Asian order, surname preceding personal name. Chinese names and words are treated according to context. The name of the Chinese restaurant in "An Evening Conversation" is rendered in Sino-Japanese: Tōtōtei, not Táotáo-díng; on the other hand, the word that the narrator in "Cogwheels" would presumably have pronounced as Sino-Japanese *kirin* is represented in *qílín*.

A brief note about the Romanization of Japanese and Chinese names may be in order. The macron over vowels (e.g. ō vs. o) indicates length for

Japanese words. For Chinese words, the four tones are marked, e.g. ō, ó, ǒ, and ò. For Japanese words, n before m, p, and b is pronounced m.

Resisting a propensity widespread among academics, I have kept the notes to a minimum. Particularly for "The Life of a Fool" and "Cogwheels," where literary references and autobiographical allusions abound, the temptation to "explain" has been strong – and thus partially placated with "Additional Terminology" at the end. Curious readers may avail themselves of that appendix, though it is not – and is not intended to be – complete. Not even Akutagawa's own Japanese contemporaries would have understood all of his fragmentary and troubled musings at the end of his life, and to relentlessly render factual – historical or biographical – what should be left as literary would surely spoil the story.

I wish to express boundless gratitude to Jill Schoolman for her wisdom and patience over several years as I struggled to complete this work, and to Masako Nakamura, from whose keen eye, extraordinary linguistic sense, cross-cultural learning, and unending generosity I have undeservedly benefited for more than twenty years. Finally, to my family and above all to my wife, Keiko: *Arigatō gozaimasu.*